SHE WAS THE
PRIZE HE STOLE
FROM ANOTHER
MAN'S ARMS.

HE WAS THE ENEMY SHE
WAS BORN TO LOVE. . . . .

THE SEDUCTION

"Thing is," he said, kissing her eyelids very gently, then leaning back to gaze intently down into her wide eyes, "I wonder if you've had many men . . . any men."

"I'm not going to answer that question." Indignation and alarm made her struggle anew. "Cal, let me up right now."

"Sure," he said easily, his breath warm on her cheeks. But he made no move to let her go. Instead he nibbled at the corner of her ear, sending a flame of sensation through Melora that seemed to her would set the hay on fire. "If you want me to," Cal added smoothly.

A wild, throbbing ache took possession of Melora as Cal's mouth branded kisses across her helpless throat. It was torture, sweet torture. She had to get away from him, so she could think, so she could wrest back control of her own body, which was betraying her as it never had before. . . .

FOREVER AFTER

CHERISHED

JILL GREGORY

GREGORY

ALWAYS

YOU

A DELL BOOK

To Larry and Rachel—my favorite, and most beloved characters of all, with love forever

And to Karen A. Katz, Marianne Willman, and Ruth Ryan Langan—dear friends and most splendid kindred spirits, with enduring love and friendship

Published by
Dell Publishing
a division of
Bantam Doubleday Dell Publishing Group, Inc.
1540 Broadway
New York, New York 10036

ISBN: 0-440-22183-8

Printed in the United States of America

Published simultaneously in Canada

April 1996

RAD   10 9 8 7 6 5 4 3 2 1

RAWHIDE, WYOMING

Prologue

He'd never stalked a woman before.

He didn't much like it. But there was no other way.

As he sat with his hat pulled low over his eyes and his long legs stretched out beneath a small square table in the Ginger Horse Saloon, the tall, quiet stranger drank whiskey and let the talk swirl around him, talk as thick and heavy as the tobacco smoke that drifted over the baize-topped gaming tables and the gleaming mahogany bar.

The place was like many others he had passed through in Arizona, New Mexico, Nevada. Flocked red-velvet wallpaper, brass chandeliers. A big, crowded room teeming with cowboys and ranchers and townsmen. There were some gamblers and a half dozen red-lipped women in cheap, gaudy dresses and strong perfume—heady floral fragrances that vied for attention with the odors of tobacco, whiskey, and sweat. A piano player pounded at the keys of the instrument in the corner; coins clinked; boots scraped against the floor.

A typical place, the stranger thought, full of colors, sounds, smells.

And talk.

Talk about Melora Deane.

She was the belle of the town, maybe even the belle of the territory, from the sound of it. Daughter of rancher Craig Deane of the Weeping Willow Ranch, one of the largest spreads around.

He'd already seen the ranch. But not the girl—not yet.

He finished his whiskey, ordered another, and listened some more.

Almost everyone in the Ginger Horse had something to say about her. People talked openly, admiringly. They said she was a handful. A beauty. They said she was every inch her father's daughter.

And they said she was getting married tomorrow to Wyatt Holden.

The stranger was the only one who knew she wasn't.

Because tomorrow at this time Melora Deane would have vanished. And the stranger in the gray shirt and sleek black pants, with the silver handled gun belt slung low on his hips and the dark blue neckerchief loosely knotted at his throat, was the only one who would know what had become of her.

He didn't want her. But he was going to take her anyway.

Because there wasn't going to be any wedding for this talked-about happy couple; there was only going to be a funeral.

An uproarious burst of laughter erupted from the poker players near the window, followed by someone shouting for another round of drinks.

The stranger paid for his whiskey, glanced neither here nor there, and strode out the double doors into the Wyoming dusk.

It was time.

WEEPING WILLOW RANCH

1

Melora Deane hunched her tired shoulders over her father's desk and frowned down at the sea of payroll ledgers before her.

A cold, hard lump of rage rose in her throat. "Those damned rustlers! I'd like to string up every single one of them single-handedly!"

She brushed back several loose strands of dark gold hair that had escaped from her ponytail and forced herself to read the figures over again. Maybe there was a mistake.

There wasn't. Melora closed her eyes, the lump in her throat tightening into a thick knot.

Outside the window a meadowlark sang, a beloved, familiar song she'd heard all her life. The sound was both lovely and painful, ripping through her heart.

She took a deep breath and compressed her lips, thinking of the vast, beautiful Wyoming rangeland that stretched for miles in every direction, of the cattle grazing freely across the rolling Deane property.

Anger flooded her.

She and Jinx were rooted here, to every inch of grassland and foothill that encompassed the Weeping Willow. It was their home, their birthright. And they were in danger of losing it forever.

First we lost Pop. Now we're in danger of losing the ranch. I won't . . . won't . . . let it happen.

She dropped her head and scrubbed her knuckles across her wet eyes. *Don't cry, think!* she told herself furiously. But it was hard to hold back the tears. She loved the Weeping Willow with every fiber of her being, and so did Jinx. It was their legacy from Pop, it represented everything he had built, everything he had been, but now the rustlers who had murdered him were destroying the ranch too.

And so far she hadn't found a way to stop them.

"For a girl who's getting married tomorrow, you're working much too hard." Aggie Kerns scolded her from the study doorway.

Melora glanced up, then shook her head at the slim, tiny woman who had taken care of her and her sister since their mother died eight years ago. Nearly sixty, with small shell blue eyes and gray curls that sprang out all over her head, Aggie was a reassuring presence, firm and practical and loving. She possessed a brisk manner and a warm heart, and she was wonderful with Jinx. Especially lately, since the accident.

"Don't lecture me, Aggie." Melora grimaced. "I just have to go over another set of books—"

"No, you don't, Mel. Not tonight. Why, tomorrow this time you'll be on your honeymoon, and you haven't even done all your packing yet, I'll wager." As the girl conceded this with a guilty nod, Aggie sighed. Melora Deane was a beautiful, spirited young woman, and at twenty she had more energy than five cowhands put together, but since her father's murder she'd darn near worked herself to death. Enough was enough. Aggie bustled into the study and placed both her spider-veined hands on the mahogany desk.

"Just as I thought. Now listen to me, honey. You let Wyatt take over all these financial matters for you after you're married. See if he can't sort things out. My word, you've done enough worrying about stock and rustlers and expenses to last you a lifetime."

"We'll see." Melora opened the center drawer and replaced the ledger books. "I don't want the Weeping Willow to be a burden to him, Aggie. It's my responsibility. But at the very least," she added as Aggie opened her mouth to argue, "I'll get his advice."

Wyatt had already offered to go over all the books with a fine-tooth comb for her, to turn his considerable business acumen to the task of straightening out the affairs of the Weeping Willow Ranch. He had even offered to invest money in more stock and to hire on more hands so that the range could be patrolled at night. *He's wonderful,* she thought, her heart fluttering as she pictured the lankily handsome black-haired man she was going to marry in only a few hours.

But Wyatt had all his town businesses to look after, and his own neighboring ranch, the Diamond X, which he'd inherited four months ago from his uncle. *Keeping the Weeping Willow solvent is my job,* Melora told herself. She just had to figure out a way to do it.

But Aggie was right about one thing. The mounting debts would have to wait until after her honeymoon. First things first. She was just rising from her chair to go upstairs and pack when she heard the clatter of approaching hoofbeats.

"Goodness, who can that be?" Aggie demanded.

It was Melora who strode to the study window and saw the tall gray-hatted rider approaching, handling the splendid black stallion with the confident ease of a man long accustomed to being in control. At the sight of him the smile that had won Melora Deane countless hearts sparkled across her face.

"It's Wyatt!" she exclaimed, and shot out the door like a firecracker.

Aggie watched from the window. She smiled contentedly as the slender gold-haired young woman dashed down the porch steps and across the yard to greet her intended. Even after a long day, wearing only a black and red checkered shirt and Levi's, Melora cut a striking figure. Running lightly through the charcoal shadows of falling dusk, she glowed with the vibrancy and radiance that had always commanded admiration.

And tall, dark, roguishly handsome Wyatt Holden was the perfect complement to her slim, vivid beauty. As he dismounted and swept Melora into his arms,

Aggie felt happy tears prick behind her eyelashes. It was about time Melora settled down with a man who would take care of her and help share her burdens.

Yes, indeed, they were the perfect couple.

"LET'S take a walk," Wyatt said, after thoroughly kissing her. "I've brought you a present."

"Give it to me right now, Wyatt. You know I can't bear to wait for anything!"

He chuckled, drawing her along with him into the grove of cottonwoods beyond the corrals. "After tomorrow, honey, neither of us will have to wait for anything," he said in a deep, low tone.

Melora grinned, and a faint blush stained her cheeks. She knew what Wyatt was referring to. Their first night of lovemaking. It would be so strange to lie in bed with him . . . and it would be beautiful too, she told herself quickly.

Anticipation tingled through her, with only a little bit of anxiety thrown in. *Married!* she thought in wonder, studying Wyatt's smooth profile as hand in hand they strolled beneath the cottonwoods. *Tomorrow night this handsome man with the charming drawl and the adorable dimples will be my husband.*

She'd known him only a few months, but it was all the time she needed. Wyatt had arrived in Rawhide after his uncle Jed Holden, the Deanes' neighbor, had succumbed to pneumonia and left the Diamond X Ranch to him. From the moment Melora set eyes on him at the May Day town dance, she'd known that he was different from all of the other men who'd pursued her. Those others, both at school in Boston and here in Wyoming, had been boys. Wyatt Holden was a man. A self-assured, intelligent, sophisticated man, who didn't fawn over her or show off in front of her or drive her loco trying to steal a kiss. That wasn't his style.

He had quickly become one of Rawhide's leading citizens, respected even by her father's friends, the older, established ranchers in the valley. He had investments all over the West, he'd told her, a fleet of fishing boats in San Francisco, a freight company in Kansas, and a saloon in Nevada. He'd bought a livery stable in Rawhide already and was considering taking over the Paradise Saloon as well.

"I'm investing my future in Rawhide," he'd explained the night he proposed. "*Because I love you.*" He'd gone down on one knee in the ranch house parlor, gripped both her hands in his, and urged her to share that future with him.

Now the future was about to begin. *At last*, she thought, thinking with shivery anticipation of the extravagant pink satin nightdress she had splurged on from Lacy's catalog, which she intended to wear tomorrow night. She imagined herself gliding toward Wyatt in that lovely floating confection, pictured the way his eyes would light as he studied her. He would sweep her into his arms. And they would kiss—a long, dreamy kiss. And then he would untie the silk ribbons holding the bodice together and—

Her thoughts broke off abruptly as Wyatt halted beside a fallen log. "Have a seat right here, Melora. And close your eyes. Now, give me your hand."

Into her outstretched palm he placed a small box wrapped with a yellow velvet bow.

The sight of it almost made her forget her worries about the ranch. Melora's gold-flecked brown eyes shone with anticipation as she lifted the lid. Then she caught her breath, and her mouth formed a perfect O. "Wyatt, it's lovely!" she gasped, carefully lifting out the exquisite ivory cameo nestled inside. Its thin gold chain glistened in the fading light. "I've never seen anything half as beautiful."

"I have." Wyatt tipped her chin up and gazed down at her, his expression so intent she felt her pulse begin to race. "Every time I look at you, Melora, I see the most beautiful treasure on earth."

Was there ever a sweeter, more wonderful man? Melora flushed with pleasure as he fastened the clasp for her. His touch was warm, sure, and gentle. She imagined those sure hands touching her tomorrow night in their hotel suite. Imagined them undressing her. And a quivering warmth spread through her, filling her with a leaping anticipation.

Wyatt's smile was full and satisfied as he studied the cameo circling her throat. Pleasure gleamed in his deep-set, piercing blue eyes. "There now. It's not half as pretty as you are, honey, but as a little prewedding token of my affection, it'll do. Are you excited about tomorrow? All packed for the honeymoon, I hope."

"Actually I have a little more to do. I've been working on the payroll . . . oh, let's not talk about it."

He sat down beside her on the log. His dark eyebrows drew together as he smoothed back a strand of her silken hair, which had fallen over one eye. "I hate to see you tiring yourself out and worrying endlessly about the ranch. After the wedding I'm going to take over for you."

"I can't ask that of you. The Weeping Willow's debts are my responsibility—" she began, but Wyatt cut her off, frowning, placing a finger against her lips.

"And you're my responsibility, Melora. Don't you trust me to straighten out your affairs?"

"Of course I do!" Distressed at this very notion, Melora threw her arms around his neck. "It's not that at all! Wyatt, I just hate to bother you with my problems." She searched his face anxiously. "You've had your own share of troubles to deal with; the rustlers have been stealing from the Diamond X as well. And you have all your other businesses to keep track of."

Wyatt paid no heed at all to the squirrels chasing one another through the brush or to the purple darkness gathering all around them. His vivid blue eyes fixed themselves upon her intently, and his voice was low and strong. "There's nothing more important to me than your happiness, Melora. Nothing. And I know you won't be happy if you lose the Weeping Willow. Believe me, honey, I'll do everything in my power to help save it for you."

Gratitude swelled within her. For so long she'd wrestled alone with the burden of keeping the ranch going. It still took some getting used to, the notion that she was going to have a husband who wanted to help her, a man whom she could depend on to stand by her and Jinx. Relief, gratitude, and love poured through her as she tightened her arms around Wyatt's neck and kissed him.

"Thank you, Wyatt. I can't thank you enough. I promise not to dump all my problems in your lap, but I would appreciate some help. Some advice . . ."

"Whatever I can do." His lips nuzzled hers, warmly, excitingly. "We'll tackle all these problems right after the honeymoon. In the meantime," he told her, tracing a finger across her delicate jaw, "I don't want Mrs. Wyatt Holden worrying her head over matters that her husband can attend to. You'll have your hands full searching out the right doctor for Jinx and making her travel arrangements—"

A shrill cry rang out from the ranch house, breaking into the fragrant peace of the night.

"That sounded like Jinx!" Melora jumped up, fear darkening her eyes. They heard something carried on the wind that sounded like a sob. "Something's wrong!"

She started to run, with Wyatt right after her. Terror struck deep in her heart as she darted back the way they had come, past the bunkhouse and the stables, the outbuildings and corrals. Suddenly the cry came again, and this time she could make out the words.

"Mel . . . Aggie . . . *help*!"

Wyatt pounded across the porch before her and swung open the front door. Melora bolted inside. "Jinx, where are you?" she shouted frantically.

"Here, she's in the kitchen," Aggie called, and together Mel and Wyatt sprinted through the hall and the parlor and halted as they reached the kitchen door.

Huddled there on the floor was Jinx, a small, bony vision of waist-length red-gold hair and huge olive green eyes brimming with tears. She was lying a few feet from her invalid chair, sobbing heartbrokenly as Aggie knelt beside her and cradled her in her arms.

"I t-tried to walk. I wanted to s-surprise you . . . to walk down the aisle at your w-wedding." The little girl wailed as Wyatt moved forward and lifted her from the floor.

Melora pushed the cane-backed invalid chair out of the way. "Wyatt, please bring her into the parlor," she cried distractedly, and seized Jinx's hand, hurrying along with them as Wyatt carried the eleven-year-old across the kitchen.

"Are you hurt?" she asked anxiously, scanning the small pale face as Aggie followed close behind.

"N-no, I banged my elbow, but—"

"Anything else hurt?" Melora sat beside her as soon as Wyatt set the child upon the chintz sofa mounded with pillows.

"No. I'm sorry to . . . scare you, but I wanted to surprise you. It was going to be my w-wedding present!"

"And it would be the best present in the world!" Melora assured her, fighting to keep her own tears from spilling out of her eyes. "But it can wait, Jinx. There's no hurry. Why, when the doctor finds out what's wrong, I'm sure you'll be walking in no time!"

Jinx hadn't taken a step since that early morning last spring when Craig Deane had been shot by rustlers on his own south range. Jinx, who had been riding, had made the horrible discovery by herself, stumbling across their father's body lying in the brush. He'd been shot in the head.

In horror and shock at finding him Jinx had fallen from her horse and been knocked unconscious. Though no bones were broken and aside from some bruises she had no apparent physical injuries, the little girl had been unable to walk since that day.

"I wish I could have done it; you would have been so surprised. I have only one sister, you know, and she'll have only one wedding," Jinx whispered, her head drooping.

Melora's heart ached with love and pain. If her willpower alone could have made Jinx walk again, the girl would have been running by now, fleet as the wind. But she couldn't heal what was wrong with her sister; all she could hope to do was ease the sadness. "It doesn't matter, silly puss. The only thing that matters is that you get better." She hugged Jinx, gently squeezing her delicate shoulders, and smoothed the soft red-gold curls back from the pointed little face.

Watching them together, Aggie thought how different they were, yet how alike. Melora, with her dark gold hair cascading past her shoulders, her tawny eyes and silken apricot complexion, looked like a delicate fairy-tale princess, but she had a will of steel and a temper from hell. She had inherited her father's strength of purpose and his iron determination, while little Jinx was the image of their sensitive, dreamy mother, Alexandra Deane. Jinx possessed the same wide green eyes as Alexandra, and the same lush, fiery curls. Only her freckles were her own, a perky sprinkling across her turned-up nose. She loved to draw delicate, fine-lined pen-and-ink sketches, she dressed up her three cats in bonnets and tiny vests that Aggie taught her to sew, she spent hours with her horse, Sir Galahad, and she often stayed up reading until nearly dawn.

Just as Melora had been, she was bright and quick in school, but since the accident she had stopped attending the bustling schoolhouse. She didn't want visits from any of her friends. Melora was distressed to see her cutting herself off more and more, but Aggie sensed that Jinx didn't want anyone pitying her or staring at her. "She needs time, time to recover from the shock of finding your poor father, time to heal from the inside. She's got the Deane spirit in her, Melora, so there's no need to fret about it. She'll snap back, you'll see."

As she watched them now on the sofa, heads bent together, touching, Aggie's heart thrummed with affection for both of them. Such good girls, going through such difficult times. But they both were tougher than they looked, she reflected proudly, each in her own way. They loved each other and this ranch with the same fierce devotion their father had shown, and Aggie sensed that there was enough fight in both of them to conquer every obstacle in their path.

Her gaze shifted to Wyatt Holden, smiling tenderly down at Melora. Bless the man. He would help them, both of them. His arrival in Rawhide a few months ago had been a godsend.

"You will get better, Jinx," he told the child firmly, much to Aggie's approval. "That's a promise.

We're going to get you the best doctors the East has to offer, whether they're in Boston or Philadelphia, Chicago, or New York. You'll have the very finest care. And then we'll find out exactly what you're up against.''

"And whatever it is, young lady, you'll lick it," Aggie put in confidently.

"You sound just like Pop!" Jinx smiled, looking up at last, and her enormous olive green eyes shone with a glimmer of hope.

"Well, he was always right, wasn't he?" Aggie asked, wagging her finger.

"Except when he argued with me," Melora pointed out, grinning.

"Speaking of arguments, I don't want to hear any about what I'm going to say next. But it's getting late, and you young ladies both should be getting along toward bed." Aggie glanced meaningfully at Wyatt. "Your bride has to get her beauty sleep, mister. Unless you want a bleary-eyed hag to walk down the aisle tomorrow."

"Heaven forbid—not that my own true love could ever look like a hag," he added with a laugh as Melora's mouth dropped open in protest.

"No, I don't reckon she could, but her head's already been turned quite enough with all the beaux she's had, so there's no sense in you adding to it," Aggie told him crisply, though her eyes were warm. "Besides, poor Mel still has to pack! So you go ahead home, Wyatt, and let these girls get some rest."

An hour later, after Aggie, Melora, and Jinx had had their fill of milk and strawberry pie in the kitchen,

Aggie thoughtfully retired to her own room on the second floor, leaving the sisters alone. Melora pushed the invalid chair along to Jinx's room to help her get ready for bed; she was well aware that these were the last moments alone she and her sister would spend before she was married.

After the accident they'd converted the small back parlor into a bedroom so that Jinx would not have to be carried up and down the stairs. It was snugly appointed, with Jinx's own brass bed and bright patchwork quilt, yellow curtains, and a collection of favorite books and dolls on the shelf beside the window. Two of Jinx's kittens snuggled at her feet, while the other held court on her lap as the girl sat upon the bed, her legs stretched out before her as Melora brushed her hair.

"Isn't Wyatt the dearest man, Jinx?" Melora drew the brush lovingly along the blaze of curls, thinking of the moment when Wyatt had placed the ribbon-wrapped box into her palm. "It was so sweet of him to give me this cameo tonight."

"It's very pretty."

"And he's certainly the handsomest man ever to set foot in Rawhide—next to Pop, of course," she added, her eyes misting over. "And he's so thoughtful and kind. Oh, sweetie, how did I get to be so lucky?"

"Umm."

Melora paused, brush in hand, and peered suddenly, warily into her sister's face. " 'Umm'?"

"I mean, I don't know," Jinx said.

Melora stared at her. "Jinx! What's wrong? You do like Wyatt, don't you?" she asked anxiously.

There was a small silence.

"You mean you *don't*?"

She looked so crestfallen that Jinx immediately bobbed her head. "Oh, I do, Mel. Really, I do." She swallowed. The kitten rubbed its face against her knee. "It's just that we haven't known him all that long, and you know how it takes me a while to warm up to people, but I think he's handsome as could be, and nice and—"

"He'll be good to us, Jinx, you'll see." Melora spoke quietly. She set the brush down and sank beside her sister on the bed. "We'll be happy. All three of us. The sad times are behind us now."

Jinx chewed her lower lip the way she did when she was worried. "Don't get me wrong," she said, sounding so serious and so much like their father that Melora hid a smile. "I do think Mr. Holden is nice. But, Mel, are you sure you want to marry him?"

"Of course I'm sure. Don't I seem sure?"

"Ye-es, but—"

"But what? Out with it!" Mel exclaimed.

"I just wonder if you're marrying him because of . . . me."

"You!"

Jinx nodded. "You know what I mean," she said slowly. "Because of my legs . . . because he's rich enough to send me to the best doctors and—"

Melora reached out and gently grasped her shoulders. "Oh, Jinx, no. Don't ever think that. Of course

I'm happy that Wyatt is rich enough so that we'll be able to afford to take you back East, and do you know what else? He's going to help us save the ranch! But I'm not marrying him because of that.''

"You love him, then?"

"I do." Melora's eyes shimmered like topaz in the soft light of the kerosene lamp. "I enjoy his company more than any other man I've ever met."

"But that's not love," the little girl protested. "Love is . . . when your souls touch."

Melora laughed and lightly pinched her cheek. "Silly puss! How do you know anything about love? Your head is always buried in your books. People's souls don't really touch, and they don't see stars when they're together. Believe me, Jinx, nothing like that happens at all! Love is pleasant, very pleasant! It makes you want to spend your life with someone because you know that he's the only person in the world meant just for you."

"Yes, but, Melora, you thought you were in love with Walker Hayes too."

"That was different." Melora's cheeks pinkened, and she gave her head a toss, sending her ponytail swinging. "I was fifteen then—and ridiculous. Too flattered by the attentions of a boy three years older than I was to know any better."

"What about Linc Bowden?"

"That only lasted two weeks! Then I couldn't bear any more of those dreadful love songs he kept braying under my window."

"And Mr. Rivers?"

"He was our schoolteacher, Jinx. Ten years older

than I was! Goodness, I had no idea he was going to come to Pop with a proposal of marriage.''

Jinx giggled. "Must be downright inconvenient having every man within miles tell you you're the prettiest girl in the territory, asking you to dances, and trying to win your picnic lunch at church socials,'' she murmured, and Melora chuckled.

"That's all over now. I'm going to be a married woman.'' She reached out impulsively and clasped Jinx's hand. She held it tightly within her own firm, slender fingers. "And the three of us are going to be a family.''

Jinx nodded, but the sadness deep within her eyes struck Melora like a rock lodged in her heart. "Is there something else, honey?''

"I wish," Jinx whispered, a catch in her voice, "that Pop were here to walk you down the aisle.''

"Me too." Taking a deep breath, Melora struggled to swallow down her own still-fresh heartache. She'd been at school in Boston when the news had come that her father was killed. All during her grief-stricken train journey home she'd fought to contain the tears that would have drowned her if she'd let them flow. Never to see Pop again, to hear his hearty, cheerful voice, to kiss his rough, sage-scented cheek, or bring him a late-night glass of whiskey when he was doing paperwork until midnight. It was almost more than she could bear.

But I still have Jinx, she reminded herself as she sat now in her sister's softly lit room, listening to the night breeze play at the curtains. *And Aggie. And Wyatt.* She straightened her spine. "Pop will be watching,'' she told Jinx softly. ''He'll be watching from the doorway of heaven, with Mama right beside him. I know it.''

The words seemed to comfort her sister. Later, when Jinx was tucked in and ready for sleep, her kittens curled around her, Melora made her way up the wide oak staircase and entered her pretty rose-papered room, carrying with her the hope that Jinx would keep that comfort close when all their friends were gathered around them for her wedding day.

Tomorrow night, tomorrow night, I'll be a bride, tomorrow night. The refrain ran through her mind all during her bath. She was humming as she patted herself dry with a towel and when she slipped into a gossamer white cotton nightdress and began to brush her hair. She dipped and whirled before the mirror, admiring the delicate cameo still clasped about her throat and studying the way the low-cut nightdress clung to her curves. This was the last night she would sleep alone, the very last night. After this she and Wyatt would make love every single night; they would wake up in each other's arms, kissing, touching. . . .

She twirled toward the closet where her hatboxes were stacked, her heart light. She never saw the man who glided like a dark ghost through her open window; she didn't hear even a footfall until it was too late. . . .

The hand clamped down hard across her mouth, stunning her. Out of the blue she was seized ruthlessly from behind and yanked savagely backward against an iron masculine frame.

Melora struggled wildly. Surprise and terror crashed over her as she tried to scream, tried to get away. But the strong hand over her lips dug in even harder, and her cries were muffled with merciless efficiency. Her fear grew, sweeping through her like a gale wind as she struggled desperately to twist around, trying to see the silent man who held her, to wrest free, to kick or strike him, but it was useless. She found herself imprisoned by arms far stronger than her own.

Who is this? Melora wondered wildly, dread ripping through her as she struggled with all her might. Who had come into her room and seized her like this? Was it a rustler? One of the rustlers who had murdered her father?

A single thought obsessed her mind. She somehow had to break away, to reach her carpetbag, where the small Colt pistol she'd packed lay atop her riding habit and traveling clothes.

She slammed an elbow backward, catching her attacker, she hoped, smack in the ribs.

He flinched, cursing softly, but didn't loosen his grip even the tiniest bit. Matter of fact, he tightened it, his fingers digging into her with the strength of rawhide.

Kick, bite, hit, Melora screamed silently to herself, but he was too strong. He held her helpless, and before she could do more than give out a stifled yelp of outrage, he had thrown her facedown on her bed, was holding her down, her face pushed against the coverlet, while he dragged her arms behind her and began tying her hands together.

Fresh terror bubbled up into her throat. She couldn't breathe, couldn't see, couldn't move. Panic swept over her.

And then he slipped a blindfold over her eyes, stuffed a cloth into her mouth, and yanked her up again, none too gently. Melora drew great breaths of air into her nostrils. While before she had fought wildly, now her legs trembled so violently it was difficult to stand, and she felt clammy with an all-encompassing fear.

Locked in darkness, Melora suddenly realized that another set of footsteps was moving about her room. There were scuffling sounds, whispers. *How many men are with him?* she wondered, her heart racing like a runaway bronco.

Then a low, cool voice spoke into her ear. "Not one sound. We don't want to disturb your father or sister, do we? That might prove unhealthy."

He dragged her ruthlessly sideways. Ten, fifteen, twenty steps. Stumbling blindly along with him, barefoot, Melora stubbed her toe and let out a muffled oath. She felt him stiffen. Then abruptly she was swept up in strong arms and carried down the stairs. Her heart pounded with fear as next she was borne across the hall and outside into the yard.

Frantically she tried to keep some sense of her surroundings, but a cloud of terror descended on her when she was tossed up sidesaddle onto a horse, and her abductor immediately swung up behind her, his arms enclosing her like steel bars. She felt the solid pressure of a hard-muscled body against hers and shivered as the horse's rough coat scraped her bare legs.

This can't be happening. I'm getting married to-morrow, she thought in horror as the horse moved forward, its trotting strides quickly lengthening to a gallop. Through the roaring in her ears she heard one—no, two—other horses galloping alongside.

Sharp night wind slapped through the sheer night-gown, chilling her skin, whipping her hair. Behind the blindfold her eyes ached to see. She wanted to spit out the vile gag but could not. She couldn't even move her fingers; they were growing numb already from the rope.

Melora bit back tears of fear and frustration. Her whole body trembled. Below her the horse gathered speed.

And the stranger behind her tightened his arm around her waist and spoke again.

His voice was even colder than the wind.

"Sit back and enjoy the ride, Miss Deane. We've got a long ways to go before we make our first camp."

2

They rode for hours through oblique, windswept night.

By the time the horse beneath her at last slowed to a canter and finally halted, Melora was so cold and so weary she felt she would stiffen up like a fence post and simply die. Only the warmth of the man riding behind her shielded her at all from the biting wind. The heat and strength and vitality of him surrounded her but gave her no comfort, for he was not her ally but her enemy. An enemy who would demand from her . . . only God knew what.

She shivered from her neck to her ankles, and her senses spun dizzily when her captor dismounted and without warning yanked her down from the saddle.

She nearly fell, her knees crumpling beneath her

weight, but strong arms caught her and kept her upright.

"Take it easy, Miss Deane." That cool, deep voice again. She wanted to see the face it belonged to; her fingers itched to slap it. She was afraid, afraid of what was in store for her and of what would happen next, but rage curdled beneath the fear. And she made a vow to herself: She would not cry, would not plead, would not show the terror that tasted sharp and metallic on her tongue. No matter what this man and his companions did to her she would show no weakness. None!

Steeling herself as she felt him loosen the gag, she tensed her shoulders. Pop had always said: *Hold your ground, Mel, and fight for what you believe.* He'd lived and died by that code. And so would she.

They'll find out quick enough that they cannot intimidate Melora Deane, she thought harshly, summoning all her wits and her courage.

Her heart thumped in double time as her captor stripped off the gag. Coughing a little, she swallowed several times and flexed her cramped throat muscles. Her tongue dabbed over dry, cracked lips that were so sensitive they quivered.

"You all right?" The voice sounded gruff.

"All right? Of course I'm not all right. I've never been treated so abominably in my entire life! Take off this damned blindfold now—this instant!" she ordered in a hoarse croak so unlike her own usual tone it infuriated her even more.

"I think the lady likes to give orders," she heard

that same cool voice drawl, and it was full of mockery. From a few feet away she heard guffawing.

But she felt hands at the back of her head, un-
knotting the blindfold.

Melora blinked rapidly as her captor whipped off
the silk neckerchief that bound her eyes and her vision adjusted to her surroundings. She was in a clearing, in the middle of nowhere. An icy canopy of stars
glittered overhead, and their light along with that of
a crystal half-moon revealed low surrounding hills
and trees etched in darkness and an expanse of open
plains beyond. Faint moonlight cast an eerie glow
upon the clearing in which she stood and partially
illuminated the shadowy figure of the man standing
before her.

"You low-down cowardly bastard," Melora grated
out, her mouth and throat so dry and raspy that the
effort of speaking brought tears to her eyes, but that
did not affect the unstoppable torrent of words that
poured out.

"Just what in the world do you think you're doing?
Do you know who I am? Do you realize what you've
done?" She coughed, then spoke again, her voice
stronger, fueled by the outrage that poured through
her in crashing waves. "How *dare* you do this to me?
I demand that you untie my hands this instant, give
me a horse, and let me go."

He merely stared levelly at her, this man who had
so callously trussed her and taken her from the safety
of her own bedroom, who had brought her here to
this lonely, chilly place wearing only her nightdress
and a cameo necklace from the man she loved.

"Bastard, untie me!" she shouted when he continued to make no move. Her eyes blazed with hate as
she stared into his face.

He set his lips together, shooting her an implacable
look. He was a complete stranger to her, a six-foot
cowboy in snug-fitting black pants, a wide-brimmed
black hat, and a gray shirt, whose demeanor radiated
cool nonchalance. Melora took his measure quickly,
noting that he was perhaps twenty-five or thirty, sun-
bronzed and hardy-looking, with a day's growth of
beard stubbling his strong jaw. He was rangily built,
lean but with a muscled chest and broad shoulders.

And strong arms, which were firmly holding her
around her waist, supporting her.

His face was not at all handsome, she decided, her
eyes narrowing. Especially in comparison to Wyatt's
vivid, chiseled features. It was a blunt, tough, rather
ordinary face, she observed angrily, the features even
and clean-cut, unexceptional—except for his eyes.
These were intelligent and unusually keen, of a light,
clear green color that reminded her of a frozen river.

And they were fixed on her with unrelenting calm.

"Didn't you hear me?" Melora flushed as he still
made no move to cut her bonds. "I said untie me—
now!"

"I heard you."

Fury flared in her eyes. She wanted to kill him.
Her wrists, bound behind her, were chafed raw; they
were probably bleeding. The cold night air was slic-
ing right through her sheer nightdress, and she knew
that if it weren't for his arms around her, holding her
up, she would most likely collapse. And she knew

that he knew it too. That made her only more furious as she stared up at him with undisguised scorn, hating the intimate feel of his corded arms around her, and the nearness of that maddeningly steady countenance, and, most of all, the raw strength and ease that radiated from him.

"Look, you obviously know who I am." She bit out the words, using the tone of a schoolteacher whose much-tried patience with her wayward pupils is nearly exhausted. "But you may not be aware that tomorrow I am getting married. Not just to anyone, but to one of the most prominent men in the territory. *Do you understand what that means, you three lame-brained half-wits*?" Her voice rose on the words. She shook her head to toss her windblown hair from her eyes and sent a searing glance around the group to encompass the two men standing behind him as well. They were gaping at her as if they'd never seen an enraged female before. Melora ignored her captor and fixed them both with her most commanding stare and spoke slowly and distinctly so there was no mistaking her meaning.

"If you don't let me return home this very minute, I guarantee that my fiancé will have every man in Rawhide searching for me by morning. And when they catch up with you, you'll wish you'd never been born!"

The two other men said nothing, just stood there like mangy dolts, watching her with a mixture of amusement and pity on their ugly horsey faces.

Then the cowboy gave her a shake. "Simmer down, Miss Deane. Your threats don't impress us;

your tantrums neither. You're with us now, so you can forget about your fancy fiancé and your fancy wedding. Zeke, cut the lady's ropes," he said, and the taller of the other two stepped forward. "Keep an eye on her while I give Ray a hand with the horses."

He released her then and turned away. Just like that he turned away. Melora watched his broad back in furious amazement as he strolled across the clearing and busied himself with the horses, moving about with brisk, smooth purpose, as unconcerned as if she were a passerby he had casually encountered in a general store, someone with whom he had discussed the price of potatoes.

"Who is he?" she demanded in slow, frigid accents as Zeke sawed at her bonds.

"Guess you could call him the boss."

The last of the rope fell away. Zeke watched her wince as she rubbed the raw skin of her wrists, his long, bony face impassive. Then he led her to a tree stump. "Here, have a seat, Miss Deane. Take it easy. Reckon you're all tuckered out. And while you're at it," he added in an almost friendly tone, shuffling his big booted feet in the grass, "let me give you a word of advice."

His eyes glistened down at her like wet black grapes. "Don't cause no trouble, and you won't get hurt."

"That's your advice?"

"Yep." He nodded and swatted at a mosquito. "You've got nothin' to worry about; the boss ain't got a mean bone in his body."

"Not much he doesn't," Melora muttered. This

man was obviously an idiot, in the pay of the other, with no personal interest in her or the kidnapping. She wondered if he could be persuaded to give her some answers and maybe, possibly, bribed to help her. "Zeke, please," she said in a low, heartfelt tone. "I don't understand. Who are you? Why did you kidnap me?"

"That's for the boss to say. This here is his deal."

"Please tell me. I don't understand. Are you rustlers? What can you possibly hope to—"

"We're no rustlers!" He interrupted her indignantly, snatching off his hat and scratching his ear. "Never heard anything so insulting."

"I'm sorry, forget I said that. I didn't mean to insult you." She hurried on, keeping her voice low enough so that the others couldn't hear. "Zeke, it's clear that this wasn't your idea, and that *he's* in charge. So I'll tell you what. If you let me go tonight, I'll see to it that no one arrests you. You won't get in any trouble—none at all. Just let me slip away. Distract him for a few minutes so that I can get to one of the horses and—"

"Aw, keep quiet." He sighed, waving his hat at her in disgust. Then he plopped it back on his head. Beneath it his thatch of rough brown hair hung to his shoulders like a clump of dirty straw. "No one's going to let you go, so quit wasting your breath. If you just wait a bit and don't try anything stupid, he'll probably let you have some water soon, and maybe some coffee. Then, missy," he added, slanting her a warning glance, "you'd best get yourself some shuteye. Tomorrow's going to be a real long day."

Frustration washed over her as she stared at this gangly, homely man in the brown shirt and overalls. There was no mistaking his sincerity. He would not help her. She felt the last shreds of her self-control slipping away.

"Why are you *doing* this?" she asked, her voice carrying in a low, frenzied wail that reached the other two men. Through the gloom she saw them glance over their shoulders at her.

"Ask *him*," Zeke replied, jerking his thumb backward with a shrug. "Cal's in charge of this outfit."

Cal. So that was his name. "What does he want with me?" Melora persisted, desperately clutching Zeke's sleeve as he started to turn away.

"That's for him to say."

"Who is he? An outlaw?"

"Reckon so. Me and Ray met up with him in jail. But that's all I'm going to say," he added, glaring. Then his expression softened to one of wry concern. "Say, you're lookin' mighty cold there. I'll just get a fire goin'."

And with that he shambled off and started gathering twigs and sticks, leaving Melora alone on her tree stump, her arms crossed around herself in a futile attempt to keep warm—and to preserve some minuscule shred of dignity.

Her thoughts raced ahead as Cal and the others went about the business of making camp. *Look around. Think. Maybe you can slip off and disappear into the brush,* she told herself desperately, even as the numbing cold crept through her bones, and clouds above obscured the moon, shadowing the clearing in deeper darkness.

She'd have to do some fancy hiding to keep them from finding her, but it *was* dark, and if she found the right place to conceal herself—

"Don't even think about it."

Cal's tall form loomed over her. His booted feet were planted apart, his thumbs casually hooked in his low-slung gun belt. *How had he appeared like that, out of nowhere?*

Melora stared up at him through shimmering, hate-filled eyes, taking in the rough stubble on his dark face, the brown hair that just touched his shoulders, his straight, arrogant nose, and his sensual mouth, which curled ever so mockingly as he studied her. But most of all at that moment she noted his eyes, those striking, miss-nothing eyes. His gaze was clear and shrewd as a puma's.

"Don't think about what?" she asked through clenched teeth.

"Running away. It won't do you any good. I'll just find you again."

"That so?"

"That's so." Cal reached out and cupped her chin to tilt it upward, noting as he did so the trembling of her lips and the heat of those incredibly beautiful golden brown eyes beneath their thick fringe of lashes. "I'm not letting you go, Miss Deane," he said quietly. "Not until I'm good and ready."

She snapped her chin back from his hand. "When will that be?"

"I'll let you know."

She vaulted off the rock, her fingers clawing for his eyes, his cheeks, his neck, but he grabbed her wrists before she could inflict any damage. She winced as his fingers pressed into her raw skin.

He saw the pain flicker across her face and glanced down. Beneath his fingers, the tender skin of her wrists was scraped and bruised from the rope.

Cal swore under his breath. He released her and forced himself to step back a pace. "Sorry I hurt you."

"If you were sorry, you'd let me go," she cried bitterly.

He shook his head, and for a moment she saw a fleeting sadness in his eyes, a glimpse of pain that softened the infuriating arrogance of his demeanor. Then it was gone, and the flat calm was back.

"You've had a rough night, Miss Deane," he said curtly. "Let's not make it any rougher. Looks like you could use some blankets and a cup of coffee." He took her elbow and steered her toward Zeke's campfire. "You won't be much use to me if you freeze to death."

His words stirred more questions and rekindled her fear. *Use to him? What possible use could I be to him?*

But suddenly Melora was too overwhelmed by cold and fatigue to argue anymore. She let him lead her to the fire, sit her down near the glowing opal flames, push a mug of steaming black coffee into her icy hands. She felt the heavy woolen saddle blanket he draped around her shoulders and gave a tiny, quivering sigh as she snuggled into its thick, scratchy warmth.

She was tired. Bone tired. And utterly confused by what was happening to her. A few hours ago she had been home, safe and secure on the Weeping Willow Ranch, looking forward to her wedding, and now . . .

Now she gulped coffee at a strange campfire in the middle of nowhere, the prisoner of this quiet-voiced, cold-eyed outlaw. Now she had no idea what the future held for her or if she had a future at all.

Melora kept her gaze fixed blearily toward the flames, though she could sense Cal watching her. Let him. She was too weary to glare back, too worn out and despondent to fight or protest anymore or even to try to escape.

At least not tonight.

She'd sleep and then perhaps tomorrow . . .

Tomorrow. Her wedding day.

Tears scalded hot and salty behind her eyes. She bit her lip and blinked them back, focusing hard just above the bright dancing flames.

CAL saw their glitter across the firelight, and the knot of tension inside him tightened.

Why did she have to be . . . like this? Beautiful beyond belief. Sharp-tongued yet fragile. And possessing more spirit and more courage than any other girl he'd ever known.

Seated in the shadows just behind the flames, Cal set his hat down beside him and raked a hand through his hair. This whole business was a lot dirtier and a lot more complicated than he'd planned on.

He wished it were over.

It all had sounded so simple when he'd drawn up the scheme. So just and so fitting. But now that he had Melora Deane right where he wanted her . . . aw, hell.

He couldn't afford to let emotions get in the way.

She was just a pawn, he reminded himself, clenching his fists. She was a tool for getting what he wanted. He couldn't afford to start thinking of her as a girl, a beautiful, fragile, radiant girl, or to start feeling sorry for her or worrying about her. He had to remember why he had started this and why he would do whatever it took to finish it.

Sitting several feet away from her, he watched as she closed her eyes and a delicate shudder passed through her shoulders. The skin around her eyes looked shadowed and drawn.

She'll be fine when she gets some sleep. And she'll settle down and accept things by tomorrow.

Meeting Ray's questioning glance across the campfire, he nodded, signaling that Ray and Zeke could turn in; he would take the first watch. At least for tonight they'd have to guard her to make sure she didn't try to escape.

Cal tore his eyes from the girl and stared moodily into the flames. He drank the coffee from his cup without tasting it. Hell, he had expected her to be pretty, but not like this. She was lovely. Enchanting. That sweep of glorious dark gold hair that cascaded down her back—the strands felt like silk when they brushed against him. Nor had he expected such slim, delicately expressive brows to frame large, vivid eyes as splendid and fiery as topaz.

Her attitude had caught him by surprise too. Far from being cowed by her predicament, she had the temper of an exploding shotgun. He sure hadn't expected that. Tears, yes, pleas, yes—those he had expected. But not hard-hitting questions, demands for her freedom, and that proud, stinging fury.

The fact that Cal sensed she was keeping her fear well hidden and well under control only brought out a grudging respect in him.

Why did she have to be so appealing? To have a heart-shaped face with the delicate bone structure of a royal princess, or that stubborn, thrusting, adorable little chin he found sexy as hell.

And why in hell did she have to be almost naked, with the lush softness of her breasts and hips tantalizingly outlined by nothing more than a flimsy wisp of silk?

Something twisted sharply, painfully inside him.

He pushed the something away.

He had no choice. He'd started this, and he'd finish it. Or die in the process.

He forced his thoughts to the following day, when his enemy would discover that his beloved intended bride was gone. Vanished. A decidedly cold smile wrenched at Cal's mouth.

We'll see how you like losing what's yours.

The game had begun. It was an ugly, deadly game. Still, it was a game he had to win, no matter the cost.

He got to his feet, tiredness now beginning to wear

on him. But his stride was long and purposeful when he retrieved the extra bedroll he'd brought for her and threw it down on the ground near where she sat by the fire.

"There you go, Miss Deane. It's all yours."

"You've thought of everything, haven't you? A neat, well-laid-out plan. Too bad you'll live to regret it," she snapped, eyeing him with loathing.

Cal didn't bother to answer. His glance dropped to the cameo glowing at her throat. He'd been too distracted by everything else to notice it earlier, but now the sight of it narrowed his eyes. It took every ounce of self-control he possessed to fight the deadly rage that swept him.

She can keep it until tomorrow, he told himself, turning on his heel and stalking to the edge of the clearing before he was tempted to snatch the cameo from her throat. *But no longer. First thing in the morning she hands it over.*

Pure hatred poured through Melora as she watched him stride away. *Wyatt, I'm counting on you*, she thought frantically, her heart twisting painfully. *I'm counting on you to find me and bring me back home, to kill this outlaw Cal and his partners for what they've done to me. And if not, I'll find a way to do it myself. All of it. By God, I will.*

She cocooned herself in the bedroll, clutching the blanket up to her chin. The darkness around her loomed heavy as coal. She had never felt more alone.

By the flickers of the fire she could see Zeke and Ray, already settled down to sleep, but Cal sat nonchalantly in the shadows, his back against a tree trunk, smoking a cigarette.

Tomorrow I'll make him sorry he ever started this—whatever this is. Tomorrow he'll find out he's made a huge mistake.

Sleep claimed Melora almost instantly, blotting out the image of Cal's tall, strong form, his ruthless calm, and his ice green eyes, plunging her deeply, thankfully into the safety of sweet black oblivion.

She never stirred until the morning.

3

Morning arrived all too soon for Melora.

She heard the scrape of boots on rock, the low rumbling of men's voices, the shuffling sounds of horses being led about and saddled. And at once the memory of last night's ordeal flooded back.

She didn't open her eyes at first. She waited, motionless in her thick, warm bedroll, pretending to be still asleep while Cal talked quietly with Ray and Zeke.

"I'm not taking any chances; we have to wipe out every trace of our camp," she heard him say in a low tone. A gust of damp wind drowned out his next words, but when it died down, she strained to pick up the rest. "... even though with luck the rain'll hit soon and wash away our tracks, we've got to make sure no one can pick up our trail."

"Don't you worry, Cal, there ain't no one going to have a notion where to start looking for that little lady. Not until you give 'em one, that is." It was Zeke's voice. Melora recognized its scratchy timbre at once.

"When we going to split up, Cal?" she heard Ray ask, over the clatter of what sounded like pots and pans. Was it her imagination or did she smell fresh-brewed coffee and frying meat and biscuits?

Then Cal spoke again. "We'll split up at Thunder Pass. If we ride hard, I reckon we ought to reach it before sunset."

As they moved off, too far away for her to make out their words, Melora thought of home, of Jinx at the breakfast table, asking Aggie where she was, of Aggie going upstairs to her room and finding her gone, her bed not slept in, of Wyatt learning that his bride had disappeared. . . .

Don't think about it, or you'll start to cry. Think about escaping, about finding your way back. You can outsmart Cal what's-his-name and those two idiots he's got working for him. You're not some namby-pamby who doesn't know how to shift for herself; you're Craig Deane's daughter and don't forget it.

Taking a deep breath, Melora opened her eyes and surreptitiously looked around.

The men were clustered near the horses, not looking her way. She lifted her head a moment, glancing swiftly about to get her bearings. This morning the clearing looked different from last night: larger, grassier, yet more secluded against the wall of the mountain. The sky was overcast, the air damp and chill.

In every direction were plains, vast rolling plains, rising gradually in the far northward distance to buttes and mountains.

The urge flashed through her to scramble up before anyone realized what was happening and to sprint through the copse of trees to her left in a bold dash for freedom. But something told her this was not the time. They had horses and guns. And daylight.

They would certainly find her.

But maybe after Thunder Pass, when Zeke and Ray had gone their separate ways, and there was only Cal to contend with . . .

Cal turned and saw her then. She gritted her teeth, sat up, and tossed her sleep-tousled curls from her eyes as he headed across the clearing with Zeke and Ray dogging his heels.

"Reckon you'd best get a move on, Miss Deane. We're headed out." His voice was as flat as the expression in his eyes. With his brown hair combed, wearing a fresh black shirt, vest, and trousers, and with the blue neckerchief knotted around his neck he looked refreshed, tough and alert, and more than ready for a hard day's ride. The thought flashed into her mind that he seemed to be a man who would always be ready for what life might throw at him.

"Yep," Ray added, rubbing his mustard yellow chin whiskers, "if you don't get some breakfast now, you won't have any grub till lunch." He slapped his hat against his portly thigh. "And riding all morning sure is hard enough work without doin' it on an empty stomach."

She shifted her gaze to Zeke, who was swilling coffee from a tin mug. His long, mousy face looked even thinner in the morning light than it had in the darkness, his black eyes peering sleepily out at her from over the rim of the mug.

"Well?" Melora barked at him. "Aren't you going to put in your two cents' worth?"

He seemed oddly distracted. "Why, sure, Miss Deane, if you want—"

"I *don't* want." Then Melora realized, too late, that the bedroll blanket had slipped down when she sat up. All three men were eyeing her and her sheer nightdress with decided interest.

Her cheeks flamed as she clutched the blanket to her. "The least you barbarians could do is provide me with some decent clothes!" It came out as a shriek.

Zeke peered at Cal. "Think maybe we should get her the stuff we brought along?"

"Might as well. Otherwise she'll shout the hills down." Cal shrugged, and threw Melora one flinty glance before turning back toward his saddlebag. Deliberately ignoring her, hoping she couldn't see his irresistible interest in her every move, he busied himself stowing various utensils and belongings in his pack and reminded himself that the less he had to do with his stunning kidnap victim, the better.

In truth he couldn't wait for her to get herself dressed in some decent clothes. It had been damned distracting last night, seeing her in that flimsy night-dress, but today was somehow even worse. By all rights she ought to look haggard today—pale, exhausted, and yes, damn it, frightened.

But Melora Deane, with her flushed cheeks, her sunshine hair, and her flashing eyes, seemed every bit as defiant and willful as she had last night.

This might not be as easy as I thought, Cal admitted to himself uneasily. *If I don't cow her into cooperation right quick, this could be a mighty long and unpleasant journey until we get where we're going.*

He swore under his breath as he slung his pack over his shoulder and headed toward his bay horse, Rascal.

When Melora saw Zeke carrying her rose and gray floral carpetbag and her small brass trunk, she scrambled up in disbelief, hauling the blanket with her. Well, thank heavens for small favors—she'd at least have her personal toiletries and some clothes. What very civilized kidnappers to have brought her traveling bags along, the traveling bags she'd packed to bring on her honeymoon!

At this thought, Melora's rage mounted until she felt she would choke on it. Before Zeke could hand the carpetbag to her, she snatched it from him, then glared as he and Ray shook their heads and chuckled.

"Don't you two smelly idiots have anything else to do than stand there and leer at me?" she demanded. "Go water the horses or shoot yourselves in the foot or . . . something!" Her gaze seared them with contemptuous loathing.

They just grinned, shrugged their shoulders, and

Zeke set the trunk down before he and Ray lumbered off.

Clutching her two bags, Melora started toward the trees. Pain shot through her thighs and calves with every step, but she resolutely ignored the stiffness and hurried forward until Cal's sharp voice stopped her in her tracks.

"Where do you think you're going?" Just as he had last night, he sprinted to her side and stepped in front of her, blocking her path.

"I have need of a few moments of privacy. You don't expect me to get dressed or to—to perform my toilette here, do you?"

His thumbs were hooked in his pockets. He was studying her suspiciously, his hat pushed back on his head. He'd changed to fresh clothes, but he hadn't bothered to shave, she noticed, and the rough stubble on his jaw and chin was darker and thicker than it had looked last night in the moonlight, giving him an even harsher aspect. But his words were surprisingly mild. "There's a stream just past those cottonwoods. Be my guest."

"Thank you!" she said sarcastically, but as she started to brush past him, his hand shot out and gripped her arm.

"Not so fast. There's something I want first."

Something he wanted? Melora tried to yank her arm away and failed. What could he possibly want?

As she usually did when she was uncertain or angry, she attacked. "There's something I want as well. To understand who the hell you are and why you've done this to me. Just what are you after?"

"There's no need for you to know that now. But I do need something from you."

Her heartbeat quickened as his eyes dropped from her face and flickered briefly down to the pulse throbbing in her throat.

"And what might that be?" she demanded in a low, dangerous tone.

"The cameo," he said grimly.

Surprise twitched through her. "What about it?"

"Give it to me."

She dropped both the carpetbag and the trunk, and her hands flew to her throat, cupping the ivory cameo protectively.

"Never. You can't have my cameo!"

Suddenly he looked even more dangerous than he had the night before, when he'd first taken off her blindfold.

"Can't I?" he asked so ominously that a distinctly unpleasant shiver needled down her spine.

Melora fought her fear. "You—you . . . Why, you're nothing but a low-down thief! You ought to be ashamed of yourself." She began backing away. "My fiancé gave me this cameo. It's precious to me. Isn't it bad enough you've ruined my wedding day? If you think I'm going to give you this—"

Cal advanced on her and seized both her hands. He pulled them ruthlessly downward. He did not let them go but held them immobile at her sides. The quiet warning in his eyes alarmed her—she had already sensed he was not a man to be lightly dismissed—and now, as she stared into those icy, determined green depths, her own eyes widened and she gazed at him in apprehensive silence.

"If you don't give it to me, Miss Deane, I'll take it. Is that what you want?"

I hate you, hate you, hate you. Melora raged silently, engulfed by drowning frustration. This tall, hard-eyed man had the inflexibility of an oak. He had stolen her from Wyatt and from Jinx and from everything she held dear. He had manhandled her and forced her to ride gagged, trussed, and blindfolded until she was more saddle sore than she'd ever been in her life. He had ruined her wedding day, he was taking her God knew where for no known reason, and now, now he wanted to steal the cameo Wyatt had given her with such love and tenderness.

Hatred and fury seared straight through to her heart. But just as Melora was about to burst out with a fiery reply, she remembered the words her father had frequently spoken to her when she was close to losing her temper beyond redemption.

Hold on to your hat, Mel. Think—think good and hard before you speak. It's smarter to use your brain, girl, and not let your tongue run away with you like a bronc that's been jabbed with a hot poker.

She swallowed back her retort and closed her eyes for a moment, trying to gather her composure. Since Pop's death she'd been working hard to correct her faults; she'd tried to grow up and run things as responsibly and even handedly as he had. She'd made an effort to learn how to curb her wildfire temper, to be patient and tolerant of others' weaknesses and stupidities, as he had been. Pop had often told her it had taken him forty years of his life to learn tolerance and control; Melora, upon taking over the ranch, had pledged to herself that she would become more like him immediately, no matter how hard it proved. So now she gave herself a lecture, struggling to subdue her instincts to lash out in anger.

Compose yourself. Think first; then speak.

So she thought. She thought about this lanky, despicable Cal with his cold green eyes. She thought about him swinging from a hangman's noose. She thought about his face turning a ghastly mottled purple, about him being cut down after a good long time and buried in a cheap pine casket on Boot Hill.

She thought the entire notion absolutely lovely.

Melora was smiling grimly as she opened her eyes. "Fine," she said, mimicking the tone he had used with her earlier. "If you want the cameo, here. Take it." Yet her trembling fingers fumbled on the clasp. "And I hope you're cursed every moment you have it. Which won't be long. When my fiancé catches up with you—"

She broke off at the sudden nasty gleam that entered his eyes. Melora stared at him, silent, trying to read the keenly attuned, deadly set of his face.

"Yes?" Cal prodded. He cocked his head to one side, mocking her. "Don't you want to threaten me with the dire punishments Mr. Wyatt Holden will exact?"

She studied him, her heart suddenly thudding. "I never told you Wyatt's name," she said slowly. "How do you know it?"

"I know lots of things, Miss Deane, and none of

them concerns you." He reached to take the cameo, which dangled in her hand.

Melora made a small moue but didn't try to cling to the cameo. It was so fragile she feared it would break in a struggle. But as Cal's fingers grazed hers, heat singed her, and she dropped the cameo into his hand as if it were a live coal.

Cal appeared not to experience any such sensation. He stared down at the delicate ivory cameo for a moment, then slowly closed his callused fist around it.

When he looked at her again, his gaze flicked over her with dismissive coldness. "Go get dressed."

His expression aloof and unreadable, he watched her gather up her carpetbag and her trunk and hurry off toward the trees.

Beneath that steely gaze, she was only too glad to escape to the shelter of the trees.

LESS than a quarter of an hour later Melora had washed in the stream, combed the tangles from her hair, and dressed in the only garments that would be serviceable in her present predicament. The mulberry traveling dress she had packed for her honeymoon would not do, nor would her aqua silk faille, nor the cream-colored walking gown with its delicately embroidered lace sleeves; all were left neatly folded within her brass trunk. She had to make do with her lace-up boots and the dark green velvet riding habit she'd originally worn at school in Boston; her father had bought it for her right before she went off and left him and Jinx for the very first time.

"You'll be riding in pretty parks now, Mel, not on

the ranch," he had told her, his eyes glistening with proud tears. "I don't want those eastern girls turning up their noses at my little girl. So you must have a right and proper riding habit, the kind they wear in the East. According to the catalogs at Naughton's, this here velvet thing is it."

The "velvet thing" had served her well. It was tightly cut, with black lace at the throat and wrists, and its fitted bodice and long split skirt accentuated the soft curves of her figure. The brilliant dark green was stunning with her deep golden hair, her tawny eyes, and her pale apricot coloring. No one in Boston had laughed at her. She had been courted and petted and invited to ride in the park so often one of her suitors had jokingly christened it Melora Park.

But little had she ever guessed she'd be wearing the very same riding habit during her kidnapping. *At least it's more appropriate than this damned nightdress,* Melora thought despondently as she folded the filmy white garment back inside her carpetbag atop two other traveling dresses. Suddenly she saw the barrel of her gun sticking out from beneath a rolled-up pair of clean drawers.

Her gun! She'd forgotten all about the little Colt pistol she'd packed in her carpetbag. And she had another gun in her trunk, Melora suddenly remembered, muffling a whoop of excitement, the tiny hideaway derringer she'd tucked beneath the jewelry pouch days ago.

How thoughtful of Cal and his pards to present her with her very own weapons!

Melora clasped the little Colt in her hand, the cool

steel sending a flow of confidence back into her. Pop
had always stressed to her two things: Be self-reliant
and be prepared. To that end she'd decided that one
small gun in each bag while traveling through rough-
and-tumble country to San Francisco for her honeymoon would be a prudent precaution. Now it seemed
like brilliant foresight.

But as she knelt beside the trunk to fish out the
derringer, voices from the clearing made her pause
and listen.

Those were Zeke's and Ray's voices, raised enough
so that she could hear them arguing about when the
rain would most likely start and whether they would
be setting out for the day's ride before noon. They
sounded edgy and impatient as they waited for her,
and she suddenly realized that at any moment one of
them—or Cal—would come to get her.

*Forget the derringer. You have to get out of here
now.* Springing to her feet, she surveyed the vicinity
with a darting glance. All her senses felt as if they
were on fire.

She'd already determined that there was little cover
in the sagebrush-studded plains north of the clearing.
But ahead, where the stream trickled past some rocks
and curved down an incline, she saw thickening
clumps of alders and what looked like the beginning
of a wood. The ground was nearly level here, and the
denser overhang of trees was only a hundred yards
ahead.

She had to try. She had her Colt, her wits, and her
knowledge of the land. And with any luck she might
also have a precious few moments' head start.

Like a squirrel, she dashed along the stream toward the thicker line of trees, her boots flying across the short grama grass. When she reached the beginning of the wood, she threw a glance over her shoulder.

Not a soul in sight. They hadn't started looking for her yet.

Run.

Heart pounding, she plunged ahead.

4

"**I** *know* when rain's comin', Ray; my bunions tell me every damned time, and I guarantee you, there'll be a downpour before noon, or my name ain't Zeke McCloud."

"You're wrong, Zeke. Wrong, wrong, wrong. I'll bet you any damned thing you want, I'll bet you ten dollars that it don't rain till after sunset."

"You know I don't bet money, Ray," Zeke shouted, stomping directly up to the other man, glaring into his face. "My ma taught me never to bet money. Now if you want to bet, I'll bet you somethin' else, something like your saddle. I fancy that new saddle of yours—"

"Quiet!" Cal thundered.

They stopped arguing and stared at him.

"How long has she been getting dressed?"

"Oh, I'd say a quarter of an hour, mebbe," Zeke answered, tapping the face of his pocket watch.

"Half an hour or I'm a mule," Ray countered, bristling.

"You're wrong, Ray. Wrong, wrong, wrong. It's only been—"

"Will you both shut up?" Cal stalked furiously around the clearing. "I just don't know. How long does it take a woman to . . . get dressed and all and make herself presentable?"

"Beats me. Long time, I reckon, based on what I remember from that wife I used to have—"

"Ray, you were never home long enough to know how long it took her to get dressed," Zeke pointed out disgustedly, then broke off upon seeing the wrath etched across Cal's usually calm face. "Don't *you* know, Cal?"

"I don't know a damned thing about women, or I wouldn't be asking the pair of you," he muttered, his gaze fixed on the spot where Melora had disappeared with her bags. "But I'm getting suspicious of our little Miss Deane."

"You mean she might have tried to get away?"

"That's exactly what I mean." Cal paced back and forth again, his scowl deepening as several crows circled over the clearing, cawing loudly in the heavy gray sky. The horses whickered, a damp wind sent tumbleweed rolling, and still there was no sign of Melora.

"I'll wring her damned neck." Cal started toward the trees.

"She wouldn't . . ." Zeke protested doubtfully.

"Naw, how could she hope to get away?"

"She's gone!" Cal shouted through the trees.

Zeke and Ray gazed at each other in horror and then dodged after him.

As Cal neared the brass trunk and carpetbag left abandoned near the stream, he caught a fleeting glimpse of green cloth disappearing within the wood up ahead. A muscle in his jaw tensed as he sprang forward.

This is what I get for giving her privacy, for trusting her at all, he thought as he bolted in pursuit of the slender fleeing figure, which he could just keep in sight as it darted through the tight maze of trees. *Well, from now on, it'll be a whole different story,* he vowed. Red-hot anger churned through him as he shouldered past branches and whipping leaves. He'd keep her in sight every minute; he wouldn't give her another chance to do something so foolhardy and troublesome as to try to escape—on foot—in the middle of the wilderness, without so much as a cabin or an outpost for at least thirty miles.

Behind him he could hear Zeke and Ray scrambling to follow, but he didn't bother looking back. His legs were long and powerful; he was faster than she was, and he was gaining on her. It was loco for her to think she could get away for long. When he caught up with her, he'd teach her not to try.

Melora plunged frantically through the trees and brush, heedless of the branches slapping at her face and clothes. She could hear Cal crashing after her and risked one precious second to glance wildly back at him. He was catching up!

Fear leaped like a flame within her. She fired a warning gunshot over her shoulder, then kept running, frantic as a hare being ruthlessly hunted down by a hawk.

Her breath came in short, heaving gasps, her lungs ached with the effort of running, but she kept on, plummeting ahead with a wild, delirious need to escape, to be free, somehow magically to rescue herself and return to the way things were yesterday. To the happiness of her wedding day, and the company of her sister, and the comfort and security of home . . . and Wyatt's arms.

She gave a half sob. Cal was gaining on her.

Thighs aching, she ran faster, her hands out before her as if in supplication to the land to swallow her up.

But suddenly, just as she half turned to fire again, a huge weight hit her and knocked her to the ground. She toppled with an anguished cry.

Cal broke her fall with his own body, twisting in midair so that she landed half atop him. But they didn't stay in that position for long. Swiftly he rolled her over, wrenched the gun away, and pinioned her beneath him, catching her arms above her head in a viselike grip.

"Just what in hell do you think you're doing?" he demanded. "I'm damned if I have time for these stupid tricks!"

"Let me up!"

"No chance, lady. You're in a lot of trouble."

Desperately Mel tried to buck, to twist and wrench and somehow squirm free, but her spirits sank as she realized the futility of it. He was far larger and stronger than she, and like it or not, she didn't have much choice but to lie there beneath him and wait for him to decide what to do with her next.

She went perfectly still.

Cal shifted slightly, pinning her all the more securely. The hardness of his body pressed against hers sent a strange tight heat through her belly.

"Well, what are you waiting for?" she cried at last, wishing she could wipe the faint sheen of perspiration from her face or somehow toss aside the heavy coils of her hair, which had fallen across her cheeks in her struggle and were now dangling before her eyes and twisted around her nose and jaw. But she couldn't move.

"Go ahead and get on with it!" she continued, biting her lip. "Aren't you going to hog-tie me again or shoot me with my own gun or—"

"I'd like to take you over my knee."

At this, panic set in, and she started struggling again. "Don't you try it, you greasy, disgusting saddle tramp, you . . . kidnapper, you thief! I'll make you sorry you were ever born!"

With his jaw set, Cal watched her lovely face twist and contort with the hopeless effort of trying to free herself. She was a spunky little hellion—he had to admit that, and he could almost admire it—but he was wondering just what it *would* take to intimidate her.

Maybe a herd of stampeding buffalo. Or a charging cavalry regiment. Then again, maybe not.

She went still again, exhausted and breathing hard. Her hair drifted in tangled skeins across her face.

Releasing one of her hands, Cal reached down and shifted the heavy golden tendrils aside, laying bare once more the finely chiseled features, which were so dainty and so feminine, the straight, firm nose, the lush lips the color of baby roses, and the alluring eyes that blazed at him from beneath slim, gracefully arced brows. Whew. He felt his breath choking deep inside his lungs.

She was something all right. An enchantress. Her magnificent hair slid through his hands like the finest silk. The finest, most richly textured, unbelievably soft silk, and despite all of the hardships she'd endured since last night, those lush curls still smelled faintly of lavender.

And so did she.

No doubt Miss Melora Deane of the great Weeping Willow Ranch bathed in perfumed water with flower-scented soap, he thought harshly. No doubt she was accustomed to the finer things in life, to being petted and indulged, and to getting her own way. He'd seen *that* plain enough; she was obviously as spoiled and headstrong as they came.

Well, now she'd just have to get accustomed to a rougher life—at least for a while.

And that was that.

Grimly he stared down at her defiant face as she lay beneath him, her skin damp with sweat, her wide-set eyes fixed on him with a mixture of hatred and apprehension, and suddenly, unexpectedly, pity stirred.

She was putting on a good front, game as could be, but he'd have bet every gold piece he owned—which was not too many, unfortunately—that beneath it all, right at this very moment, she was scared to death. He could feel her softness, all the delicate curves and hollows of her body, and her ultimate feminine vulnerability touched his conscience. She probably was wondering right about now if he meant to rape her, Cal realized abruptly. He adjusted his weight so as not to crush her, and—he admitted to himself—to lessen the risk of growing even further aroused in case she decided to start once again with those enticing, wriggling movements. Yet he kept her securely pinned, his long frame heavy upon her. He had no intention of letting her up until they had a few things straight between them.

"I order you to get off me right now!" She tried again, clearly desperate.

Cal shook his head. "Calm down and listen to me, Melora," he said, surprising himself and her by the use of her given name. But at that moment Zeke and Ray rushed up, panting and sweating like a pair of flogged pigs.

"Need any help, Cal?" Zeke rasped out, coming to a halt a few feet from where Cal and Melora were lying on the ground.

"Does he look like he needs any help?" Ray snapped in exasperation. He yanked his hat off and began fanning his face. Sweat droplets glistened in his yellow whiskers. "Since when would Cal need help with a mite of a female like this? Zeke, you're a damned fool."

"Miss Deane and I are about to come to an understanding." Cal spoke roughly, his eyes still riveted upon Melora's. "You two go back and finish packing up the camp. We're riding out the moment we get back."

"D-don't go," Melora called out feebly, turning her head to gaze imploringly at the other two men. "He's going to strike me. Beat me . . . Please save me . . ."

They stopped in their tracks, taken aback, and threw uncertain glances at Cal.

"I threatened to spank her," he said impatiently. "It was just a warning, not an intention—*so far*," he added meaningfully, fixing her with a scowl.

To her dismay, both Zeke and Ray nodded, grinning at each other, for once in agreement.

"Sure, reckon we know you better than to think you'd strike a woman, Cal," Zeke said respectfully.

"No, he'd just kidnap one," Melora said.

Ray shook his head, staring down at her sorrowfully. "Cal here is a fine person, miss. Fine as they come. And I can tell you he's got more patience than half the men in this territory all put together. But he's hell when he's crossed. My advice to you is: Don't cross him."

"Yep, behave yourself," Zeke advised her anxiously. "Do what you're told. And when Cal's through with this here plan of his, he'll take you home safe and sound."

Cal flicked an amused glance between the two of them. "I reckon I couldn't have said it better myself, boys." He grinned. "And now, let me straighten out a few things with the lady so we can make tracks before sundown.''

Melora waited apprehensively as Zeke and Ray tramped away. Once again she found herself alone in the woods with Cal, alone but for a squirrel nibbling a nut in the tree branches high above.

"Are you ready to listen to reason?"

I'm ready to spit in your eye, she thought, her chest swelling with indignation at being treated in this manner, but she remembered in time and with great bitterness that it wasn't always wise to speak one's mind, so instead she gave him a stiff nod.

"Then get up and listen to me," Cal said shortly. He shifted off her and got to his feet, scooping up her Colt and pocketing it in one deft motion. Immediately Melora pushed herself up to a sitting position, rebellion simmering in her eyes.

Cal noticed how her fingers were splayed in the dirt below; he half expected her to grab a handful of it and fling it in his face. Or try to.

But she didn't. She took deep breaths, obviously trying to keep a lid on her temper.

"Let me explain a few things to you before we ride out. It'll make things easier on all of us."

"I'm listening."

"Believe it or not, Melora, I don't want to hurt you. None of us do. But you're not getting away, and you're not going back home until I say so."

"And when will that be?"

"When I've accomplished what I've set out to do. Maybe a few weeks from now."

"A few weeks from now?" she cried, surging to

her feet and confronting him with her hands on her hips. "Today is my wedding day, you ignorant jackass!"

"No, ma'am, it's not."

"Well, it's supposed to be!"

"That's the point," he said softly, a gleam entering his eyes.

Melora stared at him as he hooked his thumbs in his gun belt and looked smug. "You're not doing this to hurt me," she said slowly, her face paling as the truth hit her. "You're doing it to hurt Wyatt. *Why*?"

Cal regarded her in silence a moment. Then he shrugged, but not before she'd seen the taut anger register in his face at the mention of Wyatt's name. "That doesn't concern you."

"Doesn't concern me? What in hell are you talking about?" Unconsciously she repeated her father's often used phrase. "You drag me off from my home, from my little sister, from my wedding—and you say it doesn't concern me?"

"My reasons are my own business," he rejoined coolly, and pushed his hat farther back on his head. "The only thing you need to remember is that if you cooperate, don't make any trouble, and don't try any more stupid attempts to escape, you'll be fine. But let me ask you a question."

"Can I stop you?"

He ignored this and stepped closer, watching her face. "Do you think your father will set up a search party for you, or will he leave it to Wyatt? Or will they join together?"

All the color drained from Melora's face. Her lips

were dry. Suddenly she remembered that odd comment he had made last night at the ranch, about not disturbing her father while he was smuggling her out of the house.

"My father is dead," she whispered.

Now it was Cal's turn to stare, to go still and white as a statue. "Craig Deane? He's dead?" She saw the shock register, saw his sharp intake of breath. "I swear I didn't know," he muttered, and paced away from her, then hurried back. "I thought you were . . . living under his roof, that you—do you mean you're running that ranch by yourself?"

"More or less. And I'm also responsible for taking care of my little sister," she informed him bitingly. Still, she was puzzled by his reaction. He looked stunned. And upset. "What difference does it make to you?" she asked stiffly.

"Maybe if I'd known you were living at the ranch all alone, without any male protection, I wouldn't have taken you." He shook his head ruefully. "Despite what you think, I'm not the kind of bully who goes around picking on lone women. But I thought— Oh, hell, it doesn't matter now."

"Yes, it does. Because you can still make things right—by letting me go."

"No. Sorry, but I can't do that." His expression was grim. "Now that this thing is started, I've got to see it through to the end. I reckon there's no turning back, Melora, not for either of us."

He took her arm. "Come on. Time to break camp."

"I can walk back myself if you don't mind." She

shook off his hand. "But I'm not going anywhere until you tell me exactly and in detail what this is all about." Sticking out her chin, she kicked at the dirt for emphasis and smiled tightly when some of it landed on his boot. "I won't give you any peace until you tell me why you kidnapped me and what you have against Wyatt, so you might as well do it now rather than later. You see, it runs in the Deane blood never to give up."

His scowl told her he was losing patience. *Good*, she decided. The sooner he lost patience, the sooner he would just give in and tell her what she needed to know. She'd learned long ago that with her indomitable will most people found it easier to placate her than to oppose her. She estimated that this idiotic Cal with whatever lamebrained scheme against Wyatt he was hatching would do the same.

"My fiancé happens to be one of the finest men I've ever known"—she went on, tossing her head—"and if you think I'm just going to stand by and let you continue with whatever low-down, dirty plan you have in mind for him, you're dead wrong! I won't let you use me to hurt Wyatt. I'll stop you dead in your tracks."

To judge by the icy mask of his features and the glitter in his eyes, she'd touched a nerve. And when he spoke, his voice held a distinctly unpleasant edge that further confirmed it. "Don't bet your ranch on it, Miss Deane."

"I would bet my ranch on it. I'd stake everything on it. And if you won't tell me what you're up to, we can just stand here all day because I'm not going anywhere until you—ohhh!''

Before she realized what was happening, he suddenly seized her and with a low grunt tossed her like a sack of grain over his shoulder.

"What are you *doing*? Set me down this minute!"

Ignoring her, he stomped back through the trees toward the stream.

"Set me down! You obnoxious, arrogant, insufferable snake, you stop and set me down right this very minute! I'm perfectly capable of walking! I demand—"

"Shut up." He ignored her ineffective attempts to land blows upon his broad back and continued to stride past rocks and shrub. "You are by far the most spoiled, insufferable, irritating woman I've ever met, and I don't have either the time or the stomach for your tantrums," he said grimly. "Now behave yourself, or when we reach the stream, instead of letting you retrieve your bags, I'll throw you and them into the water."

"You wouldn't!"

"Try me."

Melora stopped struggling. She bit her lower lip furiously and closed her eyes tight as her teeth clacked in her mouth at the jostling movements. She tried very hard to picture Cal dead in a coffin on Boot Hill.

Her demeaning and uncomfortable posture only heightened her already severe loathing for this man. Right now she should be at the church, twirling about

in her wedding dress; instead she was stranded in the
wild with a pair of no-good saddle tramps and with
Cal no-last-name, who was by far the most detestable
man ever to breathe air.

Wait. Wait for the right moment, she told herself,
her eyes sparking with vengeful designs. *Then you'll
show him he can't do this to Mel Deane and get away
with it.*

When at last he lowered her down beside her bags,
he set her on her feet with a thump that rattled her
teeth.

"Hurry up. If you want those bags to come along
with you, pick 'em up and bring 'em," Cal instructed
coolly.

"Let me close this one first." Mel flung out the
words between gritted teeth, but instead of closing her
trunk, she dipped her hand inside in one quick movement, shoved aside her jewelry pouch, and yanked out
her derringer.

"Freeze, mister."

She pointed the gun at his heart. All around them
hung an early-morning gray mist. A spray of drizzle
dampened Melora's rapt face as she came slowly to
her feet, the gun held steadily, aimed at his chest.

Cal sighed. "Don't you ever give up?"

"It's loaded. And I'm an excellent shot."

"I'll wager you are."

"My father taught me himself." She clicked off
the safety deliberately. "Now you're going to talk and
I'm going to listen. And when you've explained the
reason for this little adventure to me, if I decide not
to shoot you, I might just let you live long enough

to turn over one of those nice rested horses to me
and—"

"Go ahead and shoot," Cal ordered.

Her smile was thin. "Don't tempt me."

To her fury he took a step toward her. "I don't
think you have it in you."

A taunt. The man was taunting her. Melora kept a
lid on her temper with an effort. She had to stay calm,
to remain in control. There was a fine sheen of sweat
on her upper lip, despite the coolness of the day, but
she spoke with utter composure. "Then you're loco,
Cal. Because I'd as soon shoot you as let you go
further in this plan to hurt Wyatt."

She nodded at him, her hands perfectly steady on
the gun. "I'll shoot you to protect myself and him,
and it will give me immense pleasure to do it."

"You're going to have to prove that."

And with that he took another step toward her. And
another.

Damn him! Melora backed up several steps. She
was breathing hard. "Halt!" she commanded as the
color fled her cheeks.

He kept advancing.

There was a roaring in her ears. For just an instant
her finger trembled on the trigger. "Damn you, halt!"

Suddenly he leaped at her, lunging for her gun
hand just as Melora did the only thing she could do.
She squeezed the trigger.

Her shot missed by inches as he seized her wrist
and twisted it, then yanked the gun clean away.

A wail of frustration shrieked from her throat.

"Just for that," Cal said evenly, "we leave the

bags. You'll have to get by with that fancy riding outfit and nothing else for the next few weeks."

"No!"

"I gave you a chance."

"You would have done the same thing!"

The truth of it flickered momentarily in his face. Then his hard features closed up, becoming impenetrable as granite once again.

"If you want them, bring them." He snapped out the words like a cavalry captain. "But do it fast."

And no sooner did they reach the clearing, she trudging along with both bags in tow, Cal stalking behind her, carrying her gun, than Ray and Zeke brought up the horses, and the sun showed at last a sickly glimmer in the grayish blue sky.

And off they rode.

NO breakfast. Not even a sip of coffee. Melora's stomach rumbled its protest as she gripped the reins of the extra horse her kidnapper had so thoughtfully provided for her. Cal had everything figured out. He rode ahead of her, Zeke and Ray behind. There was nothing for her to do but keep going.

They rode for hours across sagebrush plains dotted with wildflowers. When they finally stopped at noontime, Melora sat off by herself under an aspen, hungrily devouring the hard biscuits and dried meat Zeke brought her.

Then more riding. They were headed northeast, she realized sinkingly. Toward the Black Hills? The hours dragged on, and the grayness of the sky lifted. The sun grew stronger, arcing across it. Melora's stiff body ached with weariness.

But Cal and the others showed no sign of slowing or stopping.

Then, at last, the beautiful sunset light cast its radiance across a sky of dusky purple and rose. At a place called Thunder Pass the party halted, and Zeke and Ray prepared to leave.

"Where are they going?" she asked Cal, suddenly realizing that tonight she would be all alone with him under the stars.

"Home." He then surprised her by adding a bit more information—rare for him. "They've done me a good turn by helping me get things under way, but now it's time to strike out separately. Of course," he added cryptically, "they'll do me one more little favor along their journey, and then their part in this is done."

In silence she watched as Zeke and Ray shook hands with Cal. She couldn't help reflecting on how different they were from him. Yet she sensed a warmth, a special bond between Cal and these two shambling, grimy pards of his.

"We'll never forget you, Cal," Zeke muttered, his voice thick with emotion.

Ray nodded in agreement. "Anytime you need somethin', Cal, you just send for us. You know we can never do enough to repay you."

"You have repaid me. The slate's clean." Cal locked gazes with each of them in turn, and then suddenly he grinned, a grin so boyish and open it transformed his face. "Try to keep out of trouble, you two. I might not be around to save your scrawny necks next time."

There were answering grins and chuckles and some more banter exchanged. She sensed their comradeship, their reluctance to part.

Yet eventually part they did. But not before Zeke and Ray gave her a few words of advice.

"Don't cause him no more trouble, you hear? He's too nice a feller. If you'd just stop fretting so much and go along, why, the two of you might even become friends. A pretty thing like you and a nice young feller like that?" Zeke winked.

"I reckon I'd rather jump off Devils Tower," Melora retorted.

Ray wagged a finger in her face. "Well, maybe you can't be friends, exactly, but don't complain so much and don't keep yammering at him either. Cal doesn't like that. He's a quiet sort."

"Is he?" Melora's eyes lit up. "Well, then I'll have to see to it that I chatter day and night and make his life every bit as miserable as he's made mine."

Sadly they shook their heads at her. "Good-bye, Missy Deane. And good luck."

Wish your precious Cal good luck, Melora thought savagely, yet as she watched them ride off due east, apprehension set in.

Now she was alone in the middle of nowhere with Cal. She might have been able to wheedle or bamboozle the other two somehow, if given half a chance, but she doubted Cal would fall prey to any tricks.

As she stole a sideways glance at him while he

grabbed hold of her mount's reins and started off again, a new thought passed through her mind.

He would have to sleep, wouldn't he?

Somewhere inside her, hope awoke.

Now there wasn't anyone with whom he could trade off keeping watch. And while he slept, she might find a chance to escape. No, she *would* find a chance to escape.

Jinx, Wyatt, I'm coming home, she vowed silently.

And as the horses galloped toward the darkening line of hills in the distance, she wondered what they all were thinking in Rawhide, if a search party was combing the area for her, if anyone had a clue to what had become of her.

Poor Wyatt, she thought in dismay as she pictured how desperate he must be. *And my poor frightened Jinx.*

Her chest tightened with anxiety as she thought of her sister. Jinx had only Aggie to hold her and soothe her now. *But Wyatt will take care of them*, she told herself as the last rays of light glowed feebly in the sky. *He'll take care of both of them. Together he and Aggie will reassure Jinx and do their best to allay her fears.*

But Melora knew her sister. Jinx would be so lonely, so scared. She had lost Pop, she'd lost the use of her legs, and now she'd lost Melora.

"*I hate you*," Melora screamed, and Cal turned in the saddle to stare at her.

Tears streamed down her face, but Melora didn't care.

She saw his gaze narrow in the fading light. Then

he swung back around and resumed the business of
riding.

Tonight, Melora promised herself, her hands tight
on the reins as she choked back her sobs. *I'll get away
from him tonight—or die trying.*

5

Aggie wiped her hands on her apron as Jinx stared disinterestedly down at the bowl of beef stew before her on the kitchen table.

"Jinx, honey, try to eat. Starving yourself won't bring Mel home any quicker."

"Not hungry."

"But it'll do you good—"

"Please, I'm not hungry, Aggie." The child's voice came out in a tortured whisper.

Sighing, Aggie put her arms around the girl in the invalid chair. "There, there," she murmured, not knowing what else to say. She exchanged a sad glance with Wyatt, who'd arrived at the ranch a few moments earlier with nothing to report.

He'd been combing the valley all day with several

dozen men from town and some neighboring ranches. No one had found anything.

"Wyatt, how about you? You really ought to sit down and have yourself a decent meal too—" she began, but he held up a hand.

"You're sure that nobody heard anything? Anything at all?" he demanded for the twentieth time. "Aggie, Jinx, you're sure?"

They both nodded. Jinx idly picked up her spoon, then set it back down on the gingham tablecloth, fighting back tears.

"Melora would never have gone away on her own—never. She wanted to marry you so much. And she'd never leave on purpose without saying goodbye," she added, biting her lip.

"That's right," Aggie murmured, smoothing the girl's long red-gold curls. "She sure wouldn't."

Wyatt wheeled away from the table and strode back and forth across the gleaming wood floor. *Poor man*, Aggie thought, ready sympathy welling in her chest. Exhaustion was stamped across his vividly handsome face, his eyes were bleary, and his boots were caked with dust. He'd been in shock when he'd heard the news that Melora was missing, and he hadn't stopped searching for her since.

Beyond the white lace kitchen curtains, darkness cloaked the land and the distant sound of coyotes filled the night.

"I have a bad feeling about this," Wyatt muttered.

Aggie glanced at him in alarm and cleared her throat. "Wyatt, please."

He continued as if she hadn't spoken, pacing with

long, leonine strides, his long-jawed, darkly handsome face oblivious of the child watching and listening so attentively.

"Those tracks we found showed there were several horses. Add that to the fact that Melora's reticule and money pouch were still on her dresser, and it's clear as blazes someone took her." He spun toward Aggie, burning anger in his eyes. "Someone came right into this house and grabbed her!"

"Who—who would do that?" Jinx's small fingers whitened on the invalid chair. "And why?"

"I'm not sure, honey, but I do know Melora is going to be all right," Aggie said quickly. "Wyatt, stop scaring the child," she added, and at last the sharp note in her voice penetrated his self-involvement.

The cold, frightening fury left his face, and he visibly forced his muscles to relax. Suddenly he looked once more the friendly, charming man they both knew, the one who'd come calling on Melora all spring and summer.

"You're right, Aggie. My apologies." He went to the girl and knelt beside her chair. "Jinx, honey, there's nothing to worry about. The other search party will be checking in soon, and if they haven't found her, then I will. I'll start again first thing tomorrow, and I swear to you, honey, no matter what the cost, no matter how many men I have to hire or how far I have to search, I'll bring your sister home."

"Promise?" Jinx looked so hopeful, so desperate to believe that Aggie's heart nearly broke.

"Promise." Wyatt stood. "She will be my wife,"

he said, the purposeful light glinting bright as cold metal in his eyes.

Jinx leaned back in her invalid chair, and a small shudder trickled up her spine. Instead of making her feel reassured, something about Wyatt Holden made her feel uneasy. But she didn't know why. He was tall and strong and nice. He was smart and knew how to get things done. And he was promising to find Melora, so he could marry her after all.

But she was uneasy all the same.

"I'm going to say a prayer that Melora comes home safe," she whispered, and then peered at Aggie. "Can I go to bed now?"

"You sure can. Wyatt, I'll be right back after I get Jinx tucked in nice and cozy."

"Take your time, Aggie. I'm going back into town to meet with Sheriff Coughlin."

When Aggie had pushed the invalid chair through the kitchen doorway, Wyatt Holden slammed his fist down on the counter. Cursing under his breath, he strode out onto the porch and surveyed the encompassing blackness with a scowl.

Layers of emotion churned beneath his stolid exterior. Fury, bewilderment, disbelief that his bride had been snatched almost out from under his nose all roiled through his blood.

This was by far the most humiliating day of his life. Right now he and Melora should be in their hotel suite. She should be in his bed, naked and writhing beneath him. She should be all his, his alone.

Instead she was out there with some other man or

other men. What the hell were they doing with her—
to her?

They're all dead men, he vowed to the stars glowing above.

Dead men.

Because no one touched what was his. No one in-
terfered with his plans. And no one—no one—took
anything of value from him and lived to tell the tale.

And Melora Deane, he reflected, as he surveyed
the dark breadth of the Weeping Willow Ranch with
eyes hard as stones, was valuable indeed.

Too valuable to lose.

He would find her.

6

Cal halted at dusk on a plateau shaded by pine trees. Just beyond the trees, a stream murmured over smooth stones. *A soothing sound*, Melora thought wearily as she slid from the saddle and her feet touched hard earth.

"Collect some wood for the fire," Cal ordered without sparing her a glance. He was already leading the horses toward the stream.

As Melora picked up a long, thin stick, she thought how dearly she'd like to hit him with it. But for now she'd best lie low and comply. Better to allay his suspicions and give the impression she wasn't going to rebel anymore; then he might relax his guard enough to give her the opportunity she needed.

Besides, after no breakfast and a quick, unsatisfying lunch, she needed a good, hearty dinner to give her strength for whatever scheme she concocted tonight. If she refused to help with making camp, Cal just might take it out of her rations.

But that wasn't entirely fair, she told herself. Despite all he'd done to her, he wasn't cruel—only pigheaded and determined to carry her off for some idiotic reason. Eyeing him as she stooped for another twig, she studied his lanky frame, the deep muscles of his chest and shoulders, the unruly mop of chestnut hair that fell into his eyes as he lifted the saddles from the horses. He was the picture of tall, cool efficiency, she decided, wishing he were as muddleheaded as Zeke and Ray. He was quick yet gentle with the horses, she noted, watching as he stroked the muzzle of his bay, Rascal.

What did he want from Wyatt? Why had he spoiled their wedding and dragged her off this way? The questions plagued her all through the time she gathered the twigs and made preparations for their supper. But until Cal let slip a bit more information, she knew she would have no answers.

It was a delicious supper. Cal shot a rabbit and roasted it on a spit, and with it they had canned beans and hardtack and coffee. She and Cal didn't speak at all during the meal, and that suited her just fine. She was thinking, thinking of how she would escape.

And by the time she licked the last bit of rabbit meat from her fingers and drained the final drops of coffee from her tin cup, she had a plan.

She wouldn't fall asleep tonight; she'd only pretend to sleep. She'd wait until Cal dropped off, and then she'd put one of the saddles over her shoulder, make her way to the horses, and take the mare she'd ridden today, Sunflower, who knew her and, she hoped, wouldn't whicker or snort or some such thing. It would be necessary to lead Sunflower off a ways as quietly as could be before saddling up and mounting, but she would do it.

And then she'd be off.

Melora knew that they'd been headed steadily north and east, so she'd ride back just the opposite. It might take a few days without food and water, but if she were lucky she'd hit a town or run into some friendly traveler who'd point her in the right direction and perhaps share some rations with her. . . .

It's a stupid plan, Melora told herself frankly, seeds of fear sprouting inside her as she stared into her empty cup. She knew how easy it was to get lost, to end up dead of starvation or thirst when you set out without maps or supplies, or you could run into outlaws or Indians, you could end up with vultures picking at your bones. . . .

But a voice inside her told her she had to try to get away. Melora Deane could not allow herself to be meekly borne off from her home and her family like some kind of helpless lamb. She had to fight. She had to get back.

At least she had to *try*.

Sighing, she tried to think of the bright side: She was strong, she was an able rider, and she knew this land. For the rest, she'd have to rely on luck and her own wits.

The cleanup chores were finished, and the deep

violet night sky bloomed with tiny silver stars when Cal finally spoke to her, other than to tell her to scrub the plates in the stream and repack the cantina.

"Time to turn in. We'll be making an early start tomorrow. Sunup."

I'll be starting out earlier than that, Melora thought, but she only nodded to him and watched from beneath her eyelashes as he threw down his bedroll not far from the fire. Before she could make a move to fetch hers and unroll it, however, he did it for her, placing it right beside his own.

"I don't think so, Cal," Melora told him haughtily. "I'll be sleeping as far from you as I can get—"

"Which isn't very far." He cut her off, and suddenly her blood froze as she saw the rope in his hand.

"What—what are you doing with that? You're not going to tie me up again?"

"Just at night," he said grimly, deliberately not looking into her dismayed face. "So we can both get some shut-eye. Otherwise I'll have to sleep with one eye open so you can't escape, and you probably won't doze off at all, watching for an opportunity. This way both of us can just relax."

"No!" She scrambled up and backed away from him, her gaze fixed in dread on the rope. "No, don't do this, Cal. I promise not to try to escape. So there's no need."

"I can't trust you, Melora. There's no point in arguing. You see, in my family I'm known as the stubborn one. That ought to give you a clue. So let's not waste time."

Even as Melora thrust her hands behind her back

and pressed her lips together, determined not to make things any easier for him, he seized her, yanked her hands before her, and wound the rope around them in a flashing movement that made her eyes darken with anger. She couldn't follow the pattern of the knot, and when he secured the other end of the four-foot rope around his belt, she could have spit with frustration.

So much for escaping.

And just how would she manage to get any sleep at all, tethered to this arrogant outlaw, who probably snored to raise the dead?

When he dropped down without warning onto his bedroll, she was dragged down to her knees. Tears of desolation and helplessless pooled along her lower lashes.

But I'd rather die than ask him for mercy or pity or anything at all, she thought fervently. After all, she was a Deane, and the Deanes were as tough as old boot leather.

She threw herself down on the bedroll, stifled a sniffle, and closed her eyes.

But, oh, she was conscious of Cal's long, hard-muscled frame beside hers. Strange, she ought to be sleeping alongside Wyatt in a feather bed tonight, feeling the warmth, the solidity of his body, know-ing the gentleness of his hands, his kisses, and learn-ing what it was to love a man. Instead she was freezing to death on this godforsaken plateau, trussed up like a calf waiting to be branded, sleeping beside a stranger with no heart and the coldest eyes she'd ever seen.

Suddenly she felt a hand grip her shoulder, and

lightning seemed to strike through to the bone. She drew in her breath as he rolled her over, and Melora tensed, every muscle taut for battle.

Cal held her by the shoulders, studying her face. "You're crying."

"Don't be ridiculous!"

In the waxy starlight she saw his lip curl. "Uh-huh."

"I don't understand," she said in a low tone, wishing she could wipe the moisture from her eyes, "how you can tear a bride away from her groom before their w-wedding. Haven't you ever wanted to get married?"

He gave a scornful laugh. "Can't say as I have."

"Haven't you ever loved someone?" Melora cringed as her voice broke, but she forced herself to continue. "Loved someone so much it hurts inside?"

"No." Cal's tone was as hard as the gates of hell. "No one besides my family."

"Family? You mean *you* have a family?"

Silence. Then he answered at last. "A pretty big one, matter of fact, though it used to be bigger." His thumb gently stroked away the tears that had slipped down her cheeks. "Look, Princess, I may not have grown up rich and spoiled like you, the owner of a huge, prosperous spread, but we're not all that different. I have family that I care about, just as I imagine you care for your . . . sister?"

"Yes," she whispered. "Her name is Jinx."

"What I'm doing right now, I'm doing for *my* family. Because—oh, hell, it's a long story, and you're not interested anyway. Let's just say that maybe in the end I'm doing you a favor. Maybe your not marrying Wyatt Holden is the best thing that could ever happen to you."

Melora jerked away, a deep, shuddering breath running through her. "You're crazy!"

"Could be." Cal restrained the urge to stroke her hair. It glinted like spun gold in the faint light that crackled off the campfire. He wanted to plunge his fingers through those thick, glorious strands, to bend close and kiss the back of her neck, to inhale the flower fragrance of her . . .

There was something about her, something that was getting to him. Something besides her beauty, her spunk, the graceful, decisive way she moved, the elegant tilt of her head.

No, he'd never loved anyone. He'd known plenty of whores and plenty of virgins; he'd slept with the former and steered clear of the latter. But a woman whom he could talk to, understand, tell his troubles to, take care of, kiss, hold . . . love?

Never.

What the hell was she doing to him? Why was he thinking about all this now, when he should be getting shut-eye, so they could make an early start in the morning?

Sunup, he'd told her, and sunup it would be.

"Get some sleep. We'll cover rough country tomorrow."

"Where are we headed?" she ventured to ask, still trying to sort out what he'd said about his family and about Wyatt.

He hesitated for a moment before answering. "Guess you might as well know. The Black Hills."

"Cal, *why*?" She lunged up, shivering in the frosty air that whistled through the pines. The wrenching note in her voice was not from cold or fear but from sheer tortured frustration. "What's the point of all this? What do you want from me—or rather, from Wyatt?"

Cal pushed himself up to sit beside her, and suddenly he looked fierce and frightening. "I don't want anything from you, ma'am," he drawled with cool mockery, "except your company for a ways. But your precious fiancé, that's another story. I want to hurt him. To make him suffer. To twist his insides with worry and pain and loss. And in the end to watch him die." Cal finished with awful, brutal calm.

Melora gasped, all the color rushing from her face, leaving her smooth skin as pale as ice and her golden brown eyes wide with horror.

He reached out to grasp her shoulders again and gave her a shake. "That scares you, doesn't it? Well, then don't ask me any more questions about it because I guarantee you won't like my answers. But you can stop thinking about marrying that son of a bitch because it will never happen. He's a dead man."

"You're going to murder him?"

His mouth curled unpleasantly, sending twisting fear through her. "I'm going to see that he gets what he has coming."

"Damn you, what did Wyatt ever do to you?"

Suddenly, as he stared back into her eyes, she saw the wariness, the iron purposefulness close down in a harsh mask over his features. Everything about him tightened. If he'd been planning to answer her, he changed his mind.

"It's a long story, Melora," he said curtly. "Go to sleep, unless you've got something else in mind."

His taunting tone and the sudden hard gleam in his eyes told her exactly what he was hinting at. Melora flushed to the roots of her hair, apprehension squeezing through her blood as she gazed at the lean outlaw beside her.

"The only thing I have in mind," she retorted, shaking with a fury that shared space with fear, "is getting back to my fiancé and going on my honeymoon with *him*. We were going to San Francisco. And you've ruined it. You've ruined everything. But Wyatt and I will get married, and you'll be the one who is dead!" she assured him, her eyes flashing.

Cal, looming over her, with that scornful, almost amused sneer on his face, seemed more unmoved than ever.

Because Melora was unnerved and at a distinct disadvantage, she forgot her resolve to master her temper and did what she usually did under such circumstances: she attacked.

"And when Wyatt's killed you—or I have—I'll take my cameo back off your carcass!" she hissed.

Suddenly a ghost of a grin flickered over his face. "Reckon I'd like to sit here and jaw with you all night, but we'd both better get ourselves some shuteye. Sweet dreams, Princess."

"I hope you have nightmares."

"How could I, sleeping next to you?"

Melora slumped back down on the bedroll as Cal slouched down beside her and closed his eyes. Odious, disgusting man! If her hands were free, she'd claw his eyes out. If she had her gun . . .

Oh, what's the use? she thought, breathing hard as she lay there on the ground, her body convulsed with hatred. *Your hands aren't free, and you don't have a gun, and you're not going to be able to escape tonight, so you may as well go to sleep. Because as smart and cunning as Cal thinks he is, and as much as he believes he's thought of everything, one of these days he's going to let his guard down, he's going to slip up, and when he does, you'd better be ready.*

She closed her eyes, no longer feeling sorry for herself. She was filled with a deep, passionate purpose. If it was the last thing she did, she'd turn the tables on this loathsome desperado.

SHE didn't know when she drifted off to sleep; she only knew when she came awake. It was still dark, the cool, deep blue darkness well before dawn, when the night is at its lushest and most dangerous. A rough hand covered her mouth, and an arm across her chest held her shoulders still.

Her eyes flew open to see Cal leaning over her, his broad chest crushing her breasts, his fingers digging against her lips. ''Shh. Horses. Someone's coming this way.''

Melora heard. Muffled sounds in the brush, hoofbeats over rock, a low, guttural voice, another one answering.

Quick as a wink Cal cut her bonds and the rope that bound them together, and the next moment he was standing, with his rifle pointed at the two riders who broke through the trees.

"Hold it right there." His rifle fixed itself in a businesslike way upon the broad chest of the man in front.

Melora couldn't see his eyes, but his clothes looked dirty and tattered, and with his wide red face partially covered by a bushy black beard and the big rifle at his side, she knew instinctively he was trouble.

"Not another step, stranger," Cal warned.

But the bushy-bearded man didn't seem to notice Cal's rifle. He halted his big gray horse, held up a ham-size hand to his companion, a sullen, unkempt-looking scarecrow in a greasy duster, and spoke in a soft, clever voice.

"Hold your fire, mister. Name's Strong—Otis Strong. Me and Jethro here, we're not looking for no trouble. But we seen your smoke from your campfire a while ago and headed this way. Lookee here, Jethro?" He smirked, half turning toward his companion. "We sure never expected to see a pretty lady out here in no-man's-land, now did we?"

"Keep moving," Cal said calmly. "My wife and I don't take kindly to strangers."

"We're running mighty low on rations, mister. Maybe we could share your campfire tonight and buy some coffee off you and maybe some hardtack if you and the little lady can spare it—"

Before he could finish speaking, there was a dull

thud. Melora, who'd been watching the bearded man closely with growing distrust, turned in time to see Cal topple forward and hit the ground.

She gasped in terror as she saw the third man. He stood over Cal, studying his prone form with a satisfied smirk, and she realized with a jolt of dismay that he had evidently sneaked around the camp in silence and coldcocked Cal from behind.

Melora sprang toward Cal, horrified by the blood seeping into the dirt beneath his head. He wasn't moving, and his eyes were closed, and the fear that he was dead struck her like a fist in her stomach, but before she could reach him, the third man barred her way. With a grunt he grabbed her around the waist.

"Good work, Lomax," Jethro, the scarecrow, whooped.

Lomax looked to be about fifty, a potbellied and foul-smelling goat of a man with long, greasy red hair and lashless eyes the color of river mud. Instinctively Melora kicked him in the shin, and he released her with a bellow of pain.

"Git her," Strong commanded as she bolted. Jethro spurred his pinto forward.

She got no farther than the shadow of the pines before Jethro whipped the horse around her, cutting her off. With her heart in her throat, Melora changed direction, darting to her left, but found Lomax blocking that path, his arms outstretched. Strong slid from the gray and sauntered over, stepping over Cal's unmoving form without even glancing down.

"I told you boys I'd find us a woman to keep us entertained while we're hiding out," he said smugly, grinning around the group. He approached Melora, beaming like a skunk eating cabbage. "And a real looker she is, too."

"You leave me alone." She retreated a step as he bore down upon her. "If you let me tend to . . . my husband, he might live. If not, you'll all be hunted down for murder! So if you don't want to get yourselves hanged—"

"Hell, we're already bein' hunted for murder," Jethro broke in, guffawing, shrugging his bony shoulders. "And they kin only hang us once, so why the hell should we give a damn about your poor ol' husband there?"

The chill that swept through Melora froze her blood like creek water. She knew there was no point cajoling or arguing with these men. She recognized their ilk. Suddenly she dodged past Strong, whipping by him so quickly he didn't have time to grab her. She ducked beneath the pine boughs and ran through the thick, soft blackness toward the stream. From behind her came the noise of pursuit, and her feet slid ever faster over the rough ground.

Was Cal dead? Horror churned through her. My God, she was trapped out here with these three murderers! She knew what they would do to her, and shivers convulsed down her spine as she plummeted forward in a desperate run for freedom. She'd rather die than be caught; she'd rather break her neck running through this thick, pillowy blackness than submit to them.

But as she spied the glint of the stream and pelted toward it, a rope slithered around her shoulders, slid nearly to her elbows, and then tightened so swiftly she gasped in pain. She was flung to the ground as the rope jerked sharply, and then Jethro leaped off his horse and trod over to her, grasping the rope between his hands.

Lomax and Strong appeared out of the darkness and leered down at her as Jethro knelt, grabbing a handful of her hair as she struggled to sit up.

"Hope you're worth all this trouble, lady."

"Bring her back to the hideout," Strong ordered without further ado. "Me and Lomax'll check out the camp and get their horses and supplies and finish off that hombre. Then we'll meet up with you straight away. And lookee here, Jethro," he added, jabbing a finger at the scarecrow twisting the rope in his hands. "You'd better make damn sure she's still alive and kicking until we've all had a turn with her. Don't you forget."

Fighting back the nausea rocking through her, Melora presently found herself wrenched up before Jethro on his horse, the rope still taut about her shoulders, crushing her bones. She had to bite her lip to keep from crying out. The fear was now a living, breathing thing inside her, consuming every thought. She tried to keep from trembling as the pinto galloped through the darkness, crossing a short gully, then veering west beneath the shadow of a series of buttes.

Strong and Lomax had gone back to finish Cal; that meant by now he was almost certainly dead. And she, instead of finding herself the prisoner of one man, someone at least who had demonstrated no desire to hurt her, was now the captive of three cold-blooded murderers, three disgusting animals who planned to do far worse than shoot her.

She closed her eyes as they rode, picturing her little sister, recalling all the happy times she and Jinx had shared in their home and out on the range. She remembered their picnics at the swimming hole, the days spent watching Pop and the ranch hands breaking in newly caught mustangs, evenings with Pop and Aggie on the porch drinking cool lemonade while the sun set over the golden prairie. What she wouldn't give to be back there right now, riding across her own belovedly familiar rangeland, breathing in the sharp tang of pine, the sweet night air, with her own stallion, Dusty, galloping beneath her.

The pinto halted so suddenly Melora jerked forward.

"Here you go, lady," Jethro drawled with mocking politeness as he pushed her off the horse, sending her tumbling down into tall, stringy weeds. He dismounted and yanked her up by the rope, grinning as she cursed at him.

"Guess I might as well tell you, I got only one use for women, and aside from that, I don't like 'em much. Lomax or Strong don't neither, so if you think we're goin' to coddle you, you're dead wrong. *Dead* wrong," he reiterated, chuckling over the emphasis he placed on the word.

A shack loomed out of the murky grayness of the night. Dingy and ramshackle, with boarded-up windows and peeling logs, it looked about as inviting as a coffin. He pushed her inside and lit a kerosene lamp set on a small table sticky with spilled whiskey. Gray and black rats fled to the corners of the room, deserting a pile of filthy tin plates piled in the sink. Other than several bedrolls flung down on the earthen floor, the cabin contained only three chairs, the little table, and a fireplace half filled with blackened logs.

Melora took a deep breath. "If you let me go, I'll see that you're well rewarded—" she began, but Jethro again grabbed a handful of her hair and twisted it until she cried out in pain.

"Right now I don't care much about money. We've got enough stashed away to last us awhiles, and when we want more, we kin just rob us another bank. What I really want is right here lookin' at me with big brown eyes. See, little lady, I haven't had a woman in 'bout three years now. I've been stuck in a damn hellhole of a prison. Had to kill me a couple of guards to get out, but I made it. And now I figure I deserve a little fun."

"I'm sorry," Melora managed to croak, trying not to cringe as his fingers left her hair and groped to her breast. He grabbed it and squeezed. "I didn't know. Of course you want to have some fun. If—if you take the rope off me, I'll t-try to be n-nice to you. I'm sure you're just lonely and—"

"Yeah, real lonely." He hooted, grinning from ear to ear as if showing off the rotten yellowing teeth that gleamed like those in a jack-o'-lantern. "Well, why not?" Suddenly he let go of her breast. He studied her eagerly, his small, wolfish eyes gleaming with an unbridled lust that curdled her stomach. She tried to remain still and calm beneath that insulting scrutiny, but it took all her willpower to manage it.

"Let's take off this here rope, and then that fancy outfit you're wearing, so's I can see what you really look like."

She nodded wordlessly, her eyes downcast so he couldn't see the venom in them. As Jethro began tugging the rope up toward her shoulders, she kept her gaze lowered.

"Let's see. Why, I haven't looked at a naked woman since . . ."

The rope lifted over her head. And Melora dived for the big Colt in his holster.

She jumped back with it in one deft leap. "Don't move, you bastard, or I'll kill you where you stand."

She leveled it straight between his eyes.

Jethro gaped at her; then, slowly, deep crimson rage suffused his cheeks. "You ain't got the stomach fer it," he snarled, and lunged at her.

Melora fired twice. Blood spurted all over the shack as he jackknifed to the floor. She staggered back, gasping as horror rose uncontrollably. From the corners of the shack she heard the rats scurrying, and before her on that earthen floor Jethro lay in a sickening, widening pool of his own blood, bone, and flesh.

She swallowed hard and looked away.

Get out. A voice inside her screamed through the shock that gripped her. *Get out before Lomax and Strong show up.*

Not looking down at Jethro, Melora reeled toward the door and flung it wide.

Otis Strong stood on the threshold, his bulk filling the narrow space, his eyes glittering dark and dangerous as he barred her way.

7

Melora screamed and fell back, frantically jerking the gun up again, but before she could shoot, Cal shoved Strong into the room, and she saw that the big man was Cal's prisoner.

She'd never thought she'd be glad to see Cal, but relief hit her like a flood tide when she realized he had his gun digging into the other man's broad back. There was a bloody cut on the back of his head and blood all over his shirt, but other than that, he looked fit and ready for battle. The fierce darkness in his eyes almost made Melora feel sorry for Strong. She'd never seen Cal look like that.

"You all right?" His voice was curt. His eyes never left Strong.

"Yes, I—I thought you were dead . . . that they killed you—"

"They tried."

She lowered the gun, suddenly weak with relief. "Where's Lomax?"

"Dead." Cal flicked a glance at the bloody form on the floor. "Nice work with Jethro."

Then two things happened at the same time. Cal saw Jethro's hand twitch and spotted the small black hideaway pistol that must have come from his boot, and at the same moment Strong saw it, too.

"Look out!" Cal shouted, and as Jethro aimed his hideaway gun at Melora, Cal fired three bullets into him. That stopped Jethro cold, but Strong took advantage of the distraction to seize Melora. Savagely he twisted the gun from her grasp and jammed her up against him as a shield. He tossed a beefy arm around her neck and pressed Jethro's Colt against her temple.

"Get out of my way, boy, or I'll blow the lady's head off."

Cal's cut was bleeding again, dripping down through his chestnut hair and onto his back. He seemed oblivious of it. His eyes were fixed on the mean, triumphant face of the other man.

"Let her go, Strong."

The big man sneered at him. "Ha. She's too purty to leave behind. I'm takin' her with me. And there ain't a damned thing you can do about it."

"Don't count on it."

For answer, Strong jammed the gun harder against

her temple, and Melora cried out in pain. She saw Cal's jaw clench.

Her glance flew wildly from Cal to the door as Strong began edging her toward it. The barrel of the gun dug coldly into her flesh, and she felt that at any moment it would go off. He would kill her just for spite. But no, not yet, she thought wildly. He needed her until he got away from Cal.

Her feet dragged as Strong forced her along with him, but Melora couldn't risk resisting. At this moment she scarcely dared breathe.

Cal watched them through narrowed eyes, yet he made no move.

"Drop your gun, boy, and kick it over here," Strong ordered. "*Now.*"

As Melora whimpered again in pain, Cal obeyed. Strong kicked the gun out the door, sending it thudding into the weeds.

"So long, boy." He chuckled. "I'll take real good care of your woman for you."

Then they were out in the deep purple night, and Strong was breathing hard in her ear as he propelled her toward his horse.

But as he hoisted himself into the saddle and reached down to haul her up before him, Melora saw her opportunity and took it. She bit the filthy hand that grasped her, bit it with all her might. Strong snatched his hand away with a scream of pain.

It was all the chance she needed. Melora leaped away and plunged toward the trees.

Suddenly she heard a crash, and as she peered back, she saw Cal and Strong fighting on the ground.

The gray horse shied away from the scuffle as the men rolled through the weeds, grunting, punching each other in the darkness. The night was alive with flying fists, low curses and groans, and sickening thuds. Melora crept back toward the fray, thinking of Cal, injured, thinking of how he'd forced Strong to bring him to the cabin—to rescue her. With her heart in her throat she tried to discern who was winning this fight to the death. She saw Strong atop Cal, hitting him again and again with a powerful right fist.

Dear God, she thought on a sob, *where's the gun?*

Hurtling through the darkness she began to search, her fingers grasping and clawing through the thick, tangled weeds near the door as she listened to the awful sounds of thudding fists and grunts.

She found it at last and lifted up Cal's big Colt. She whirled toward the two men.

"Strong! Stop! Stop right now or I'll shoot!"

But both men were so consumed by their battle that neither heeded her. Melora saw that Cal had somehow rolled free of his opponent and was now on his feet, throwing deft, savage punches, one after the other. He ducked to avoid a blow aimed at his chin and threw a vicious right that slammed into Strong's midsection.

The big man sank to his knees.

"Get back, Cal! I've got him covered!" Melora shrieked, planting her feet apart and aiming at Strong, but Cal paid no attention to her. He followed up with two more blows, and Strong went down.

Cal threw himself on the other man, pinning him,

and rained one punishing blow after another down upon his opponent.

Melora had never seen anyone fight like that before—with such ruthless, single-minded brutality.

Strong was a bigger man, heavier, perhaps more experienced. But Cal, with his deft, hammerlike blows, fierce strength, and blinding agility, was by far the more ferocious and determined opponent.

And suddenly it was over.

Cal's fists fell to his sides. He appeared to be carved from granite as he stared down at the man sprawled senseless beneath him.

"Is he dead?" Melora whispered, fighting the nausea that rose in her throat.

"No. But I reckon he won't be bothering anyone for a while." Matter-of-factly Cal pushed himself to his feet, glancing down one last time at the battered ox of a man crumpled in the bloodstained dust.

Then he limped toward Melora and took the gun from her numb fingers. There were cuts and bruises on his face, and he looked weary beyond belief, but his cool green eyes were clear and steady as he holstered the pistol. "Come on. Let's get out of here."

But reaction had set in upon Melora, a reaction every bit as dizzying as one of those vicious punches. Her knees wobbled, then buckled. She sank toward the ground. Instantly Cal's arms swooped around her, lowering her gently.

"Did they hurt you? Tell me the truth."

"N-no. I'm f-fine."

But tears began to roll down her cheeks. His arms

tightened, feeling almost like an embrace, she thought in dazed wonder. She saw concern in his eyes and quickly averted her face.

She wouldn't cry in front of him; she wouldn't! He was the one responsible for all this. If he hadn't taken her from the Weeping Willow, none of it would have happened. Completely humiliated by her own weakness, she gulped cold night air and yanked free of his arm, struggling to her feet.

Cal stood too, gripping her gently by the shoulders and forcing her to face him. The concern in his eyes as he tilted her chin up made her dizzy.

"It's all right, Melora," he said quietly. "You can cry. You've been through a lot, more than any woman should ever have to go through."

"I'm *fine*, but I want to go h-home. I want to see my sister and Wyatt and—"

"You can't do that."

"Why not?" she cried, and tried to break away from him, but when he caught her arm, she suddenly threw herself against him and began to sob.

Stunned by how soft she felt nestled against him, Cal held her. The fragility of her bones beneath his hands had an unsettling effect deep inside his gut. He closed his eyes as she dropped her head against his chest and let the awful, racking sobs come.

Her tension, her fear, her agonizing loneliness—he felt them all vibrate through her and into him, felt them seep into his chest, into his heart, and he knew in that illuminating moment the depth of her pain and of her bravery.

A gust of wind caught at the strands of her hair

and blew them up to drift like silk threads across his unshaved jaw. He sighed and smoothed the thick ribbon of curls, stroking them gently as he blamed himself for all that had happened.

"I'm sorry, Melora. Sorry for all this. I never meant for you to get hurt."

She lifted her tear-streaked face and gazed up at him, her body still trembling beneath his hands like a flower in a windstorm. "Let me *go*," she whispered, pleading.

The muscles in his chest constricted. *Let her go. Maybe I should.*

And then he thought, *To him? To the man she plans to marry, her precious Wyatt Holden?*

He gritted his teeth. The thought of her locked like this in the arms of that black-haired lying, murderous bastard filled him with a rage that brought ice to his eyes.

"*No*," he said aloud, so savagely she jerked her head back, studying him with wide, newly frightened eyes.

"No, Melora," he repeated more calmly, though his voice was tight with purpose. "You can't go back—not yet."

She pushed away from him. Slowly she wiped the tears from her cheeks with the back of her hand, like a child. "You came for me." Her gaze pondered him with gradual comprehension. "You made Strong bring you to the hideout so you could find me. So you could rescue me from Jethro."

"Of course. You don't think I'd leave you to him, do you?"

"No," she whispered, hugging her arms around herself. Misery filled her pale, lovely face, shone beneath her wet lashes. "No, you wouldn't. Because of your plan. You need me. You weren't ready to give up on whatever scheme you've embarked on just because three outlaws attacked us. Not because you . . . cared what happened to me, only because you needed me."

Cal scowled. It would be so much easier if what she said were true. If he didn't have feelings, a conscience, if he didn't have this strange, savage need he'd discovered tonight, a need to protect her from everyone, everything . . . even himself.

Let her think it's true. It's better for both of us.

"You're right, Melora. Nothing is going to make me give up my plan. Nothing is going to interfere. Now do you understand that?"

She did. Oh, she did.

Dawn was tinting the sky. Amber light glowed across the tops of the huge black buttes that jutted up from the prairie as Cal led her toward the horses.

"No sense trying to get any more shut-eye now. Let's get out of here, and we'll stop for breakfast later. Reckon you'd better ride with me."

She nodded dully. What did it matter? He'd go ahead anyway, even if she argued that she needed to sleep. How she longed for sleep! Weariness tugged at her, and she yearned for the oblivion of slumber to wash away everything that had happened these past few hours and the impossible, hopeless predicament in which she found herself. But there was no respite and so far no escape.

As the sun shot up over the mountains, Cal helped her into the saddle, mounted behind her, and off they rode.

8

"**A** storm's brewing—a bad one." Cal slowed Rascal and spoke to Melora over the rising wind. It was several days after the attack by Strong, Lomax, and Jethro. They'd covered a lot of ground since then, but he'd barely spoken to her since they'd left the desolation of the outlaw shack.

"Unless I miss my guess, we're not far from a little town called Devil's Creek," he told her shortly, glancing ever so briefly at her weary, dust-filmed face. He quickly looked back at the sky. "We'll spend the night there. But I'm warning you, Melora, don't cause any trouble."

She nodded, dread dancing down her spine as she too scanned the sky. She hoped Cal hadn't seen her dismay. As her horse snorted and followed Rascal along a wide rocky incline, she studied the black storm clouds, which had been growing ever more ominous these past few hours. The sun had vanished behind them sometime after noon, leaving an eerie dim greenish glow in the sky. She'd been watching that glow, and the distant lightning slashes, with trepidation.

Cal was right; the storm looked to be a bad one. A sick all-too-familiar tightening began in her stomach.

Ever since Melora was a little girl, she'd been afraid of storms. Pop had often said that Mama had been the same way. But it was Melora's most hated weakness, the one she was least successful in fighting. As the clouds darkened and the wind picked up, flinging bits of dust and small stones into a stinging whirlwind, she clenched her hands on the reins and kept a worried eye on the darkening clouds.

More than ever she wished she were home, but instead she was farther away than ever. The land had changed dramatically since the previous morning. No longer were they riding through sage- and grass-carpeted plains dotted with buttes and pine-capped ridges. Since early yesterday they'd been in Black Hills country, crossing sunflower-dotted valleys lined with bur oak, galloping across wide emerald meadows, and skirting the aspen- and pine-forested hills that led to the darker line of green hills ahead. Great ponderosa pine forests loomed on these distant hills, making them appear black and forbidding, thus earning them their name, the Black Hills.

The land was stunning here, sharply different from

the rangeland of the Weeping Willow, Melora thought with a flash of homesickness, though she could not help being awed by the spectacular beauty of this huge open country, with its rocky hills, its enormous forests cresting in the distance, and its jewellike flowers glistening in the meadows below.

Last night they'd camped near the Belle Fourche River, less than a mile from Devils Tower, and from their little ridge had gazed in silent awe at the huge rock column and had watched it glow a flaming golden red long after the sun had set. Afterward the moonlight and starlight had seemed to glisten brighter, whiter, milkier than ever when illuminating that strange giant spire that stood guard over the flatland below.

Cal had studied it in silence, his thoughts seemingly far away. That wasn't unusual. He'd spoken only a few dozen words to Melora since they'd ridden off from that rat-infested shack; by the very next morning he'd made it clear that whatever compassion he might have felt for her during that ordeal had been completely stamped out.

His attitude had been brusque, distant, and aloof. In fact he'd barely glanced at her in all this time.

But Melora's thoughts had returned over and over to those few mesmerizing moments when he'd held her, stroking her hair. His hands had felt so gentle. So protective. And there had been concern, real concern, not cool mockery in his eyes; she was sure of it.

An odd, fluttery sensation whirled through her when she thought of it. And what was it he'd said?

I never meant for you to get hurt.

But she couldn't believe that, not really. Maybe he hadn't intended that she fall into Strong's or Jethro's clutches, maybe he hadn't meant for her to be in danger of getting beaten or raped or murdered, but he *didn't* care about her, not really, she kept reminding herself.

If he did, he wouldn't have kidnapped her in the first place, and he wouldn't be subjecting her to this grueling cross-country trek, and he wouldn't be forcing her to be away from Jinx, and he'd let her go home, where she belonged, so she could marry Wyatt.

Yet she couldn't stop thinking about how he had come to that shack to rescue her, to save her from Jethro. Was it only because of his stupid plan?

Yes, she told herself, studying his tall vest-clad frame astride Rascal some ten feet ahead of her. *He's an outlaw, remember? Zeke told you that he and Ray met Cal in jail.*

Biting her lip, she wondered what crime he'd committed. And where. Remembering the savage ruthlessness with which he'd beaten Strong, she couldn't help shivering. There was a dark, unreachable side of Cal that she knew was dangerous. He'd made it clear that he would do whatever he had to do, no matter how pitiless, to achieve his ends.

Yet somehow, much as she tried, she didn't hate him—not in the fervent, desperate way she had in the beginning.

Cal wasn't cruel; there was no viciousness in him, at least not directed toward her. He was stubborn, and smart, and utterly dogged in this mission of his, whatever it was.

But that was the problem. What the hell was it?
Melora wondered for the thousandth time, frowning as she galloped between him and the packhorses for Devil's Creek. Studying the back of his head, the thick brown hair touching his shirt collar as he steered Rascal toward some aspens, she wondered if it might not be time to abandon the silent treatment and try to reason with the man. To find out what made him tick and why he was so damned set on dragging her across the country, clear to the Black Hills, and possibly—from the looks of it—over the border into South Dakota.

Because knowing what she had gleaned about Cal thus far, she now thought there had to be a reason, a damn good reason, at least in Cal's pigheaded mind.

Instead of trying to escape, maybe she'd try to figure out what it was.

And then she had no more time to explore this idea because Cal turned again to speak to her.

"Devil's Creek is a rough little town, but it's got one halfway decent hotel. We'll be able to pick up some supplies in the morning, and then, if the weather clears, we'll head out to the cabin."

"Cabin?"

"Where you'll be staying for a while."

She drew in a breath as she realized he hadn't said, "Where *we'll* be staying for a while." Did he mean to leave her at this cabin *alone*?

Melora had a vision of herself tied up in some

filthy, godforsaken shack like the one Jethro had taken her to while Cal went off to carry out heaven knew what plan against Wyatt.

"No! No, Cal. This is it!'' she exploded, pulling her mount to a halt. "I'm not going one more step until you tell me exactly what you're up to."

Cal circled back and studied her, his expression grim.

"This isn't the time to cause trouble, Melora." As if to punctuate his words, the wind gusted then, swirling dirt and tumbleweeds around them and biting into her skin with a sting like gnats. "This town I'm taking you to, Devil's Creek, it's not nearly as civilized and law-abiding as what you're used to in Rawhide. If you're smart, you'll keep quiet, you won't talk to anyone, you won't stir up any trouble. There's no law within thirty miles of the place,'' he warned, his eyes narrowed. "It's filled with men like our friends Strong and Lomax—and Jethro. No one there's going to listen or believe a word if you start blabbering out some foolish story about being kidnapped . . .''

"It's not foolish, damn you. It's the truth!''

"But no one's going to care. Or stick their neck out to help you. Savvy?''

"Perfectly,'' she snapped. Her chin thrust out. "I'm not stupid.''

"Then prove it,'' he said roughly. "Come on.''

"No.'' Melora's lower lip came out in a pout. "I won't go on—not another step—until you—oh, damn you, Cal, what are you doing?''

He seized her without any further ado and yanked her off her horse and into the saddle before him. He slid one lean arm tightly around her waist as his other hand grasped her horse's reins.

"If you think I'm going to waste time arguing with you, Princess, you're wrong."

He spurred Rascal to a gallop, and they thundered through the aspens, even as the first few sprinkles of rain began.

Fuming, Melora bit back all the stinging retorts that sprang to her lips. What good would they do? Cal was too infuriating, too bullheaded, too arrogant and mulish ever to listen to reason.

She hated him anew, suddenly and passionately, her frustration and rage boiling to the surface all over again.

Worse than everything else, she was blisteringly aware of the intimate pressure of his arm around her waist, of his long, taut calves against hers. His closeness, the strength of him, the musky male scent and proximity of him created a tingling sensation everywhere their bodies touched. It caused her heart to speed up like a locomotive, and her cheeks to flame with heat.

Damn you, Cal.

THE town of Devil's Creek was every bit as ominous-looking as Cal had described. It consisted of nothing more than a few false front buildings, most of them saloons or brothels with broken shutters or boarded-up windows. As she and Cal rode down the street, squint-eyed men lounging against storefront walls and hitching posts viewed them with suspicion and glinting interest. Suddenly, as those intent, wolfish gazes scrutinized her, Melora found herself very glad of Cal's solid presence.

And why not? she told herself, fighting against this sensation. *He has a gun and you don't. If you were armed as he is, you wouldn't worry a whit over any of them.*

But a small voice inside her whispered that she would. There was something raw and decaying about Devil's Creek, a sense of lawlessness, of cruelty and violence that permeated the dusty streets and even the tumbleweeds blowing through the alleys. It creaked in the broken wooden boardwalk and in the partially hinged shutters that banged in the wind. She found herself unconsciously leaning back in the saddle, brushing against Cal's tall frame, reassuring herself that he was there and she was not alone.

They stopped before a crumbling two-story building that looked as if it had never seen better days. WICKE'S HOTEL read the yellowed sign overhead.

When they walked inside, Melora surveyed her surroundings in dismayed silence. Dirt encrusted the lobby's peeling green walls; the steps were uncarpeted; the dining room to the right looked dingy and uninviting.

She could just imagine the dampness of the bed linens, the shabbiness of the rooms. *But it's better than sleeping outside in the storm,* she reminded herself uneasily as thunder roared outside.

A huge, scowling clerk with the shoulders of a small mountain squashed a fly on the counter with his fist before handing Cal a key.

"Room two-oh-three," he barked. "That'll be two dollars. Pay in advance."

Cal peeled off the bills and thrust them at the man, whose menacing demeanor lightened a bit as Cal met his stare with steel-edged calm.

"Enjoy your stay in Devil's Creek," the clerk added sourly when they started up the stairs. Just then a thick-necked cowboy in soiled buckskins, black leather vest, and a plaid bandanna hurtled down the steps two at a time, nearly crashing into Melora. Cal yanked her out of the way just in time. He seized the man's arm as the bruiser went past and hauled him up short.

"Ought to be more careful, mister. You almost knocked down my wife."

"So?"

"So I think you should apologize to her."

The cowboy gave a short laugh. He looked as if he were about to sneer something unpleasant, but suddenly he actually peered into Cal's lean, hard face, and whatever he saw in those icy green eyes made him think better of it. He cleared his throat, then threw a milder glance Melora's way.

"Sorry, ma'am."

"That's better." Cal released him in disgust and took Melora's arm, escorting her up the remainder of the steps.

"I thought you said we should keep our mouths shut and not look for any trouble," she remarked the moment they were locked into the tiny, dank-smelling room.

Cal shrugged, amusement flickering briefly in his inscrutable face. "I said *you* should keep quiet," he pointed out, flashing a glance about the grimy, dimly lit premises. "I've never been able to keep out of trouble much myself."

"Me either. Look at me now."

"Must I?" he drawled, hooking his thumbs in his gun belt as he studied her from beneath the wide brim of his hat. Some devil made him bait her. "You're not nearly the illustrious creature you were when I nabbed you out of your bedroom in your pretty little nightdress."

Mouth agape, Melora whirled to face him beside the narrow bed. Her cheeks flamed a bright poppy as she balled her hands into fists.

Yes, her once-lovely green velvet habit was now soiled and disheveled, the beautiful lace sadly torn and limp, and her cravat coated with travel dust. Yes, she felt vile and filthy and smelly and as unattractive as a bale of hay, but what Cal seemed to have forgotten was that it was all his fault. Now he had the gall to add insult to injury by reminding her of just how scruffy she looked!

"You did this to me, you mangy outlaw, you kidnapper! You and your disgusting friends, you've reduced me to a—a hag, a filthy hag. Before I met you, for your information, half the men in Rawhide had proposed to me or were planning to do it. They fell all over me—before I met Wyatt, that is," she added hastily, coloring an even deeper shade of red. "And by rights, at this very moment, I ought to be on my honeymoon, in a sumptuous, opulent, *beautiful* hotel

suite with my beloved *husband*, sharing a bed and—
and other things with him—''

''If it's a honeymoon you want, Princess,'' he shot
back, eyebrows raised, ''I reckon I can try to oblige.
After all, I told the clerk at the desk we were married.''

''If you so much as touch me, I'll—''

''You'll what?'' he demanded. For some reason
Cal couldn't fathom, he stalked over to her, placed
his hand beneath her adorable, stubborn little chin,
and tilted it up.

She promptly smacked his fingers away.

''Princess,'' he growled, ''I can't have you thinking you're no longer a desirable woman. Because
even as you are right this very moment, you're hardly—what did you say—a hag.''

''A compliment of the highest order,'' she retorted,
her eyes sparkling with anger. ''Why, if that's an example of your form of address, you must be downright *beloved* by the ladies, Cal. In fact now I
understand why you snatched me from my bedroom;
you must have to kidnap a woman to get one to notice
you.''

She thought he'd be angry, but instead he laughed.
A spontaneous, rumbling laugh that emanated deep
from his broad, solid chest. And he was grinning from
ear to ear. ''Well, you're not far off, Melora,'' he
admitted ruefully. ''I'm not exactly a ladies' man.''

She threw him a scathing glance from beneath her
lashes. ''No!''

But her sarcasm bounced off him. Cal was too
busy noticing the fetching picture she made in her

crumpled green velvet riding habit, travel dust and all.
"Maybe I need some lessons in proper courtship,"
he heard himself say. Then he groaned inwardly.

Why was he talking to her like this? He'd never
flirted with any woman in his life, had never known
the first thing about how to make amusing small talk
or to throw out flattering compliments. That had been
Joe's specialty, he thought. *I'm the tongue-tied one,
the one who always went solo to those town dances
or who made up excuses not to go at all.*

And to flirt with Melora Deane, of all people, the
woman pledged to his enemy, a breathtaking beauty
he'd made up his mind to dislike before he ever met
her, one who'd had an army of suitors, who'd proved
to be as headstrong and annoying as any female that
had ever walked the earth, and who was his prisoner.

It was wrong-headed and thick-skulled. Bordering
on lunacy. He'd never been able to pay a compliment
without stuttering to anyone but little old ladies and
maiden aunts back home. How in hell did he think to
trade flirtatious sallies with the belle of Wyoming?

As thunder cracked through the charged air outside
the window, and Devil's Creek shook with a rising,
howling wind, and a gust as cold as mountain snow
swept through the pitiful little room, Cal forgot all
that. He forgot his awkwardness with women, his
damned shyness. He was aware only of how close he
stood to Melora Deane and how utterly, bewitchingly
exquisite she was. Even with her thick gold hair cascading in wild tangles over her slim shoulders, even
with her smart outfit looking more like beggar's rags
than what it truly was, even with all that, she was

purely, heartbreakingly lovely. Those startling, vivid tawny eyes flecked with gold, the rich texture of her hair, the luminous glow of her skin that no amount of caked-on trail dust could diminish. And her lips. Cal caught himself staring at her lips.

Naturally pink and full, gracefully shaped like a satin bow, they looked more luscious than ripe strawberries, and he suddenly wanted fiercely to taste them.

He didn't realize what he was doing, but his arms went around her faster than a rattler springing at its prey. Then slowly, watching her eyes widen with disbelief and fury, he lowered his head and touched his mouth to hers.

Shock coursed through him at the explosive contact. At the same moment lightning rent the night outside the window, filling the sky. But not only the sky, Cal thought in astonishment. It had struck them, both of them, sure as he stood here.

Hadn't it?

His shoulders shook. And his loins tightened. Heat soaked through his denim shirt.

A current had flashed between them, soldering them together, him and this woman he'd been determined from the start not to care about. Yet here he was, his mouth locked on hers, burned and searing. As rain began to pelt down upon the dust and debris of Devil's Creek, the slender fragility of Melora Deane was branded against his frame, and the soft thrust of her breasts against his chest knocked his breath away.

Wonderingly he kissed her, exploring the luscious

honeysuckle taste of her. He entwined his hands in the velvet thickness of her hair, hair more golden than the sun, and kissed her some more. Kissed her thoroughly, hungrily. Consumingly.

He'd kissed only whores before now. But this was so entirely different, sort of like the joy of riding an unbroken bronc, Cal determined, knowing somehow Melora would have skined him alive if she had heard the comparison. He deepened the kiss as he parted Melora's satin soft lips. *Yep, just like riding a bronc. It let you in for a hell of a wild ride, and the trick was to stay on till you were shook off.*

Thunder and lightning lit up the night outside the Wicke's Hotel window, but though the night tossed like a horse bucking the devil himself, Melora Deane didn't shake him off.

Didn't even try.

9

Melora couldn't breathe. She never even heard the thunder or saw the lightning slashes outside the window. But she gasped as Cal kissed her, igniting a golden wildfire inside her, a wildfire that licked through her with hot, sweetly dancing flames.

What on earth was he doing? How dare he? With all her being, she wanted to struggle against him— she actually lifted her arms to beat against him—but her limbs felt soft as butter, and her arms fluttered down again, resting instead across his broad shoulders.

It's shock, she told herself as Cal's mouth burned across hers with demanding force, stifling her resistance with a jolt of pleasure so electric it made her brain feel like a sausage deep-fried in the skillet. As she responded without conscious thought, her arms swooped around his neck, clinging, begging, tugging him nearer.

With a soft moan her lips parted, then melted beneath his. His hat toppled off as she thrust her hands through the soft thickness of his chestnut hair.

Kissing Wyatt never felt like this, she thought dizzily, and then as Cal's mouth scorched kisses across her cheek, down her neck, into the delicate hollow of her throat, she thought nothing more but merely trembled like a poppy in the wind. Then his body moved against hers, and she felt the heat and strength and hardness of him.

She looked into his eyes and became engulfed in smoky green fire. Then, deliberately, his mouth claimed hers again with rampaging kisses, kisses that brought sensations so pleasurable the floor seemed to spin away, and she clung to him to keep from falling.

She felt herself under siege, being conquered, utterly vanquished, deluged. She couldn't think, for she was rapidly surrendering. Dissolving into a thousand shards of glass, each one a brilliant rainbow of sensations she'd never experienced before—not with Wyatt, not with anyone.

And then a gunshot louder than thunder rang out from the street below, and Cal was recalled to his senses, pushing her away in shock as if she were a red-hot branding poker.

Flushing, Melora pressed shaking hands to her cheeks.

They stared at each other then until another shot

rang out, at which point Cal recovered himself and swung toward the window.

"Just some drunken fool shooting his rifle in the air, gettin' good and soaked," he mumbled as he slammed the window shut, yanked the burlap curtain across the sill, and turned back to her.

Melora's arms trembled. A drunk? *If only I were drunk right now, then I could have some excuse for what happened, what I allowed to happen. I've gone loco; that's the only explanation*, she thought wildly, fighting to ignore the tingling in her lips, the electricity that still charged through her body.

You've betrayed Wyatt! With this—this desperado who stole you away from everything and everyone you hold dear.

She clung to one thought: She mustn't let Cal see the effect he'd had on her.

And dear Lord, what an effect it was. She didn't know whom she despised more at that moment, Cal or herself.

She forced herself to move, to counteract physically the effects of Cal's kisses. Somehow she wove her way to the old bureau, on which rested a single wax-coated iron candlestick. With one motion she yanked the candle out and spun around, raising the candlestick high over her head.

"If you try that again I'll knock you cold," she vowed.

Cal came easily away from the window, but instead of approaching her, as she half expected, he flopped his body across the bed and plumped a pillow up behind his shoulders.

"Wouldn't think of it, Princess," he assured her casually.

"You shouldn't have thought of it before!"

"Didn't exactly think of it." He shrugged. He was cool. Calm. She *thought* she detected tension in the set of his shoulders, but she couldn't be sure. "It just . . . happened."

Melora ground her teeth. "It'd better never happen again! *Never*, do you hear me?"

"I think the drunks down in Hurley's Saloon can hear you," he commented dryly. He arranged the pillow more comfortably against his neck. How could he look so damned composed, so *tranquil*?

Thunder boomed, making Melora jump. She clutched the candlestick tighter as Cal continued in a smooth tone. "Only problem is, folks in town might think it strange for a wife to be shouting things like that at her husband. I'd lower my voice if I were you."

"Folks might think it strange? Strange? Don't talk to me about strange!" But Melora forced herself to lower her voice as he continued to stare at her with raised brows. "You're the strangest man I've ever met, and this kidnapping is the strangest event of my life!" she hissed. "How long are we going to go on like this? And just what do you hope to accomplish by taking me into the Black Hills?"

"Not this again." Cal frowned. He reached down to the floor and retrieved his hat, then plopped it over his face. "Think I'll take a nap."

A nap? Melora's mouth dropped open. She stared in boiling, all-consuming rage at this cretin who had ruined her life and tricked her into—into wrong behavior, into crazed behavior. Her lips still burned from his kiss, her body would never again feel quite the same after being pressed against his, and he was going to take a nap?

Her temper snapped. "You—you . . . disgusting, selfish, arrogant *cur*!" she shouted, and threw the candlestick across the room. It crashed into the door, then hurtled to the floor and rolled under a chair.

Cal lifted the hat off his face, regarding her in reproachful silence.

"There is no way you are going to take a nap! You're loco if you think I'm going to let you off that easily," she shrieked. "I said I want answers, and you're not going to get a moment's rest until you give them to me!"

She snatched his hat from him and threw it onto the floor, glaring defiantly into his startled eyes. Then, when he said nothing, she lost control of the last thin shreds of her temper and leaped onto the hat, stomping it into the floor with her boots as if it were a prairie fire that needed squelching.

"*There*, Cal, *that's* what I think of you *and* your hat," Melora panted as she stamped and squashed. "And *that's* what I think of your plan. And *that's* what I think of—ohhh!"

Too late did she notice his green eyes narrow, making him look like a tiger about to pounce. Too late did she try to jump out of reach. With one long, sinewy arm, Cal grabbed her and yanked her down on the bed, and the next moment she was pinned beneath him, trapped by his size and weight.

"That was my best hat, Melora."

"I don't care. I don't give a damn. I want answers. I want to know why I can't go home!"

"Because I said so."

"Who the hell cares what you say? My sister needs me. My fiancé needs me. And my ranch needs me."

Her words tore at him. The furious, agonized expression on her face pierced him like a knife gutting through to his soul.

When he'd kidnapped her, he'd thought Melora's father was still alive; he'd thought that Craig Deane was there, hearty and healthy to run the ranch, to take care of his family and land. He hadn't counted on Wyatt Holden's bride-to-be being solely responsible for it all or on there being a young sister at the Weeping Willow who was left all alone when Melora was kidnapped.

I didn't count on a lot of things, he realized ruefully as he studied the slenderly beautiful, very enraged woman squirming furiously beneath him. She was helpless on the mattress, caught and pinned like a mouse in the paws of a tiger, and she knew it, yet she glared up at him with that striking combination of defiance, raw nerve, and silent vulnerability that touched him more fiercely than any tears or pleas.

Cal raked a hand through his hair. He had to suppress the urge to soothe her flushed face and trembling lips with another long, sweet kiss.

Instead he suddenly shifted his weight and let her up. "Melora," he said tensely, as she sprang up to a sitting position beside him, "you win. This time."

He eased off the bed because to linger there any

longer would invite disaster. Instead he prowled to the window, pulled the burlap aside, and stared bleakly out at the wild night.

She remained frozen where she was, panting, waiting. Listening. Alert as a huntress, her head cocked to one side.

"Your fiancé did me a bad turn some time ago," he said at last. "A real bad turn. And I'm aiming to repay him." He scowled at the streaming windows. Rain ran down in flowing gray rivulets. Like unending tears, he thought with a stab of bitterness.

"So I've set a trap, and you're the bait. It's not the way I'd have picked to right this wrong," he added harshly, spinning around to meet her gaze with a level look. "But it's the only way I could think of. That's all there is to it."

Stunned, Melora could only shake her head. "Wyatt is a good man. He wouldn't have—he couldn't have . . . done anything wrong."

The cold laugh that broke from him echoed through the tiny room. "You may be a courageous woman, Princess, but you're a hell of a poor judge of character." Suddenly he strode over to his pack and removed a canteen.

"Whiskey," he said shortly. "Want some?"

She shook her head, and then, for the first time since she'd met him, she saw Cal take a long swig of liquor. "You know nothing about the hombre you were going to throw your life away on. Not one damn thing. You should be thanking me, Princess, for saving you from him."

Confusion settled over Melora like a fuzzy woolen

afghan. She could picture Wyatt in her mind's eye: tall, black-haired, handsome. Charming, smart, even-tempered Wyatt, who played with Jinx's kittens, who bought candy for the children who stopped in at Petey's General Store whenever he happened to be there. Wyatt always had a ready smile for everyone, he was always a gentleman—as Pop had been—and he was always prepared to offer a helping hand to anyone who needed it.

Aggie adored him, and so did Mrs. Appleby, the doctor's wife, and all the ranchers in the valley included him in their discussions at the cattlemen's association meetings. They respected his judgment: they listened to him and heeded his advice about the rustlers.

And he was the one who had come up with the idea of trying to find a special doctor in the East to cure Jinx's lameness, of sending her to an exclusive hospital where she could get the best medical treatment available.

He was not capable of doing anyone "a bad turn," whatever that was. The whole notion was ludicrous.

"You've made a mistake, Cal." She spoke calmly and steadily now, for her anger was evaporating. From the little she knew of Cal, she had come to believe he was not the monster she had first thought when she was dragged from her home. He had shown himself to be decent and intelligent and even, occasionally, understanding. Oh, there was anger in him, Melora conceded, but not cruelty. Not one speck of meanness. He could be unexpectedly kind, unexpectedly patient.

So now it became clear. There had been a misunderstanding. Cal apparently blamed Wyatt for something that was not his fault, and the moment she could make him understand that, he would let her go.

She tried to argue her case, forcing herself to concentrate on that and not on the storm raging beyond the window. But he cut her off, shoving the whiskey canteen back into the saddle pack, glaring at her from across the dim room, while flashes of golden lightning sliced the sky outside.

"You asked me, Melora," Cal told her coolly. "And I told you. End of discussion. I know the truth about that slimy son of a bitch. And I'm sorry, but until this little matter between him and me is settled, you're caught right in the middle of it."

"But, Cal—" Thunder made her jump and lose her train of thought. Before she could continue, he interrupted her.

"I'm going downstairs to get us some supper we can eat in our room." He picked up his battered hat, shot her a frown dark as midnight, and stalked to the door. "Stay put and don't get into any trouble until I get back. And don't try to escape," he added, with a meaningful glance at the storm raging outside, "or to enlist anyone's help. You won't find much milk of human kindness in Devil's Creek."

"Cal, don't go."

But more thunder, black and deafening as cannon fire, drowned out the desperation in her words, and he was gone without hearing them or seeing the panic in her face.

Melora jumped up off the bed. She bit her lip and

tried to stay calm. But as the windowpanes rattled and shook, and rain slashed ever harder upon the roof, she began to pace the room, her hands clenched at her sides.

She refused to look outside, but the zigzag flashes of lightning danced eerily across the dimness. Every peal of thunder knotted her stomach tighter. At one point it sounded as though the roof were going to cave in upon her.

It's only a storm, she told herself, but her breath was now coming in short, hard gasps. *It will pass.*

Her breathing grew ever more ragged as the chilling, unreasoning terror poured through her.

She ran to his pack, dug out the whiskey canteen, and took a gulp. The liquor slid like amber fire down her throat. *That's better, much better.* Melora wiped her lips with the back of a trembling hand. She took a second gulp.

Now calm down. You don't want Cal to see you like this, do you? Do you want him to think you're a sniveling little coward?

She swallowed another long swig of whiskey, then took the canteen with her as she threw herself down on the bed and closed her eyes, trying frantically to close her ears to the thunder, to the rain, to the cold, whistling wind.

Cal found her huddled there when he returned. Huddled still and silent as a corpse.

''MELORA?''

When he opened the door, he saw her curled up on the bed in a ball, her face turned away, and for an instant he thought she was asleep, but then he heard the sound of her breathing, quick and shallow and harsh, and he knew something was very wrong.

"Melora, what is it?" The tray clattered onto the table as he sprinted to her side and knelt beside her, fear scraping through him. "Are you sick?"

She only shook her head. There were no tears on her face; this was a dry, gripping terror, the kind that filled one with a soundless pain, that reverberated through the body.

"Melora, you're shaking like a leaf. Tell me what's wrong!"

Outside, thunder descended like great bells tolling death, and he saw her flinch, and her face grow ever paler. "Is it the storm?" he asked in disbelief.

She nodded and a hoarse whisper emerged. "Ever since I was a little girl—"

Lightning blazed then, and a shudder shook her. Cal's arms closed around her, drawing her close against him, so close that Melora almost sobbed with relief as she buried her head in his shoulder.

Yet she braced herself for what he would say next, something along the lines of "So . . . fierce, brave Melora Deane is afraid of a little thundertorm." But he didn't say it.

"Louisa's the same way," he murmured, his breath ruffling her hair.

"Who's Louisa?" she whispered.

"My little sister. She's seven, and every time it storms she starts to shake and sob, and we all end up sprawled together on the sofa, drinking warm milk and singing songs to try to keep her mind off the thunder. Hey, there, Princess, it's all right," he added, as another boom sent a tremble across her shoulder blades. "A little thunder never hurt anyone."

"But lightning can."

His arms tightened around her, snug and strong. "You're safe, Melora. You don't have to be afraid." His voice sounded oddly husky. "I won't let anyone or anything hurt you."

Strange words from her kidnapper, but she believed him. She had no idea why, but she believed him. The trembling lessened as he held her, stroking her hair, sliding his hands up and down her slender back. Even the glint of lightning that lit the room now and then didn't seem as terrifying with Cal's arms around her, with her head resting against his solid, muscular chest.

They sat like that for some time, until the tremors inside her ceased. "Better?"

She took a deep breath. "I think so, yes."

"Then how about some supper? There's steak and potatoes and sourdough bread, too. Also half of a pie. I thought you'd like it."

She disengaged herself from him far enough to lean back in his arms. Her eyes searched his face in bewilderment.

"You're being awfully nice to me."

"Unless I miss my guess," Cal drawled, "that's a suspicious tone I hear in your voice."

"What if it is?"

For answer, he chucked her gently under the chin, as if she were his sister, Louisa, Melora reflected wryly.

"I've got nothing against you, Princess. Nothing personal. Except for the fact that you've got real bad taste in the men you plan to marry. Otherwise this is just business for me. I'll do what I have to do, I'll see this through to the end, but I'm not out to cause you any suffering."

"So you'll feed me steak and pie and then leave me alone in some godforsaken cabin somewhere?"

He frowned and stood up from the bed and paced away from her. "It will only be for a little while. This won't go on much longer. Only until—" He set his lips together. "Let's eat. The food's getting cold."

By now she recognized that stubborn set to his jaw, and she knew he would say no more for the time being. And as he pulled out two chairs at the table in the corner of the room, she suddenly realized how hungry she was. Thankfully the worst of the lightning and thunder seemed to have moved beyond Devil's Creek and out across the high country. During the meal a steady downpour did sheet against the window, but the dingy little hotel room somehow took on the aspect of an oasis. By the amber glow of the kerosene lamp on the bureau, Cal and Melora devoured thick steak and potatoes seasoned with onions and pepper. Even the sourdough bread was warm, fresh, and delicious, Melora noted in surprise, as she lavished it with butter. And there was coffee, which Cal generously laced with whiskey from his canteen. It filled Melora with a fiery warmth that went a long way toward keeping her mind off her troubles.

"This place might be uncivilized, but someone certainly knows how to cook," she commented almost gaily, and savored another sip of the whiskey-laced coffee. She even was able to glance at the windswept blackness outside the window without her nerves jumping through her skin.

"You ought to taste my special barbecued steak sometime," Cal told her. She knew he was trying to keep her distracted from the storm. "It's got a sauce that'll wake up your innards, like old Cody used to say. He was the chuck wagon cook on my first cattle drive," he explained, fondness softening the hard planes of his face. "Boy, oh, boy, did that steak ever disappear faster than you can slap a tick. Every Fourth of July we held a big barbecue at our ranch, and my ma would bake three of her special chocolate cakes, and Lord knows how many pies, and there'd be dancing in the big parlor, and my brother Joe would play the fiddle and I'd play my harmonica—" He stopped suddenly, frowning. "Do you know much about cooking, Princess?" he asked, the glint in his eyes indicating to her that he doubted Miss Melora Deane had ever spent much time in the kitchen.

"I'll have you know I've been fixing grub for a bunkhouse full of cowhands since I was ten," Melora informed him, setting her glass down on the table with a distinct clink. "Of course I had Aggie to help me." Now it was her turn to explain. "Aggie's been almost like a mother to me and Jinx. She's lived with us and Pop and helped take care of the ranch house since our mother died. And of course, when I was away at school in Boston, she took over almost all the cooking and household work. But since I've come back, I've managed to feed quite a few hungry men on a daily basis. Although,'' she added, her eyes darkening nearly to copper, ''we only have a scant half dozen ranch hands left these days. The way the rustlers have cut into our stock, we don't need as many hands and can't afford them. Profits are down and—''

She broke off. Why was she telling Cal these personal things? She folded her napkin corner to corner and placed it beside her plate.

''None of that is important,'' she finished coolly. ''What's important is that Wyatt is going to help me save the Weeping Willow. He's head of a committee dedicated to stopping the rustlers. And he's promised to invest money in the ranch too. Soon we'll need to hire on more hands just to keep up with all our cattle.''

''Don't count on it.''

She met his icy gaze as her chin angled up. ''Don't underestimate Wyatt.'' She pushed back her chair and stood up. ''I'll wager everything I own that Wyatt and I will have our honeymoon yet.''

''Don't, Melora. You'd lose.''

What was the use? Gazing at the implacable harshness in his eyes, Melora shivered and wondered if she would ever find a way to reason with Cal about this. Still, she had to keep trying.

She couldn't bear to think about what would happen if Wyatt somehow found her, if he and Cal suddenly found themselves confronting each other face-to-face.

If that happens, I'll just have to make sure that they work things out peaceably, like reasonable men, and that no one gets hurt.

Strangely the idea of Cal's getting hurt was almost as disturbing to her as the notion that Wyatt might end up shot or injured.

She shook off the picture of either man coming to harm.

If it comes to that, I'll stop it. No matter what it takes.

Cal watched her move about the room, setting to rights the candlestick she'd thrown earlier, rifling through her carpetbag, setting out her dainty silver-handled hairbrush. Strange to see that pretty silver hairbrush and the matching ornate hand mirror in this cheap, dingy room with its burlap curtain and chipped furnishings.

Melora Deane didn't belong here. But she didn't belong on a honeymoon with that black-haired snake either, Cal reflected savagely. The very notion sent tension rippling through his muscles, made his chest constrict, and his fingers itch to shoot someone. But not just anyone.

He itched to shoot the man Melora Deane loved.

"May I have some privacy?" Her low voice broke into his thoughts. "I'd like to change."

He saw that she was holding one of the flannel shirts he'd given her to sleep in; it was warmer than that thin little nightdress she had, though not nearly as pretty to look at. Still, Cal thought dryly, that shirt looked much better on her than on him.

Then he groaned inwardly. He'd better stop thinking like that about her. It was loco. "I'll be back in a while," he said, walking to the door.

Melora couldn't help being baffled by him as she stripped off her riding habit and readied herself for bed. Cal had so many sides to him that she didn't know anything about and didn't understand. A seven-year-old sister named Louisa? A family? A brother named Joe, who played the fiddle? A ranch?

Yet he was an outlaw. A kidnapper. A man bent on some ruthless revenge against Wyatt. A man she had to escape from, to thwart, and to stop.

A man who came back into the room silently and barely threw her a glance as he prepared to turn in for the night. She was already deep down under the sheets by that time, with the lamp turned down to only a thin, feeble arc of light.

Just enough to keep an eye on him.

Rain still pattered on the window as Cal threw his bedroll on the floor. She watched surreptitiously as he hung his gun belt over the back of a chair, then stripped out of his shirt and boots, leaving on only his snug-fitting blue trousers.

He had a magnificent body. Lean, strong, toned. It was bronzed from the sun and gleamed like dark wood in the pale lamplight. He moved with sure agility, with a kind of graceful strength that she'd come to realize was as much a part of him as the thick waves in his hair or the way his eyes seemed to pierce right through her.

As she watched him hunker down and smooth out the bedroll, she remembered the feel of him when he'd held her, the hard, solid strength of him, the way his hands had glided over her, stroking, comforting.

A bewildering wooziness came over her. *It's all that whiskey*, she told herself. *You're not used to drinking liquor.*

Melora drew in a deep breath and tried to block out all these disconcerting thoughts about Cal. They were improper, as Aggie would have said. Unsuitable, as her teachers in Boston would have said. And absurd. Cal was not her hero, her protector. He was the man who had snatched her away from everything she held dear.

Yet the burning heat of his kiss branded her still. She'd kissed many boys, and a few men, but those kisses had been blandly pleasant, nothing like this. Even Wyatt's kisses hadn't affected her like this.

This was unforgettable. As the wind rattled the windowpanes and the noise of the storm settled down to a drone rather than a roar, she tossed and turned in the narrow, lumpy bed, trying to get comfortable, trying to sleep, but sleep was elusive.

She was all too aware of Cal's long frame, of his steady breathing, only a few feet away.

"Can't you sleep?" he inquired suddenly, roughly, out of the darkness.

"Of course I can sleep. I *was* sleeping. You just woke me up."

"Right. Whatever you say, Princess."

She closed her eyes and pretended to sleep. She *tried* to sleep.

But it was a long time before either of them slept.

10

Cal left first thing the next morning to purchase supplies. The moment the door closed behind him Melora sat up in bed and shoved her hair from her eyes. She'd made up her mind. She would find out if Devil's Creek had a telegraph office, and if it did, she would send a wire to Wyatt.

Excitement licked through her as she raced through her toilette. Today, instead of the riding habit, she wore another one of Cal's green and blue flannel shirts and the pair of baggy denim trousers which he'd lent her during their journey. She had to bunch the trousers at the waist and tie them with rope just to keep them from falling down—not exactly a smart Boston outfit—but as she hurried out of the hotel room early in the morning, her hair scooped into a ponytail, she didn't care how she looked.

She just wanted to wire a message for help.

They'll be so relieved to hear from me, she thought, her eyes glowing as the hotel clerk informed her that the telegraph office was next door to the Dead Man's Saloon. She composed the letter in her mind as she rushed out the hotel door and onto the boardwalk.

> *My darling Wyatt,*
> *I'm being taken to South Dakota—to a cabin in the Black Hills, not far from Devil's Creek. I haven't been harmed, but be careful when you come to find me. My kidnapper is a man named Cal, who has a grudge against you. Give all my love to Jinx. Please come soon!*

She glanced hastily up and down the puddle-filled street as she dashed along, keeping an eye out for Cal. She only hoped that when Wyatt showed up, she could keep the situation from turning violent. But she had to do this, she reasoned, striding toward the sign above the Dead Man's Saloon. She had to get home, to Jinx, to the ranch. And she had to protect Wyatt from whatever Cal had in store for him.

When she entered the telegraph office, her heart pounded as though it would burst.

"I need to send a wire immediately."

The fat, bespectacled clerk whose hair and eyebrows were the color of dried carrots shot her a darkling glance.

"You'll have to wait your turn, lady."

Melora clenched her teeth. She threw a desperate glance at the gangly brown-haired boy of about fourteen who stood ahead of her at the desk.

He seemed at a loss regarding what to write, and she stamped her foot impatiently.

"Excuse me, young man." Melora could contain herself no longer after several moments of agonized waiting. She used her most commanding tone, trying to sound the way her father had when he addressed his fellow ranchers after a rustling raid. "Why don't you let me send my wire first since I know exactly what I plan to say? And my message is extremely urgent!"

"So's mine." He flicked her a tense, distracted frown. He was twisting the pencil between his fingers, and Melora saw sweat on his brow. At another time she might have sympathized with the anxiety in his large brown eyes, but not now. When he put the pencil to the paper, only to sigh and shake his head, she couldn't restrain her impatience.

"Look, I'm sorry for whatever trouble you're having, but I don't have much time." She darted a nervous glance out the window. "I'll tell you what. You *compose* your message, while I give the clerk mine, and then—"

The boy spun toward her angrily. "If you'd shut up for a minute, maybe a body could think!"

Then, as he wheeled back toward the desk, Melora saw a familiar figure approaching the other side of the window. It was Cal.

He spotted her through the glass, and there was hell in his eyes.

Melora gulped but stayed where she was and glared right back.

What could he do to her? Shoot her right here in the telegraph office? Beat her, drag her away?

"Listen to me, mister," she said to the clerk, hoping desperately that he could be convinced to help her. "My name is Melora Deane. There will be a substantial reward for you if you will only send a wire to Rawhide, to a man named Wyatt Hol—aaah, what are you *doing*?" she cried as the brown-haired youth suddenly grabbed her arm and yanked her toward the door.

"Hey, what about your wire, kid?" the clerk barked.

"Never mind!" the boy shouted back.

Melora gasped, stumbling as he dragged her out the door. "Wait a minute, young man, just because I asked him to send a wire for me you don't have to get all—"

"Looks like you lost something, Cal," the boy announced disgustedly as he pushed Melora forward on the boardwalk.

Cal was staring at him. To Melora's astonishment, warmth and affection flashed across his face. "Well, Jesse, she tends to be a mite slippery." He actually grinned at the boy, then sprang forward and embraced the youth in a giant, emotional bear hug.

Melora looked on, too stunned to do anything else. Suddenly Cal broke away and held the boy at arm's length. "What is it, Jesse? You wouldn't have come here if something wasn't wrong."

"Something is wrong." The boy wiped a shirt sleeve across his sweaty face. "It's Lou. She's sick, Cal."

"What's wrong with her?"

"We don't know exactly, but she's got a terrible fever. I rode over to Devil's Creek to find a doctor and hoping there'd be a wire from you, but there wasn't either one. I thought of trying to find you, Cal, by wiring Zeke or Ray, but hell, I didn't know what I was going to do about Lou's fever!"

"How bad is it?"

"Bad. She's been sick three days already. She won't eat anything." He swallowed hard. "I'm scared, Cal!"

"It'll be all right. We'll be there by this afternoon." Cal seized Melora's arm and started toward the hotel at a near run, with Jesse hurrying to keep up with them. "If she's not any better by then, I'll ride to Deadwood or Cherryville and fetch a doctor myself."

"You can't. That's too dangerous, Cal. You can't risk showing your face in those towns!"

"Don't argue with me, Jesse. I'm going."

Melora digested all this as they hurried along. Obviously Cal had been too distracted by Jesse's news even to think about what she'd tried to do at the telegraph office. She could understand why. She'd already deduced that Lou must be his sister, Louisa. And she'd have bet her boots that Jesse was his

brother. There was a decided resemblance in the
strong features and the pugnacious slant of the nose.

But she had no time to ponder what Jesse'd said
about Deadwood and Cherryville because as they
reached the lobby of the hotel, Cal finally halted long
enough to speak to her.

"Change in plans, Melora. Forget the cabin. I'll
have to take you with me."

"To your family's ranch?"

"To the farm where we live now." His face was
grim, mirroring the tension Jesse had displayed at the
telegraph office.

Suddenly the urge to comfort him overtook her.
The tautness in Cal's broad shoulders and the worry
furrowing his brow filled her with emotion she didn't
fully understand. "Maybe I can help Louisa," she
said impulsively. Without realizing it, she put a hand
on his arm. "I've nursed Jinx through fevers lots of
times. And through the measles and whooping
cough."

He nodded, but his eyes held a faraway look.

"Cal, she'll be all right. You'll see."

"Grab your things, and we'll ride for the farm,"
he directed. "Jesse, you give her a hand with the gear
while I get the horses. And keep your eye on her—
she's tricky as they come!"

Melora watched him stalk away, feeling more rebuffed and alone than she'd ever felt in her life.

And so before the sun had fully begun its westward
march across a sky as blue as larkspur, the three of
them were galloping east, away from Devil's Creek,
straight toward the towering cliffs of the Black Hills.

11

Wyatt Holden yanked open the door of the Diamond X Ranch and studied the long-faced man confronting him on the porch.

"You're Coyote Jack?"

"That's me, mister." Coyote Jack spit a glob of tobacco juice at his feet, then lifted insolent coal black eyes. "So now that you sent for me and I'm here, what can I do for you?"

"Come inside to talk."

He led the Wyoming Territory's most notorious bounty hunter into the spacious oak-paneled study that had belonged to Jed Holden and shoved closed the heavy carved door.

"Brandy? Cigar?"

With his head tilted to one side, Coyote Jack

paused beside the mantel and stroked his gray mustache. A grin split his face as he nodded. "Sounds damned good, Mr. Holden. Don't mind none if I do."

As Wyatt poured dear Uncle Jed's brandy into a fine old crystal goblet, he appraised his visitor. By the time he handed Coyote Jack the brandy and a fragrant cigar from Uncle Jed's humidor, he had concluded that he was not displeased by what he saw.

The famed bounty hunter looked every inch as dangerous as his reputation. He appeared to be about forty, tall and big-bellied, and true to his name, he did bear strong resemblance to a coyote. His face was long, his nose had the length and general shape of a snout, his eyes were dark and canny, darting this way and that. Leathery skin and thin gray lips gave him a carnivorous appearance. His stringy black hair was peppered with gray and hung nearly to his thick waist. He wore all buckskin, and black boots, and a black broad-brimmed hat. Two big Colts slapped against his thighs as he sank into the deep old leather armchair opposite the desk. When he put his booted feet up on the low oak table, he was smiling at Wyatt, but there was a meanness in his swarthy face, a viciousness that showed itself in the arrogant curl of his lips, in the hellish glint of his eyes.

He looked to be the perfect man for the job.

"Now that all the pleasantries have been observed," Coyote Jack drawled, "why don't you tell me what the hell you need?"

Wyatt's glance flitted briefly over several items on the desk. He gazed at the wanted poster, then at the silver-framed photograph of Melora, then turned his attention to the mysterious wire he'd received, the one instructing him to get himself to Deadwood pronto if he ever wanted to see Melora Deane alive again. He picked up the wire and absently ran his thumb back and forth along its edges.

"I need you to find someone for me. A woman."

"And do what with her?"

"Bring her back to me. *Safely.*" Wyatt's blue eyes narrowed, fixing the bounty hunter with a tersely unmistakable warning. "I don't want one hair on her head to be harmed."

"Uh-huh. Any idea where she is?"

"My guess is she's being held in the Dakota Territory—somewhere not far from Deadwood. I'm heading that way myself."

He paced across the room, stared out the window toward the Weeping Willow property, then continued smoothly. "I'll be staying some fifteen miles from Deadwood, though, in a little town called Cherryville."

"Cherryville's a mighty rowdy place, Mr. Holden." The bounty hunter finished his drink in one swig, swung from the chair, and lumbered toward the brandy decanter. He helped himself to another generous splash of the burgundy liquid. "I'd say it's every bit as lawless as Deadwood and Devil's Creek, and some say worse even than Deadwood in its wildest days."

"That's what I like about it."

The flashing white-toothed smile that Mr. Wyatt Holden gave Coyote Jack at that moment made the bounty hunter pause and stare. Well, he'd be damned. He'd underestimated his prospective employer. Something insidious underlying that smile and his words spoke volumes. This was no simple elegant dandy, no gentleman of upright morals and pure tastes. This was a man like himself, one who dressed differently, who talked differently, but underneath they were the same.

"Yep, I know what you mean." Coyote Jack chuckled with approval. "Matter of fact, I like the Peacock Brothel in Cherryville better'n any whorehouse this side of Frisco."

"Indeed. Miss Lucille does know how to run a cathouse, doesn't she?" The answer was cool, yet there was an appreciative glint in Mr. Wyatt Holden's eyes that said far more than his words. "Matter of fact, Miss Lucille is a particular friend of mine, but I don't want you setting foot in her establishment while you're working for me. I want you searching for this woman, *my* woman. Day and night. No wasted time, do you hear me? Start at Deadwood and fan out; cover the whole of the Black Hills if you have to."

"Reckon I know that area as well as anyone." Coyote Jack downed his brandy once more and licked his lips. "If she's thereabouts, I'll find her. What's the little lady's name? And what does she look like?"

"Her name is Melora Deane. And she's beautiful," Wyatt said slowly. He turned the silver-framed photograph of Melora around so that the bounty hunter could see it. A pulse hammered in his throat

when he saw the glint of purely bestial appreciation
in the other man's eyes.

"I'm going to marry this woman," Wyatt said in
a cold, clear voice. He held the photograph up and
shook it in the air for emphasis. "She's going to be
my wife, the mother of my children. Do you understand what that means?"

"Sure do, Mr. Holden. It means you're one lucky
hombre."

"I make my own luck." Wyatt slammed the photograph down on the desk. "Don't cross me, Coyote,
or you'll be damned sorry. Now listen up." He
pushed the wanted poster across the desk.

"Here, take it. Study this man's face and study it
good. Then hunt him down. Because this is the son
of a bitch who has her; he's holding her against her
will. And when you find him, you'll find Melora."

"You want me to kill him?"

"Damned straight I do. But not until you've made
him tell you where the woman is. I want her back,
no matter what it takes. Keep him alive until you've
found her—but not a moment longer. Is that clear
enough?"

"Clear as a Montana stream." Coyote Jack stood
and thumped his glass down on the desk. His black
eyes fastened once more on Melora's photograph.
"I'll need five hundred dollars now. Another five
hundred when I find her."

"And you'll get five hundred more when you kill
the man in that poster."

Coyote Jack's mouth stretched into a wolfish grin.
They shook hands. Wyatt peeled out the proper

sum of greenbacks and then escorted his visitor to the door. "I'll be traveling to Cherryville by stagecoach, using the name Campbell. Rafe Campbell."

The bounty hunter nodded. The fact that he asked no questions pleased Wyatt Holden. He continued briskly, eager to conclude this portion of the business and move on to the other matters that concerned him.

"You'll be able to reach me at the Gold Bar Hotel. Or at the Peacock Brothel," he added with a faint, cool smile. "I'll want a report within the week."

Coyote Jack touched two gnarled fingers to his hat. "Don't you worry, Mr. Holden. That son of a bitch who took your woman is as good as dead."

Wyatt liked the man's confidence, his swagger. He sensed that Coyote Jack was a man with absolutely no scruples, the kind you could always count on to get things done. *My old pard Cal won't know what hit him,* he reflected with satisfaction. But just in case, it wouldn't hurt to have an ace up his sleeve.

A very special little ace.

An ace named Jinx.

When Coyote Jack was gone, Wyatt went directly to the stables and saddled up. His mind click-clacked various strategies as he spurred his horse toward the Weeping Willow Ranch.

Persuading Aggie to go along with what he had in mind would be no problem; the fool would do whatever he told her was best. But Jinx Deane might prove trickier. The snotty little kid didn't take much to him.

He'd have to play his cards just right or she might refuse to go along.

That couldn't happen.

He needed the kid, and he'd get her. The easy way or the hard way.

Whatever it took.

12

The farm was tucked away in a tiny, isolated valley beneath huge mountains fringed by spruce and pine. With the sun burning overhead, Cal, Jesse, and Melora charged toward the small frame house, which looked as poor and plain as an old pack saddle. Yet for all the modesty of the simple wood structure, the landscape surrounding it was spectacular.

Melora had little time, however, to drink in the splendor of towering deep green spruces or to study the craggy granite peaks that loomed up beyond the farmhouse, appearing almost to touch the glowing sky, for they reached the farmhouse in a whirlwind of dust, and before her feet even touched the ground, Cal was grabbing her arm and sprinting with her toward the door.

· Inside the small square house all was clean and tidy, if somewhat cramped. There were cheery blue curtains at the windows, and a Navajo rug brightened the floor. She had a quick glimpse of blue fringed pillows on an old horsehair sofa, some straight-backed wooden chairs, and a hand-carved bench in the kitchen, which also held a woodstove and shelves stacked with dishes and utensils. But what Melora saw first and foremost was the open doorway leading to a small bedroom in back, and through the door she could see a little girl lying in a bed, with a small, thin boy of about five standing at the foot, and another girl, with pigtails, hollow cheeks, and somber eyes, perhaps nine years of age, hovering over her.

"Cal, is that you?" The hollow-cheeked girl turned her face anxiously, her skin pale as cream in the sunlight.

"It's me, Cassie." His boots pounded across the parlor. Jesse was right behind him. "Everything's going to be all right. How is she?"

"Her fever's worse. I don't know what to do!"

Cassie threw her arms around Cal's legs and wept as he reached the bedside and stared down at the child lying on the sweat-soaked pillow.

Melora had followed Cal and Jesse to the doorway. From where she stood near the small yellow-painted bureau she could see how flushed and restless Louisa looked, tossing and turning in the bed, her pink-sprigged nightgown twisting beneath her.

"Hi there, Lou." She'd never heard his voice so gentle. "It's me, Chipmunk, Cal. I'm home. I'm going to take good care of you now. Can you hear me, Louisa?''

The little girl focused her glittery eyes on him as he knelt and grasped her tiny hand in his large, callused one. "C-Cal?"

"Yep. In the flesh. And Jesse's here too. We're all here, and we're all going to take care of you."

"Joe too?" Louisa whispered, her eyes very big.

The other girl, Cassie, let out a whimper. Melora saw Cal's shoulders tense and noticed that the thin little boy ducked his head to stare down at his shoes.

"No, Louisa, not Joe." Cal smoothed a damp, stringy tendril of hair back from the child's brow. "Cal, and Jesse, and Cassie and Will—we're all here to help you get better."

"My head hurts, Cal. I feel so s-sick. I want Ma." The child moaned and began to toss more vehemently.

"I'll sing to you, Lou, just like Ma used to. But lie still," Cassie begged. And as Cal stepped back, she came forward and clutched her sister's clammy hand.

" 'Jimmy crack corn, but I don't care, Jimmy crack corn, but I don't care . . .' ''

Little Will joined her, singing lustily, and Melora, staring around the group, swallowed back an upwelling of emotion. They all were clearly devoted to Louisa and to one another. She felt the palpable love and caring settle over the tiny farmhouse like a tightly woven quilt, and it reminded her of home.

Cal was watching Louisa, his knuckles clenched

white, his face so grim her heart went out to him. She knew exactly how he felt, the anxiety, the helplessness. Hadn't she experienced the same thing watching Jinx recover from falling off her horse, watching day after day as her sister's legs remained still and stiff and useless?

She turned and headed for the kitchen. Soup was simmering in a pot on the stove; she quickly scooped a bowl from the cupboard and ladled in a small amount of the broth.

"Cal, here take this." She spoke quietly as she entered the back bedroom, moving slowly so as not to spill the soup. "Try to get her to drink some soup. It'll help her fight the fever. And we'll need to give her a decoction of willow bark. Jesse, can you find some for me?"

"Who's she?" Will asked, gaping at her.

Cassie too was staring in astonishment. Obviously both of them had been so immersed in Louisa's illness that they hadn't even noticed her presence.

"She's a friend," Cal answered quickly. "Jesse." He addressed his brother. "Go find what she needs."

He took the bowl of soup from her hands as Jesse hurried out the door. Strain showed in Cal's eyes, but they met hers with swift, unspoken gratitude that filled Melora with a strange warmth. It radiated from her temples to the tips of her toes as she watched Cal, the kidnapper who had borne her off so ruthlessly from her home, turn back toward the small freckle-faced girl in the bed and begin coaxing her to try the soup.

But a short time later, even after Louisa had swallowed down the decoction of willow bark that Melora had steeped in hot water, the child was no better. Actually she was worse; the fever burned through her with fierce intensity. Her skin was flushed and clammy, and her eyes were wild—huge, dark, darting eyes like those of a puppy in pain. She thrashed about on the bed until Jesse and Cal had to hold her down to keep her from throwing herself to the floor.

When at last she dropped off into an exhausted, fever-racked sleep, Cal stepped back from the bed, his face drawn.

"I'm going to Deadwood to get a doctor."

Jesse grasped his arm. "Let me go, Cal. It's too dangerous for you to be seen there. Someone might recognize you—"

"No. If there's no doctor in Deadwood, I'll have to ride to Cherryville, or on to Stockton, or someplace even farther, and you don't know your way around well enough. Besides, Jesse, those towns are too rough for a boy alone. I'm sorry, but I'm not going to take a chance on losing you too!"

Jesse fell miserably silent at these words. Melora stared from one to the other of them. What did Cal mean about losing Jesse? He seemed to be saying he had lost someone else. Their mother perhaps? Or another brother?

Joe. She remembered how shaken they'd all looked when Louisa had asked for Joe. He was the one Cal had mentioned last night during the storm, the one who played the fiddle at family barbecues.

Cal was gone before Melora had time to do more

than glance at his set face. The farmhouse felt oddly bereft without him, Rascal's flying hooves leaving behind only a veil of dust that whirled up through the leaves of the spruces.

She glanced around at the sad, silent faces in the little bedroom where Louisa lay ill and found herself shepherding everyone out into the parlor, even Jesse, who shook off her hand but followed close behind.

"Everything is going to be just fine," she told Cassie and Will as they paused beside the sofa. She made sure that her reassuring smile included Jesse, but the boy didn't smile back. He merely hitched his thumbs in his pockets and watched her suspiciously, obviously the only member of the family besides Cal who knew that she wasn't really a "friend," that she wasn't present in their home by her own free will.

"Cal will bring a doctor for Louisa, one way or another, and she's going to get better in no time. Now, in the meantime, let's fix some tea and toast in case she wakes up and wants something to eat."

Five-year-old Will lifted hopeful, trusting green eyes toward her, and a pang speared through her heart. This is how Cal must have looked once as a young boy; he and Will shared the same thick chestnut hair, the same alert, dark-lashed green eyes that missed nothing and that were set beneath slashing brows. They also had similarly firm, sturdy features, she noted, and she also saw that Will's young jawline already hinted at the same strength and stubbornness his brother possessed. As a matter of fact, the resemblance among all three brothers was strong, yet each had a distinctive look about him that was all his own.

Will, for one, had dimples, two of them, that puckered his little cheeks as he smiled up at her.

"Will, Cassie." Melora continued, holding out a hand to each of them and starting toward the kitchen. "It'll be suppertime soon. Maybe you both will help me get it started."

"I know how to cook," Cassie offered shyly. "Mrs. O'Malley from the farm down the road comes now and then and helps me put up supper, and she taught me how to bake lots of things."

"Did she? Well, that was very kind of her. Then you and I will fix supper together—two pairs of hands work much quicker than one." She smiled. "When Cal gets back, he's bound to be hungry from all that riding."

"He likes fried chicken," Will informed her.

Melora beamed at him. "Well, wait until he tastes *my* fried chicken. Jinx claims it's the best in the whole Wyoming territory."

"Who's Jinx?"

"My little sister. She's a little bigger than you, Cassie. She's eleven, and her favorite Sunday supper is fried chicken and mashed potatoes, with blueberry cream pie for dessert. I don't suppose anyone here likes blueberry cream pie?" she inquired innocently.

Her grin spread as Will and Cassie clamored out, "We do!" in unison. She saw Jesse watching her from the parlor, his eyes hard and wary.

He looked so much like Cal that she almost laughed.

"Come on, Jesse. Help us." She went to his side and spoke in a low tone. "We'll leave the door to Louisa's room partially open, just like it is now, so that we can hear her if she calls out, but she needs to sleep, and the children need to get their minds off their troubles."

"All right. But don't try to get away. Cal left me in charge, and I'll have my eye on you." He said it with all the arrogant, insecure swagger of a fourteen-year-old, but beneath it Melora saw a worried boy trying very hard to be a man.

"I'm going to be right under your nose in the kitchen," she assured him. "For right now no one in this house is going anywhere."

He nodded, watching her as she hurried back to the kitchen and proceeded to delight Will and Cassie with her plans for a supper that sounded as enticing as a May Day picnic.

So while Cassie showed her the larder, and Will sliced bread for toast and brought out the teakettle, Jesse went out back to catch some chickens.

What am I doing here? Melora wondered presently, surrounded by the plucked chickens, a bowl of flour, a sack of potatoes, some carrots, and two cans of white beans. *Cal is away, and this is the best chance I've ever had to escape. If I can't figure out a way to ride out of here while Jesse's back is turned, then I'm no self-respecting daughter of Craig Deane.*

But she didn't want to sneak out. Not right now. She kept thinking about the sick little girl in the next room, whose fever was raging dangerously, and about

these hungry little children, with their worried faces
and trusting eyes.

*After I get supper going for them and check on
Louisa, I'll make my move. There's plenty of time
before Cal gets back. In the meantime perhaps I can
find out exactly how to get to Deadwood from here.
Then all I'll have to do is make sure I don't run
straight into Cal while I'm heading there.*

But somehow, when the chickens were sizzling in
the skillet and biscuits were browning in the oven,
and she was stirring beans in a pot while Cassie sliced
potatoes and carrots, with Will telling her soberly all
about his pet rabbit, Brownie, who sometimes slept
in his and Jesse's room instead of in the barn, and
Cassie confiding in her ear that she hated carrots but
always tried to eat them so as to set a good example
for Will and Lou, the opportunity never arose.

Oh, she did succeed in learning the general direction of Deadwood from the farm, and Jesse did disappear into the barn to see to his chores, and she had
a plain view of Sunflower, who'd been fed and
brushed and was now tethered outside (saddleless, but
that wouldn't stop her). Yet just as she was stepping
toward the door, reminding herself of Jinx and of the
danger Wyatt might find himself in, just then Louisa
cried out, and Melora whirled and ran into the bedroom, with Will and Cassie at her heels.

Louisa was worse. Much worse, Melora saw at
once, and fear sliced through her like a cold knife as
she lifted the girl in her arms and felt her hot, dry
skin. She was listless now, aside from that one cry,

she didn't make a sound. Her eyes were glazed with a dull misery.

"Quick, Cassie, bring cool wet cloths. We have to sponge her body and cool it."

But even as they sponged her face and neck and chest with the cool cloths, Louisa's skin grew hotter. The fever raged behind her eyes. She was so still and limp that Melora's heart quaked for her.

"We have to plunge her into a bathtub of cool water," she decided just as Jesse entered the room. She spun toward him, her hand pointing toward the door. "Bring a tub and fill it quickly. There's no time to lose!"

Louisa sobbed as they placed her in the cool water. She thrashed about and only quieted when Cassie sang to her again, this time a lullaby. Cassie had a beautiful voice, a voice that could charm frogs off a lily pad. Somehow the pigtailed nine-year-old with the serious manner of a much older girl managed to keep Louisa sitting in that tub long enough for the chill water to steep into her pores and do battle with the fire raging within.

And then, after they had managed to settle her in her own bed again, encased in clean white linens, she seemed better. Wonderfully, miraculously better.

"Her fever's broken," Melora whispered, her fingers lightly caressing the little girl's sweating forehead. She sent up a prayer of thankfulness.

"Who are you?" For the first time Louisa seemed able to focus on what was happening around her. She looked exhausted, she was damp with perspiration from the fever's breaking, but she was calmer, and the unnatural glitter was gone from her eyes.

"She's Cal's friend." Cassie grinned and squeezed her sister's hand. "I guess Cal's finally got himself a girl."

"You're Cal's girl?" Louisa asked in awe, her eyes flitting eagerly over Melora as if memorizing every detail of her appearance.

"Well, not exactly—"

"Sure you are." Will nodded vehemently and whistled through his teeth. "Cal wouldn't have brought you here if you weren't his girl," he stated with complete confidence. "He always said when he gets himself a girl he wants to marry, he'll bring her home to meet all of us and see if she passes muster."

"I don't want to know if I do or not," Melora said hastily, holding up a hand as Cassie seemed about to give her judgment. "Because I'm not—"

"Cal's coming with the doctor!" Jesse announced suddenly from the doorway, and they all turned to stare.

At once they became aware of the hoofbeats drumming toward the farmhouse, and as Melora turned to the window, she saw Cal leading the way for a rickety wagon that plummeted over the uneven land.

"You—come with me," Jesse told her roughly, grabbing her arm before Melora could even tell him how much better Louisa was feeling.

He dragged her out of the room and into the second bedroom, then stood there with his back to the door. "Don't make a sound. Don't let that doctor know you're here, or I'll—"

His voice trailed off. He obviously wasn't sure what he would do to silence her. Melora almost pitied him.

But then she remembered her own little sister. Now that Louisa appeared to be out of danger, she had to think of Jinx.

"I won't say a word," she promised, but her fingers were crossed behind her back.

She and Jesse stared at each other as they heard Cal and the doctor come in, heard the children explaining about the bathtub and about how the fever seemed to have broken.

Suddenly Melora dashed toward the door, shouting, "Help! Doctor, help me. I'm being kept—"

Jesse dived at her, trying to cover her mouth with his hands. She bit him and screamed "Help" again. But the boy was game, as game as Cal, she soon found out, for he suddenly pushed her into a closet and slammed the door.

Her shouts were muffled.

"Who's that?" Dr. Wright's beetle brows drew together as he straightened up from his patient.

"Just my wife, Doctor." Cal spoke calmly, ignoring the amazed stares of his younger siblings. "She's upset because she wants permission to come in here and tend to Louisa herself. But I'm keeping her away. You see, we just found out she's expecting a child, and she's been feeling a bit under the weather. The last thing I need is for her to come down with this fever, so you go on and tend to Lou, and don't pay my wife any heed."

As Dr. Wright bent over his patient again, Cal sent

Cassie and Will a warning glance that kept them silent in the face of his bald-faced lies. He staunchly ignored the faint sounds of Melora's fury as he watched the doctor examine Lou.

In the other room Jesse would not budge from the door. Melora, seeing that her cries were being ignored and that she couldn't push the door open, slumped down in the darkness and sat on the closet floor with gritted teeth, waiting.

At last Dr. Wright left. He pronounced that the child's fever had indeed broken, that she should get plenty of rest and take in as much soup as she could to keep her strength up.

Only when his buggy had disappeared over a rise did Jesse let Melora out of her makeshift jail. Cal was there when she stepped out, her eyes blinking dazedly in the light.

"Go away," she said dully. "I don't want to talk to you. Either of you."

"I had to do it," Jesse muttered to Cal in explanation. "She was going to tell the doctor that you'd—"

"I know." Cal cut him off as Cassie and Will appeared in the doorway, all ears. "Hey, you two, don't you have chores to do around here?"

"We want to know why your girl was yelling and why Jesse locked her up in the closet," Will piped up. Cassie nodded agreement, her hands clenched on her brother's shoulders.

"Go ahead, Cal. You too, Jesse." Melora's bitter gaze shifted from one to the other of them. "Why don't you explain?"

"Reckon I will. When the time is right." Cal went to Cassie and Will, hunkered down on one knee, and pulled them into the circle of his arms. They snuggled eagerly against him, lifting trusting faces.

"Do you remember that I told you I had to go away for a while because of what happened to Joe? That I was going to take steps making sure that the man responsible for killing him was punished? Well, I'm still working on that. And this lady is not my girl; she's someone who's going to help me."

The youngsters nodded solemnly. Cassie chewed on her lower lip. "But I don't understand. If she's helping you, Cal, why would Jesse lock her in the closet?"

"Don't ask so many questions," Jesse exploded, raking a hand through his hair.

"It's all right." Cal threw him a level look. "I don't blame Cassie for having questions. Or you either, Will. This is pretty confusing. But right now you just have to trust that me and Jesse and this lady—her name is Melora—are doing the best we can to catch and punish the man who killed Joe. And to clear Joe's name—and mine. Your job is to look out for each other, lay low here on the farm like I told you, and take care of Louisa until she's all better. Okay?"

"Okay." Will pulled impatiently out of Cal's embrace. "I'm hungry. When can we eat?"

"Oh, my gosh, supper," Cassie gasped. She broke away from Cal and, with a frantic glance at Melora, raced off to the kitchen. At a nod from Cal, Jesse shepherded Will after her.

Alone with Melora in the little bedroom, Cal shut

the door. He regarded Melora with his arms folded across his chest.

"If you wanted to escape, why didn't you leave while I was in town? I'm sure you had opportunities."

"No, I did not," she lied.

"That so?"

"That's so." But she couldn't help flushing under his relentless gaze. In the fading afternoon light his eyes were the color of a storm-tossed sea. "I was busy trying to help Louisa. I wouldn't run out on a sick child, even if she is your sister. I couldn't do that no matter what you may think of me."

"You want to know what I think of you?" Cal stepped closer.

He looked tired—exhausted, really. His hat was pushed back on his head; his boots were covered in dust; there was grime streaked across his lean face.

"No," Melora told him bluntly. "I'm not sure I do."

Suddenly Cal sat down on the bed and closed his eyes for a moment. When he opened them, he stared at her without speaking. Then he cleared his throat.

"Look, Melora, maybe I don't have any right to ask favors of you, but would you please not tell Cassie and Will—and Louisa when she wakes up again— the truth. About us. About you . . . and me."

"Don't you think your family would be interested in hearing all about how their wonderful big brother kidnapped me?"

For a moment anger flared dangerously in his eyes. Then it was replaced by that look of staunch, stubborn purposefulness that always made Melora uneasy. "They've been through enough already." He swung off the bed and advanced on her, his mouth a hard line that slashed the tough planes of his face.

"None of them has had it easy, Melora. They've lost both their parents over the years, and recently their oldest brother and their home. This farm is only a temporary refuge until I've straightened everything else out—" He broke off suddenly, frowning at her. "Don't ask me to explain it all to you because I'm damned if I will. But know this, Princess: It's my job to protect them and help put the pieces back together, and I'm damned if I'm going to stand by and watch anything else shake up their already rickety little world. So if you won't agree to keep your pretty mouth shut, I guess I'll just have to hustle you out of here and take you up to that cabin I've got all ready for you. It's a good twenty miles from here, and there's not a soul nearby, except the eagles and some deer and moose, so you can't get into any trouble— or cause any."

Her lips quivered. He meant it. There was no mistaking the cold threat radiating from his powerful frame. "I won't tell them." She turned her back on him. "But not because you threatened me."

"Then why?"

"Because I like your family. And they obviously think the sun rises and sets with you, and I don't want to be the one to disillusion them."

There was a silence. From the kitchen they could hear Cassie and Will rattling plates and cups and utensils. Outside, a rose and vermilion sunset gilded the cool blue sky.

"Fair enough, Melora." Cal spoke at last, his voice deep and quiet as the great trees lining the hills. "I'm beholden to you for that. And for what you did for Louisa today. Cassie told me and Dr. Wright how you took care of her."

She spun back toward him, shaking with anger. "You can thank me by explaining all this. By telling me why you think Wyatt is responsible for your brother's death."

"Leave it be, Melora."

"I have a right to know. To help clear up the mistake."

"There's been no mistake! Damn it!" he exploded, and reaching her in two strides, he snatched her by the shoulders, giving her a hard shake, but just as Melora gasped in fright, Jesse shoved the door open a crack and poked his head in.

"Supper's on."

"I'm not hungry." Melora was rigid in Cal's arms. She spoke between clenched teeth. "I'd like to rest."

It was true. She was worn out from the strain of the past days and, in particular, from the crisis with Louisa. And she was weary of this whole ridiculous charade, of fighting and arguing with Cal, who had to be the most muleheaded man in the world.

She didn't want to sit opposite him and pretend to be his friend. She didn't want to make small talk or eat any of the meal she had worked so hard to prepare. She didn't want to try anymore to figure out this whole mess. She just wanted to see her own little sister again, to have Wyatt cradle her in his arms and tell her that it was all a horrible mistake and that he was going to put everything to rights. That he was going to take care of her and Jinx and the ranch and she wouldn't have to worry about anything ever again.

When she glanced longingly at the neatly made-up bed beneath the window, Cal followed the direction of her gaze. He let go of her arms. "You're sure?" His tone was curt. "You need to eat, you know."

"I need to sleep. To forget everything, for a little while." To her horror she sounded dangerously close to tears.

Cal must have heard it, but to her relief he allowed her to retain some semblance of dignity by merely shrugging. "Suit yourself. Go ahead and rest. Reckon we can save you some supper for when you wake up."

He closed the door behind him without glancing back. Melora immediately threw herself down upon the blue and green checked quilt.

For a kidnapper that man was mighty considerate. And for a kidnapper he had an unusually sweet and devoted family.

It complicated everything.

He's not only a kidnapper, she reminded herself as her eyes closed and her head sank onto the pillow. *He's an outlaw. He was in prison.*

She dozed fitfully, but thoughts of Cal, of his family, of Jinx and Aggie and Wyatt swirled confusedly through her tired brain.

As she wandered through that misty gray fog somewhere between sleep and wakefulness, those same words repeated themselves in her brain. *He's a kidapper. An outlaw. An outlaw.*

Her eyes flew open suddenly. She had it. She knew why Cal blamed Wyatt for his brother's death, why he hated him so much. This had to be the answer.

If Cal was an outlaw, then perhaps his brother Joe had been one too. And perhaps Wyatt had caught them both or identified them as the culprits in some crime, and somehow or other Joe had been killed by some lawman because of Wyatt's intervention, and now Cal wanted vengeance against him.

She bolted upright, trembling. She had to get out of here. For all she knew, Cal was already making some move, was already drawing Wyatt closer to ensnare him in a trap.

She ran to the window, but it was too small for her to climb through. Frustrated, she stalked the room, forgetting her weariness, frantic only with the need to get away.

Dusk loomed, and she turned up the kerosene lamp on the bedside table, illuminating the plainly furnished little room enough so she could make out the small homemade bureau, the closet, the shelf of books along one wall. Sudden curiosity sent her to the shelf, and she began glancing through the books.

What kinds of books do outlaws read?

To her surprise, there was a leather edition of *Ivanhoe*, Mark Twain's *The Adventures of Tom Sawyer*, and *The Adventures of Huckleberry Finn,* a Bible, a much-worn volume of *The Last of the Mohicans,* and a volume of poetry. Just as she was turning away, some papers wedged between *Ivanhoe* and the Bible caught her eye. On impulse Melora reached for them.

They were folded over. As she opened them, a gasp rushed from her.

They were wanted posters.

Ice crystals formed around her heart as her gaze flew over each one in turn. Cal's likeness filled one page, his lean, taut face staring out at her, his expression fierce and stoic. The second poster contained a drawing of someone who could only be his brother—his older brother—for the resemblance was uncanny, with just the shape of the lips and the eyes and the slant of the nose and the fact that his brother wore a neat mustache somewhat different.

Her gaze riveted back on Cal's deftly sketched face. The likeness was good; it was damned good.

But it wasn't that which made her stomach feel as if she'd just swallowed ground glass; it wasn't that which made her sink down on the bed in shock, her hands trembling as she clutched the posters in numb fingers. It was the names.

Beneath Cal's image the words jumped out at her.

> *WANTED!*
> WYATT HOLDEN
> FOR MURDER AND CATTLE RUSTLING
> $200 DOLLAR REWARD.

"JOE HOLDEN" was the name boldly printed beneath the sketch of his brother.

"No." The word choked from Melora's numb lips.

''No, this can't be . . . it doesn't make . . . any sense . . .''

''Give those to me.'' Cal was addressing her from the doorway, and his tone was as hard as the fists clenched at his sides.

13

In three steps he reached her and snatched the wanted posters away. Melora perched frozen on the bed, staring at him, too shocked and bewildered to form any one of the hundreds of questions reeling through her mind.

"You—you're not Wyatt Holden," she gasped at last, fixing him with the first sparking glints of a growing fury.

"I'm not?"

"You—you used his name, you rustled cattle and used his name, and you—you killed someone—and—"

Cal's bitter, twisted lips made her voice trail off. He folded the posters and set them back between the books on the shelf, then turned toward her, his posture deceptively casual, but she could see the tension across his broad shoulders, the muscle pulsing beneath his stubbled jaw.

"Sorry, but it's just the opposite, Princess. He used my name. He's *been* using my name."

"You're lying!"

He stalked toward her again until he was so close he could have reached out and touched her ashen cheeks. But he made no move to touch her as she sat on the bed. "If you want to marry Wyatt Holden so badly," he told her evenly, "we'd best call a preacher up here to this farm and get it over with. Because if you go back to Rawhide, you won't be marrying Wyatt Holden, you'll be marrying a snake named Rafe Campbell."

His words rang like broken bells in her ears. She struggled to comprehend them, to make sense of them.

But she was lost.

"Let me out of here." Melora lashed out at last. She sprang up, facing him, flinging her hair from her eyes. "I don't believe you. You're a liar. A liar and a thief and a kidnapper. Your name is Cal, not Wyatt! Now let me pass. I will not stay another moment!"

But as she whipped toward the door, Cassie suddenly appeared on the threshold. Her eyes looked enormous, sad and scared in her pale face. She wore an ankle-length calico nightgown with a ruffled neck, and her hair, no longer bound up in pigtails, trailed loose past her thin, childish shoulders.

Melora skidded to a halt as she saw the girl. She

bit her lip, wondering how much Cassie had over-heard. Behind her Cal sucked in his breath.

Cassie peered from one to the other of them. Then her gaze jerked back to Melora. "You're not going to help us, are you?"

"Cassie, I want to help, but—"

"Didn't Cal tell you about Joe?"

"No, he didn't. But I don't—"

"The posse killed Joe," Cassie said before Cal could stop her. "And he didn't do anything wrong. And that crooked sheriff was going to hang Cal. And he didn't do anything wrong either. It was that other man—"

"Cassie, I have to leave. I can't listen to any more," Melora cried, and darted past the girl.

She fled past Jesse, who was stacking dinner plates in the kitchen, while Will played marbles on the floor. She raced past the doorway to Louisa's room, where in a flashing glimpse it appeared the girl was sleeping peacefully. She jumped over the marbles beside the rug and flew straight out the door.

"What did I say?" Cassie turned to Cal with a forlorn expression. She began to cry. "I just wanted to talk her into helping us, so this can all be over and you can stay with us for good—"

"I know, Cassie. I know." Cal patted her arm. "Stay right here now and look after Lou. I'm going to bring Melora back."

"But she doesn't want to help us," the girl wailed, and her voice echoed in Cal's ears as he bolted out the farmhouse door in pursuit of Melora Deane.

He caught her just beyond the barn and hauled her up against the trunk of a spruce. "This is a stupid idea, Melora. You can't run away in the dark."

"It's not dark yet!"

He threw a glance at the purple-shadowed twilight sky. The last glimpse of the luminously glowing sun was slipping beneath the horizon. "It will be in a minute or two. Come on back to the house, and we'll talk."

"I don't want to talk!" Melora kicked him in the shin. Cal swore but didn't loosen his grip, keeping her pinned against the tree, while his eyes narrowed dangerously at the corners.

"The reason you're so mad is that you know deep down that what I said is the truth. The truth has a way of biting people on the nose; it can't be ignored. It's *felt*, Melora; it makes itself felt. You know the truth, don't you? Don't you, Melora?"

He shook her, studying her as her face mirrored one emotion after another. All around them the final glimmers of daylight fled before encroaching blackness.

The hills sang with insect sound, and unseen animals rustled through the brush. An owl hooted from the tree above them, and beyond Cal's shoulder, on a distant peak, Melora saw a prong-horned antelope poised on the shadowy crest of a ridge. She swallowed hard as she forced herself to meet Cal's stare, forced herself to look into his eyes.

And suddenly the truth tumbled from her own lips.

"I don't know what to believe," she gasped, and

then she sagged against him, and Cal's arms encircled her as naturally as if he were comforting his own little sister.

Except that Melora Deane was not his sister. She was an exquisite young woman, one coming to grips with a terrible truth. And Cal felt something quite different from brotherly concern as he thought of how much this must be hurting her, of how Rafe Campbell could bring pain to so many, and most specifically to *her*, and from so far away.

"Melora, he's a snake. A cold-blooded, manipulative murdering snake. You should be glad you found out before you married him—"

"Glad?" Melora interrupted him, jerking back, as white-lipped and shocked as if he'd punched her in the stomach. "I'll never be glad of anything again. Either I'm a complete fool to be so taken in by him, or I'm an even bigger fool to be taken in by you." She gave a half-crazed, desperate laugh. "And I don't know which kind of fool I am! I don't have the faintest notion what to believe!"

"I think you do." Cal hauled her up against him.

With her breasts pressed hard against his chest, and his hands gripping her arms with unconscious strength that bit into her flesh, she could do nothing but stare into the intense fire of his gaze, do nothing but gasp at the heat that flowed through her, through both of them, that threatened to engulf and disintegrate her.

"Admit that you know the truth, Melora."

"No, your name isn't Wyatt." She managed to

churn out the words in a breathless voice. "It's Cal. Everyone calls you that. Zeke and Ray, your brother Jesse; so do Cassie and Will and Louisa!"

"My full name is Wyatt Calvin Holden. My family's always called me Cal ever since I was a boy. Lately I've been using it all the time, thanks to Rafe Campbell dirtying the Holden name all across Arizona. I've had to go by Cal Johnson because of those wanted posters. If I'm caught before I clear my name, I'll be hanged."

"Hanged?" She swallowed hard, searching his face. "I suppose that makes sense—because you're accused of murder."

"Accused, tried, convicted. And I very nearly was hanged already, thanks to your fiancé. The night before they were going to hang me, Jesse sneaked into town and broke me out of jail. I took Zeke and Ray out with me; they hadn't done anything but get in a fight and bust up a saloon, but the sheriff took a dislike to them and accused them of rustling. Good old Sheriff Harper." His lips twisted harshly. "The crooked bastard was in cahoots with Campbell; the two of them worked together to frame me and Joe."

"I don't understand." Dazed, with a raw, sick feeling in the pit of her stomach, she shook her head, trying to make sense of all that he was telling her.

"It's a long story, Melora. And it's getting cold out here. You're shivering."

It was true. With nightfall, cool crystal gusts leaped down the mountains and slapped icily against her skin. She hadn't even noticed until he pointed it out. "I don't mind."

"I do." He took her arm and started back toward the farmhouse, now a dark silhouette among tall trees. The cozy glow beaming from the windows seemed a beacon, as did the gray smoke pluming from the chimney. "Let's get you before a fire and give you some supper, and then later, when everyone else has turned in for the night, I'll tell you the sad saga of Rafe Campbell and the Holden family."

Everyone stared at them as they entered the lamplit farmhouse. Jesse fixed her with a wary glare, Will smiled tentatively as he clutched a fistful of brightly colored marbles, and Cassie hurried from Louisa's room, her lips trembling.

"It's all my fault, Melora," she said in a tiny voice, and hung her head. "I don't blame you for wanting to leave after I upset you."

"No, Cassie. It isn't your fault at all. I'm the one who's been worrying *you*." Melora went to the girl and embraced her, squeezing her thin shoulders. "I do want to help you—all of you." She sighed. "It's just that—"

"Melora and I had a squabble before we got here—just like one of our own family squabbles," Cal interjected from the doorway of the farmhouse. "But now everything's all straightened out."

"Did you hug and kiss?" Will asked.

"Uh, well . . ."

"You know the rule," the boy insisted. "After every squabble we have to hug and kiss and make up."

"He's right." Cassie nodded, her eyes sparkling suddenly, and even Jesse grinned, his intent green gaze flicking back and forth with amusement between Melora's delicately pinkened cheeks and Cal's red ones.

"Go ahead." Will trotted to Cal and tugged him into the cozy parlor, where a fire burned pleasantly in the hearth and everything looked tidy and inviting. "Give her a hug and a kiss."

"Can't right now, have to go check on Lou," Cal growled, and started for the bedroom door, but it was Jesse who jumped up and, grinning even wider, put a restraining hand on his arm.

"Lou's fine. She woke up, had two cups of tea, and some bread we dipped in the soup broth, and she fell back asleep. Fever's gone."

"So go ahead." Cassie gave Melora a gentle push. A giggle escaped from her lips. "Show us that you've worked out your squabble."

This is ridiculous, Melora thought, coloring up like a schoolgirl about to stand up at a dance with a boy for the very first time. *Neither Cal nor I need to do this to satisfy these silly children.*

But as her feet dragged across the floor, Cal came forward to meet her. A sweet pounding started inside her chest.

To her surprise he looked nearly as uncomfortable as she. Though he was trying to appear casual and kept his expression determinedly neutral, there was something sheepish in the way he held his arms out toward her that tugged at her heart.

But there was nothing sheepish about what happened next.

Cal seized her, swooped one arm around her waist, the other around her neck in a graceless but powerful hold, and planted a kiss on her lips that scorched through to the tips of her toes. The room spun in a dizzying circle that made her hold on to him for dear life.

It was a long kiss, a very long kiss.

At last, faintly, she heard the sound of hands clapping. Dimly she realized that he had let her go.

Slowly her dazed glance scanned each person in the room. They all were staring at her. And grinning from ear to ear.

Except Cal. He stood with his thumbs hooked in his gun belt, looking perfectly nonchalant and quite pleased with himself.

"Haven't you ever been kissed before?" Cassie piped up, giggling.

"Yes . . . of course, many times." Flustered, Melora tossed her head. This was getting to be more ridiculous by the moment. To salvage her pride, she began to speak quickly. "But I didn't expect to be kissed quite so . . . enthusiastically by Cal because I thought he was going to kiss me the way he kisses the members of his family to settle a 'squabble,' not like . . . like—"

"Not like you were his girl." Jesse finished for her helpfully, and for the first time, as she met the youth's gaze, he smiled at her with no trace of either suspicion or hostility.

"Cal's never had a girl," Will informed her importantly. "Till now."

Melora regarded Cal from beneath the sweep of her lashes, a pert, inquisitive glance. It pleased her to see that at last he looked as flustered as she felt.

"And I don't have one now either," he pointed out quickly, striding to the fireplace and adding another log. "Melora is just a friend."

"But she's so pretty." Disappointed, Will pushed his lower lip out in a pout. "If you don't want her for your girl, she can be mine."

Everyone laughed, including Melora, who threw her arms around the little boy. "I'd be proud to be your girl, Will."

"You would?"

"Yes. Proud and honored."

He beamed and tossed his older brother a triumphant look.

"Well, good for you, Will. Looks like you've got yourself a girl." Cal clapped him amiably on the back. Then he glanced at the window, noting the deep, thick darkness that had settled down like a fine wool cloak over the hills. "But now it's time for everyone to get to bed. Cassie, you'll come and get me right away if Lou wakes up in the night and needs something?"

His sister nodded and ran obediently to him for a good-night kiss. Then Cal turned briskly toward Will and scooped the boy up and onto his shoulders. "You and me and Jesse are moving into the barn, pardner, so's Melora can sleep in that second bedroom and have some privacy. Unless you want me to fix you up a bedroll in the corner, right here in the parlor."

"No, Cal—with you. I want to sleep in the barn with you and Jesse and Brownie."

Cal grinned up at the small boy atop his shoulders. "Sure thing, pardner. Hang on tight." He headed out the door, waiting for Will to duck before he crossed the threshold. "Jesse, bring some blankets and pillows," he said over his shoulder. "Night, ladies."

Later, as Melora peeked into Lou's sickroom and saw both Cassie and Louisa peacefully asleep in their beds, an odd, comfortable feeling washed over her. There was no denying it: This was a homey little house. Despite missing Jinx and Aggie she didn't feel lonely here.

She'd been lonely when she was away at school, desperately lonely for her home and family, though she'd hidden it well and concentrated on her studies, because Pop had insisted she get a good education. But each night in Boston she'd had to fight against the ache of loneliness in her heart. Here she wasn't lonely at all. Something about this house, this tight-knit little family so devoted to one another, filled a void inside her. Perhaps because Cal, in his determination to take care of them, reminded her of herself, of the way she intended to take care of Jinx. It was a familiar protectiveness, an understandable kind of love.

And to her amazement, as she wandered through the parlor and then into the kitchen, she felt a bond with him, a bond with the man she thought of as her enemy—but he was the most bewildering enemy she'd ever thought to encounter.

No longer tired, Melora brewed coffee. Restlessness seized her as she uncovered the supper plate Cassie had saved for her and proceeded to devour cold fried chicken and beans and potatoes. She had just finished her coffee and was carrying her empty plate to the sink when she spotted Cal through the kitchen window.

She'd remembered all along that he had promised to come back after everyone was asleep and tell her "the sad saga of Rafe Campbell and the Holden family." But she'd been trying not to think about it; she'd been trying not to think about anything. Deep down, she was all too aware that she would have to make a decision soon about where she stood and what she believed.

When she recalled the man she knew as Wyatt Holden, it seemed impossible that Cal's claims could be true. Wyatt's arms had been gentle, his lips soft and reassuring. Everyone thought him upright and fine. Everyone!

But when she stared into Cal's intently determined eyes and saw the sweet faces of his brothers and sisters, she was compelled to believe Cal's words. Yet his story sounded so incredible, so terrible that she shuddered at its implications.

Now she watched him as he leaned against a tree, silhouetted by bright, full moonlight. He rolled a cigarette and began to smoke, each movement thoughtful and deliberate, and she remembered the first time she had seen him. She hadn't thought him especially handsome at the time. How strange. Now he looked vitally handsome, with his dark chestnut hair glinting

in the moonlight and his stern, hard features illuminated enough to reveal their somber expression.

A powerful urge to soothe the careworn lines from
his face overtook her. She almost started forward.
Then she gripped the kitchen counter, stopping herself.

*Think, Melora. Don't be impulsive. Use the brain
God gave you. And consider.*

Was this man who had carried Will on his shoulders, ridden pell-mell for a doctor for Lou, rescued
her from Jethro and from Strong, and kissed her with
such rough thoroughness she'd trembled in places she
hadn't even known existed—was this man a liar, an
outlaw, a *murderer*?

Or was her fiancé?

Suddenly she turned and left the kitchen. She
strode into the bedroom, to the shelf with the books,
and took down the Bible. And holding her breath, she
opened it to the first page.

In fine, curving black script she read the inscription
written there: "THE HOLDEN FAMILY BIBLE."

Hands shaking, she closed it. Replaced it on the
shelf. And moved like a sleepwalker, passing through
the kitchen door and out across the neat little yard
without seeing its vegetable garden or the well or any
of the dark-petaled larkspurs growing in profusion
among the trees. She saw nothing, heard nothing. Her
mind was filled with memories: of words, embraces,
glances exchanged, plans made, moments shared.

All jumbled together in a jarring cacophony that
swelled through her brain.

Cal turned as she approached. Silently he watched

her glide through the moon-dappled darkness, thinking that no other woman he'd ever met had moved quite like that, with such unconscious grace, such artless sensuality.

"What's wrong? You look like you've seen a ghost." He wanted to catch her in his arms as she paused before him because she looked as if she might fall down at any moment, but he forced himself to continue blowing smoke calmly up into the night sky, to continue standing there as if nothing of import were about to be discussed between them.

"I've seen your family Bible," Melora whispered.

Cal threw down the cigarette and crushed it with his boot. The heart-rending catch in her throat clawed at his gut.

"The Holden family Bible." She continued so low he had to duck his head forward to hear her. "So it appears you're telling me the truth." She spoke carefully, each word like a shard of glass that could shatter at any moment. "Your family name is Holden."

"That's right."

"So that man back in Rawhide . . . is not a Holden—"

"Right again."

"He's . . . Rafe Campbell. Just like you said." She fought to breathe normally, to keep the stars and the sky from whirling dizzily before her eyes.

"Take it easy, Melora." Cal put a hand on her arm, but she shook him off.

"He's nothing but a liar!" she cried, her teeth beginning to chatter. "An impostor. He was lying to me all along!"

"Yeah, Melora, he was."

Melora braced herself against the tree, growing pale in the moonlight as she accepted his unhesitating, straightforward answer.

Something died inside her. Something like a seedling. A seedling filled with false, sickly sweet dreams. She lifted a hand to her throat, which ached with unshed tears, and stared off into the hills, her eyes unfocused.

Crickets chirped in the darkness. A nighthawk swooped and rasped out a harsh cry from the sky. "He never loved me."

She felt so empty and bereft inside that she could have wept, but she was too hollow for tears. "It was all . . . some kind of ruse. All a trick."

"Maybe not all of it," Cal said quietly. "But some. It's possible he does love you in his way—as much as Campbell can love anyone. As a possession." Cal's brows swooped together. "Something that belongs exclusively to him."

He frowned because he knew Campbell's possessive streak. They'd been friends once, and he'd observed firsthand how the man valued money, gold, fine things. And Melora was as fine a woman as any man could hope to possess—except you couldn't possess another human being. He doubted that Campbell understood that point. That was exactly what Cal had been counting on all this time: that Campbell would become so incensed at losing his woman—his personal, hand-chosen possession, and someone who had something he wanted, to boot—that he would follow her anywhere to get her back.

Even into the Black Hills.

Even into a trap.

That was the key to Cal's plan. Yet as he spoke the words, he could see how much they hurt her. And that stoked the embers of his fury. Rafe Campbell was a low-down son of a bitch who didn't deserve one drop of Melora's love.

Cal's mouth tasted bitter with the knowledge that she had truly cared for that bastard. And what he'd said was true enough. Campbell might love her in his own selfish, scheming way, but not in the way she deserved.

What sane man wouldn't fall in love with her? he asked himself jeeringly. *What man could resist such fiery golden beauty, a smile that could melt the sun, a spirit that refused to give up, even under the most trying circumstances?*

Not you, a hard, mocking voice answered inside him. And he knew he was a fool. She'd twist him around her finger like a string if he gave her half the chance, if he let on what she did to his insides, his concentration, his self-control every time he came within twenty feet of her.

So he'd better not let on. Melora Deane had lethal charm. Plenty of it. And he'd wager his hat and his saddle and his boots that she knew better than most women how to use it.

When it came to flirting and courtship and falling in love, he was no match for her, the belle of the territory.

It was almost funny that he'd fallen for her. *Her*. Because as Will kept reminding him, he'd never even had a girl. Any girl. Much less one who'd been wooed and courted as Melora Deane had been wooed and courted all of her life.

Forget it, Cal warned himself. *Don't even let yourself think about going after her in that way. You've already been Campbell's victim. Don't become hers.*

Playing the fool was something Cal Holden couldn't abide. He'd already done it once in this lifetime. He'd been Rafe Campbell's fool, believing in a friendship that had been false all along, letting himself get bested by a snake in gentleman's garb.

He wouldn't let anyone lure him into making a fool of himself again. Especially not Melora Deane.

"Look, Princess, we have to talk," he said urgently, trying to take his mind off this train of thought. Besides, she looked dazed. And sick. Another score to settle with Campbell, he told himself grimly. "You probably have some questions. If you want to know more about Campbell—"

"I do have questions—one question. Is Campbell dangerous?"

"Very."

Her face crumpled then, and she sprang forward, clutching at his vest. "I have to go home!"

"Melora—"

"At first light," she cried, her voice rising with panic. "My sister is there alone, Cal. She can't even walk! If anything happens to her, it'll be laid at your doorstep. You must take me home!"

14

Cal pulled Melora to him. One hand caught her hair and gently pulled her head back. He noted how the moonlight bathed the delicate planes of her face. Her eyes looked huge—and frightened. Frightened for her sister, as she had never been for herself.

"What do you mean that your sister can't walk?"

"She can't walk! When our pop was shot by rustlers, Jinx found him. She fell off her horse and now her legs won't work, and we don't know why. Cal, I have to get home and protect her!"

"Your sister isn't in any danger, Melora. Calm down. Campbell—"

"Campbell must have only wanted to marry me to get his hands on my ranch," she cried desperately. This was no time for pride or false dignity. "The

Weeping Willow is valuable property—even with all
the losses we've suffered lately, and it adjoins—'' She
froze and stared at him. ''The Diamond X. Dear Lord,
the Diamond X—it's not his. It's not his at all. If what
you say is true, Jed Holden bequeathed it to—you?''

''That's right. To me and Joe.''

''Dear Lord.''

''Campbell stole the deed Uncle Jed's lawyer sent
us, took it right off Joe's body after the posse shot
him down. He also stole our pay—money we were
planning to send home to help keep our own ranch
going.''

He didn't add the rest. That when Campbell and
the sheriff arrested Cal and threw him in jail after
they'd killed Joe, Campbell had proceeded to steal
every cent in Cal's pocket as well—and a silver-
handed pistol and the cameo necklace his grandmother had given Cal as a gift for his future wife.

He could spare her that at least. Melora had enough
to deal with right now without thinking about Campbell's giving her that same cameo.

He released her, watching the shock register on her
face. Melora sank down upon the cold, hard ground
and buried her face in her hands.

It was true. All of it, true. The resigned bitterness
in Cal's face and in his quietly spoken words could
come only from deep pain—pain caused by the truth.
Each word he spoke drove another nail into the coffin
that was all she had left of her betrothal.

Cal lowered himself to sit beside her in the darkness. He was aware of her shoulders trembling, of her
hair whipping about her, loose and wild in the wind.

Not looking at Melora, he plucked a wildflower that had been growing along the root of the tree and studied its delicate petals, frosted by starlight.

"You need to know this, Melora. All of it. But it's not a pretty story."

"Go on. I want to hear." No, she didn't. She wanted to run away and hide and shut out the world, shut out the truth, and the knowledge of her own stupidity, but she couldn't. She had to know all of it. She had to listen good and hard.

"Campbell knew all about the deed," he said softly. But Melora shivered at the cold steel she heard in his voice. "All about how Uncle Jed left us his ranch in good old Rawhide, Wyoming. Because Joe and I were fool enough to tell him. We'd been working for him up near Tucson, trying to earn enough money to pay off the mortgage on our family ranch in Nogales. It was a small place, a few hundred head of cattle—nowhere near as grand as the Weeping Willow—and it was a struggle to keep it profitable, but it was our home." His voice hardened. "We lost some of our cattle to disease the year after our mother died of the fever, and then the bank wanted to call in the loan. So Joe and I left Jesse and our old foreman in charge and took jobs as ranch hands for a big spread up near Tucson to make extra money. We sent nearly every penny home."

"Cal. I'm sorry. I'm so sorry."

"It's cold out here," he said abruptly, getting to his feet. "You're shivering again." He took her arm and helped her up, then started back to the house. Melora walked beside him in numb silence. She *was* chilled, inside as well as outside. She'd never felt so icy cold and miserable in her life.

"Campbell was the foreman of the ranch Joe and I worked at near Tucson." Cal continued when they were seated at the kitchen table with steaming cups of coffee before them. "When we heard about Uncle Jed passing on and about the Diamond X, we made a decision to go back to Nogales, to sell the ranch while we could still get something for it and move Jesse and the younger kids on to Rawhide for a fresh start on the Diamond X. We gave Campbell notice we'd be leaving soon and showed him the deed."

Cal picked up his coffee cup, then set it down again without drinking. His eyes were faraway. "He congratulated us. Wished us well. Which was to be expected, since we were friends, the three of us. Friends," he grunted, shaking his head.

"He can be very . . . charming. And caring."

Cal's laugh was harsh. "He damn well can."

Melora sipped desperately at her coffee, needing something hot and bracing to break the chill enveloping her. "What happened then, Cal? How did things go so terribly wrong?"

"Two days before Joe and I were due to go home, we stumbled onto the truth. That Campbell was rustling from our employer, a man named Ed Grimstock. And from everyone else in that valley," he added, pushing back his chair. He paced around the kitchen with long, restless strides like a long-caged panther.

"He and Sheriff Harper were working together. Rustling the valley dry."

Rustling. She'd heard him say the word before,

she'd seen it in the wanted poster, but this time it struck her like the claws of a hawk scratching deep into her skin, tearing through to her very blood and bones.

There was rustling in Rawhide too. But it had been going on a long time, she told herself, long before "Wyatt Holden" had come to town. Yet her hands shook a little as she lifted her cup.

Melora finished her coffee, her thoughts whirling like the grounds in the bottom of the coffeepot as she poured more of the hot, sustaining drink for Cal and then for herself.

"I think I'd better hear exactly what happened next." She took a deep breath, then glanced up at Cal. "If it's not too painful to tell."

"I lived through it, Melora. Reckon I can talk about it. And I reckon you have a right—hell, no, you have a *need* to know. So you can understand exactly what kind of man we're dealing with."

She watched him rake a hand through his hair, then sit down again and stare at his coffee cup. She couldn't tell how much of the ache in her heart was for herself and how much was for him.

"When Joe and I caught on to what Campbell and Harper were up to, we rode straight to our employer and filled him in. We were planning to head to town and wire the federal marshal, but Campbell got wind of the fact that we were on to him. He and Harper showed up at Grimstock's ranch right after we left for town. They killed Grimstock, and then they rode into town and announced that Joe and I had killed him."

"Cal, no!"

"They said we'd killed him because he and Campbell had caught us rustling."

She touched his arm. She felt sick, shocked, furious. She couldn't understand how he could tell her all this so calmly, with such quiet steadiness. But the harshness in his face as he turned his gaze to her quickly brought home to her that his anger ran deep and deadly. He kept it locked within him, but it was there, and when he faced Rafe Campbell again, it would come out.

"They caught you in town?" She prompted him, needing to hear the end of the story, needing to stop the assault of terrible words.

"Almost, but not quite." Cal ran a finger back and forth across the wood table. "There was this saloon girl who was sweet on Joe. Every girl he met was always sweet on Joe," he added with a rueful grin. Then his lips tightened. "But this girl saw Campbell and Harper rounding up a posse, and she warned us. We barely made it out of town alive."

It seemed that the insects had gone mad outside the farmhouse. The wild chirping chorus poured through the darkness beyond the windows, filling the night. But there was no other sound in the house as Cal stood, strode to the window, and stared out.

"Campbell and Harper and their posse rode us down. On the third day they set up an ambush, and Joe was shot. Killed. I got away, but they caught me a few miles later." He swung back to stare at Melora, every muscle in his tall frame coiled with tension. "I didn't even get to see my brother buried. They put me in jail, right next door to Ray and Zeke, and that was that. Oh, there was a trial, with a lot of trumped-up evidence, and I was sentenced to hang. Campbell packed up and left town a few days before the hanging—no doubt moving on to greener pastures, figuring I was as good as dead. I didn't know at the time he was eventually going to lay claim to my inheritance, and use my name to get it.''

Melora hugged her arms around herself, fighting the nausea in her throat. Her knees, her elbows, even her nostrils were trembling.

Was it possible that the man who had gone down on his knees to beg her to marry him was the same man who had rustled cattle, killed the rancher Grimstock, and framed two innocent men?

"I still . . . can't quite believe it."

"I know what you mean." Cal stood over her, his eyes hard. "I was taken in too, Melora—by the easy, upstanding way he talked, by his fine smile and booming laugh. Joe and I had been around enough to recognize most cardsharks and flimflam men, but we didn't nail this one. We trusted him; we thought he was our friend. Some friend."

"Some fiancé," she echoed in a hoarse whisper.

Cal yanked her up out of the chair so suddenly she gasped, and he held her roughly by the shoulders. "So you see now why you can't go back. I'm leading him here—to Deadwood actually. And he won't have time to bother with Jinx because he'll be too intent on getting you back. To do that, he has to follow my instructions."

"Instructions?"

"Zeke and Ray sent him a wire after they split up

from us. The wire informed him that if he wanted to see you alive again, he'd better get to Deadwood pronto. They signed my name to it. I'll wager that came as a nice little shock.''

She swallowed. "Did he really think you'd been hanged? Wouldn't Sheriff Harper have sent word to him after you escaped?''

"No," Cal said. "Harper's dead. I shot him during the jailbreak as he was about to plug Jesse in the back.''

Melora closed her eyes.

"So I reckon when that wire came, my good old pard Campbell got the shock of his life." Cal finished pleasantly, watching as she opened her eyes and struggled to take it all in.

He let her go when she wrenched away from him. Now it was her turn to pace, a churning restlessness driving her from the countertop to the stove, to the pantry, and back again to the table.

"What makes you think he'll come for me?'' she demanded, her fingers splayed on the wood surface. "He'll probably just cut his losses and run.''

"No way.''

"How can you say that? Now he knows you're alive and that you're on to him. He must know that you could show up in Rawhide and challenge his identity, that you could not only take back the Diamond X but get him thrown in jail!''

"Campbell's smart enough to know I can't take that chance, Melora. What if everyone believed him and not me—just like you did? I need proof. Proof that he was the one involved in rustling in Arizona, proof that he was the one who murdered Grimstock. Proof that he framed me and Joe. I need him to confess—fully and in front of a reliable, completely trustworthy witness. And besides," he added, giving her a hard, level look that made her heart pound faster, "there's something else. Something personal."

She held her breath as he studied her, his expression unreadable. "I wanted Campbell to lose something he cared deeply about. I wanted him to see what it felt like to have something stolen from him. Not just something, someone. Someone important. Because he stole not only the Diamond X but my brother's life. And he stole our good name."

For some reason she took a step back as he advanced on her as suddenly as a hawk swooping in on a mouse. He caught her chin between his fingers and forced her to look up, directly into the cold green depths of his eyes.

"So I stole his fiancée," he said as calmly and coldly as an undertaker. "I stole the incomparable Melora Deanc."

There was a silence. Wind soughed through the pines above the farmhouse, and the distant wail of coyotes rent the night.

"Perhaps he won't care." Her tone was equally hard. "It seems clear enough that Wyatt—I mean, Campbell—never loved me. He was merely using me. For all I know he's been planning to take over the Weeping Willow and sell it or—or . . . I don't know what, but I'm damn sure going to find out."

"We'll both find out." Cal's hand moved from her chin. It slid across her cheek, brushing aside a stray lock of golden hair. "Soon as he shows up in Deadwood and walks into my trap."

"You're so sure he'll come?"

"He'll come." His gaze traveled from her wide eyes to her full, trembling lips. It dipped down to the swell of her breasts outlined beneath the green and blue flannel shirt, then returned to lock once more with her eyes. There was a roughness in his voice and, at the same time, a kind of gentleness. "He'll come."

The wail of a coyote blasted close, so close Melora jumped straight into Cal's arms. He steadied her, his hands sure and strong. "Campbell's a skunk, Melora, but he's made of flesh and blood. He'll come for you all right. He won't let go of you without a fight. There's something in him that makes him always want to be the best—to have the best and flaunt the best."

"And what does that have to do with me?" she asked lightly, teasingly, half embarrassed by his implication, yet fascinated by it at the same time.

Any other man she had ever known would have taken her in his arms and told her in flattering detail exactly what he meant. Any other man would have kissed her and complimented her and made it all too clear how beautiful and desirable and irresistible he found her.

But Cal did none of those things. He appraised her with eyes as clear and keen as the sharp edge of a knife.

"You damn well know," he replied coolly, and

suddenly he pushed her away. After turning on his heel, he stalked to the door.

Melora felt as though he'd upended a bucket of icy springwater over her head. Twin blotches of color brightened her cheeks as she watched him twist the knob of the kitchen door.

Melora Deane was not accustomed to being rebuffed. For the second time that night shock poured through her.

"Get some shut-eye, Melora." For all the matter-of-fact brusqueness in his voice, he might have been talking to Zeke or Ray or his brother Jesse. He glanced back at her over his shoulder, his features as unreadable as weathered granite.

"It's been a long day."

The door closed behind him.

Weak in the knees, Melora sank into a chair. That man, that man . . .

She couldn't even formulate one coherent thought describing what she thought of him.

But she knew one thing. She wished she could bite off her tongue. Alone in the kitchen, with the coyotes howling mournfully in the hills, Melora stared at the closed kitchen door for a very long while.

15

Two days later Louisa Holden was up and scampering about as good as new and begging her brother Cal for permission to go to the O'Malley family's barbecue.

"Who are the O'Malleys, Lou?" Cal questioned her as he chopped wood out behind the barn, and Louisa, stringing dandelions together for a bracelet for Melora, paused a moment in her work to regard him witheringly.

"They're the nicest people around. They have five kids and a big farmhouse and Lara O'Malley is my dearest, bestest friend in the world, and her pa gave me a ride to town in their buggy and brought me three whole pieces of licorice when I only asked for one and—"

"When's the barbecue?" Cal interrupted, pausing with the ax in midair as he saw Melora rounding the corner of the barn, coming toward them, carrying two glasses of lemonade.

But Louisa never noticed and kept rattling on, intent on her plea. "Tonight. Please, please, please can we go? There's going to be pies and cakes and lemonade and—"

"Speaking of lemonade, I thought you two might be thirsty," Melora interrupted as she reached the little clearing that Cal had already piled high with lumber. She handed a glass of the cool concoction to Louisa and was rewarded by the girl's squeal of delight. Squaring her shoulders, Melora turned to Cal.

"Would you like some?" she asked formally.

He gave her a curt nod.

Trying not to stare at the hard muscles in his chest and forearms as he stood before her shirtless, wearing only his pants and boots, Melora reached toward him with the glass.

Unfortunately, he reached toward her at the same time and their hands collided, sending some of the lemonade sloshing over.

"Ooops, sorry," she gasped as she relinquished the glass.

Cal shrugged. "No harm done. There's still plenty left for a thirsty man." To her shock he suddenly seized her hand, held it up, and licked the cool drops of lemonade from her fingers.

"Delicious."

Louisa laughed out loud. Cal ruffled the girl's hair and gave her a wink.

But Melora stood still as a statue, heedless of the warm sun blazing down on her, of the scent of pine and autumn leaves and mountain air drifting around her. Her fingers felt on fire every place his tongue had swiped. She felt her face flaming. And of course Cal noticed, since he noticed everything.

He gave her a slow, lazy grin, and then he lifted his glass in a silent salute and gulped down the lemonade.

Melora didn't know quite what to do. She found herself at a loss. *Good Lord,* she thought, abruptly dropping her still-burning hand to her side with a stiff movement, *you'd better stop going all agog every time you come within ten feet of Cal Holden.*

This was getting to be ridiculous. She'd never gotten weak in the knees over any man before, but ever since that night when he'd walked out on her in the kitchen, some evil witch must have put her under a spell because she kept losing her train of thought when he was near. She kept wanting to follow him around like a puppy and wanting to make him notice her.

And at the same time she refused to let on one inkling of how she felt. She had too much pride actually to throw herself at a man, any man, and she certainly wasn't going to make a fool of herself over a man as infuriating and uncooperative as Cal Holden.

Yet . . .

Men are trouble, plain and simple, Melora scolded herself angrily. And after the fiasco of her recent judgment concerning Rafe Campbell, she'd be wise to stay away from *every* man for the rest of her life.

It had shaken her deeply to learn that as far as men were concerned, she wasn't as clever or infallible as she'd always thought she was. Common sense told her to steer clear of anyone wearing breeches, to remain an independent, wary-eyed spinster for the rest of her days, but common sense couldn't keep her eyes off Cal when he cleaned his guns, chopped wood, or played the harmonica.

Of course Cal paid no attention whatsoever to her. Since that night when he'd laid bare the ugly story of Rafe Campbell, he'd been the one steering clear. Unless it was absolutely necessary to speak to her, he ignored her. Unless they bumped into each other, he hadn't touched her. Most of the time he seemed so busy and preoccupied she might have been invisible, a ghost flitting around the rafters of the farmhouse, real only to the children.

So what had that meant when he'd had the audacity to lick the lemonade from her hand?

Was he baiting her, trying to annoy her, or something else?

You could never tell with Cal. That was the problem. He was impossible to read. Just now he set down his glass of lemonade and hefted the ax again. Melora grew breathless at the sight of all those rippling muscles.

"So, Lou, you really want to go to this barbecue?" he said just as if Melora weren't still standing there in the hot sun, the sleeves of her flannel shirt rolled up, her hands now resting on her hips.

"Yes, Cal, I surely do, and I want you to go too,

and Melora. The O'Malleys invited our entire family.''

"I'll have to think about it, Lou."

"But, Cal," she whined, her lower lip pushing out in a childish pout.

"Listen, Lou, don't argue with me about this. You know the rules. Go find Jesse and send him up here to talk to me. Then I'll let you know."

When the little girl had trotted off in search of her other brother, Cal chopped two more logs into eighths before he wiped an arm across his sweating forehead and set down the ax.

"It could be risky going to a barbecue tonight," he said at last. Melora had picked up the dandelion bracelet Lou had dropped and was fitting it around her wrist.

"Why?" She tried to sound matter-of-fact, though in truth she was startled that Cal was broaching this topic with her. This was the first time they'd exchanged words alone since the night she'd discovered the truth—the truth about him and about the man she'd been planning to marry. Every other moment they'd been surrounded by the rest of the Holden family, as rambunctious and mischievous and close-knit a family as Melora had ever seen.

That was just as well. Since she was in a state of confusion, for the first time in her life doubting her own perspicacity, she wasn't sure she wanted to be alone with him—or with any man.

She'd been taken in by a con man. She'd fallen in love with him. And now that she knew the truth, was she heartbroken, devastated?

No. She was furious. Furious with Rafe Campbell and furious with herself for falling prey to him.

She didn't understand herself.

And there was something else, something equally perplexing. She had feelings for this lean, bronzed man, who moments ago had chopped wood with such easy grace and strength, sweat glossing his chest and arms like dew on a tree trunk. Strong feelings. She wasn't ready to explore them, but they were there, as heady and mysterious as smoke from a woodfire.

She didn't understand them, and she didn't want to pursue them. But over the past few days as she'd been watching Cal, watching him with his younger siblings and as he worked in the barn and around the farm, she no longer saw her kidnapper, a stubborn, ruthless enemy. She saw a relaxed, efficient man whose chestnut hair continually fell forward over his eyes, a man who gave good-natured piggyback rides to Louisa and Will, who played the harmonica at night before the parlor fire while Cassie sang along, a man who worked hard without complaint for endless hours on the farm.

She saw a man who could make children smile, a man who had held her during a thunderstorm and somehow managed to soothe away her terror. A man who cared for his family and bore the same fierce pride in his family name as she did in hers.

She saw a man whose kisses made her burn, even when she was betrothed to another, a man whose touch seared her, whose rare smile filled her with unexpected delight.

But she didn't want to think about Cal. She

couldn't afford to, not now when she was so confused about her gullibility in falling for Rafe Campbell, so anxious to settle her score with him and get home to her sister and her ranch.

She became aware that Cal was speaking to her and forced her attention back to his words. "There's a chance someone could recognize me at the barbecue or even in town—though I have to admit, it's not all that likely. Most of the wanted posters you saw were distributed while the posse was after us. After my escape from the jail, there were some others sent across Arizona and New Mexico, but they don't seem to have gotten as far as Wyoming and South Dakota territories yet. But there's always a chance. Still, it's a small one," he admitted with a shrug. "And it sure would make Lou happy to go."

A barbecue. It sounded wonderfully normal, wonderfully festive and appealing. With pies and cake and dancing and laughter. Such an ordinary event, but one that seemed highly unusual these days. Life had not been ordinary since the moment Cal had snatched her from her bedroom. The very idea of the barbecue made her eyes sparkle, yet there was another danger for the Holden family to consider.

"What about the possibility that Campbell might already be in Deadwood?" She stooped to pick up another dandelion to add to the bracelet. "Isn't it a risk for any of us to go about right now anywhere? It would certainly spoil your plan if he spotted you— or me—or found out about the children. Can you imagine what would happen if he somehow turned up at that barbecue and saw us dancing together, talking?

I mean," she added hastily, turning the brilliant pink of the wildflowers still straggling on the hills as he turned to stare at her, one brow lifted. "I mean . . . assuming they *had* dancing there, and assuming you asked me . . . and assuming I agreed and—"

"You like to dance, Princess?"

She bit her lip. "Why, yes. I rather enjoy it—with the right partner." Melora gathered her composure enough to throw him an airy look. "And you?"

"Don't care much for it. Reckon I just never found the right partner."

He was staring at her so intently she felt the hot color deepen in her neck and cheeks. "Well, you told Dr. Wright I was your wife," she said slowly, "so if we went to the barbecue and if there was dancing and if Dr. Wright was there—"

"I'd have to dance with you." Cal finished helpfully.

She gave a light shrug. "There'd probably be no way around it."

"Probably not."

"Well, I'd hate to put you through having to dance with the wrong partner, so—"

"Whoa. Hold on there a minute, Melora." He pushed his hat back on his head and came toward her, his chest glistening in the full, hot sun. "Who said you'd be the wrong partner?"

"Who said I'd be the right one?" She'd managed to counter him, forcing herself not to stare at his chest, or his broad shoulders, or the muscles bulging in his arms. Instead she met his eyes, those vividly intent eyes that looked as if they could see right through her without any effort at all. "I mean, I wouldn't want to torment you by forcing you to—"

"It would be torment, all right," he muttered.

She went stiff as a rail. "I beg your pardon?"

"Never mind."

"Yes. Never mind," Melora spit out. "Because we'd best not go. If Campbell is anywhere in these parts—"

"It doesn't appear that he is." Cal turned away from her and reached for his shirt, which had been thrown down in the grass. He used it to wipe the sweat glistening on his face and neck. "I rode into Deadwood early this morning and checked at the hotel where he's supposed to wait for instructions. He hadn't checked in yet."

"And just what are you going to do when you've got him where you want him?" Melora hoped her tart tone disguised the fear she felt—fear for Cal, not for the man she'd once planned to marry. "A gunfight?" she demanded, a shade too shrilly. Her golden brown eyes flashed like bronze coins as she studied him. "That won't clear your name!"

He regarded her calmly. "Much as I'd like to shed Campbell's blood, I've got a better plan than that."

"What is it?"

He gave her a long look. "I'm going to get him to confess in front of a very important witness."

"Who?" Her heart beat faster as she followed him. He walked a few paces away, pausing beneath a tree to scan the granite-hilled horizon. "Who's your witness?"

"Ever hear of Federal Marshal Everett T. Brock?"

"Of course. My father spoke of him." Twisting the dandelion bracelet around and around her wrist, Melora watched his face. "My father said he was as fine a lawman as ever lived. Honest, with good horse sense and a brilliant knowledge of the law. Why?"

"Brock is retired now. Lives in Deadwood. I mean to find him, tell him the whole story, and see if he'll cooperate when I set Campbell up. If I can get Campbell to confess in front of Brock—" He turned sharply as a twig snapped behind them. Jesse was coming toward them, wearily carrying his hoe.

"How many families do you think will be attending this O'Malley barbecue tonight?" Cal asked his brother.

"Six, seven. Mostly the nearest neighbors this side of the gully." Jesse tipped his hat to Melora, then surveyed Cal with hopeful eyes. "Can we go?"

"Don't see why not."

Jesse gave out a whoop. He grabbed Melora's arm and spun her around in a quick do-si-do. "You'll go too, won't you, Melora?" he asked as she laughed. "Maybe I'll even save you a dance."

"Thank you very much, that would be delightful. But I won't be attending the barbecue."

"And why the hell not?" Cal swung toward her, his jaw taut.

"I don't have anything to wear." She shrugged. "I'd look silly going to a party in your flannel shirt and pants," she said with a rueful grin. "And my riding habit won't do either. So—"

"Hold on." Cal barred her way as she started back

toward the house. "What about the rest of those clothes you've been carrying in your trunk all across Wyoming? You must have had some dresses packed for your honeymoon."

She flinched at the word. Honeymoon. To think that she'd been planning her honeymoon—looking forward to it—with a murderer and a rustler. It took an effort to answer Cal steadily.

"Silks and satins. Far too fancy for a family barbecue. It's all right, Cal. I was just teasing you before about dancing and everything. I don't mind staying home, and you can just tell Dr. Wright if he's there that I'm under the weather because of my 'condition.'" She shrugged again. "My evening will be better spent composing a letter to Jinx. I need to let her know that I'm safe. Perhaps you would send it for me next time you go into town?"

"I can do that." He nodded. "Reckon there's no reason she should have to keep worrying about you. You'll be going home soon enough."

With that they stared at each other. There was nothing left to say. Jesse glanced from one to the other of them, then shook his head as Melora suddenly turned and strode across the grass toward the house.

Squinting against the hot sunshine, Cal stared after her thoughtfully.

"She ought to come to the barbecue with the rest of us," Jesse spoke up, kicking a log.

"You heard what the lady said."

"Just think. You'd have a chance to dance with her."

"What makes you think I want to dance with her?"

Jesse snorted. "Anyone can see by the way you look at her that you'd want to dance with her—and a whole lot more," he added with a grin. "Cal, come on. You know there's ready-made dresses in Deadwood. Some real pretty ones."

"I figured that."

"Want me to go into town and pick one out for her?"

Hefting an armful of logs, Cal started toward the house. "Reckon that's something I can do for her myself," he drawled so casually Jesse's grin widened.

"Sure, Cal," he said, following with the rest of the firewood. "After all, she's your girl."

"Not yet she isn't," Cal muttered under his breath, so low his brother almost didn't catch the words.

But he knew by the set of Cal's shoulders and the firm expression in his eyes that for the first time his big brother had set his sights on a particular woman.

And what a woman. Leave it to Cal to pick someone as pretty and feisty as Melora Deane.

But when Cal set his mind to something, he usually got it.

Jesse, who had his own eye on fourteen-year-old Dee O'Malley, whistled as he followed Cal home.

No one seemed to notice when Cal left the farm that afternoon. Cassie asked Melora to help her bake a pie to bring to the barbecue, and this they did, while Louisa and Will played tag out beyond the vegetable garden and later sprawled on the rug with the checkerboard. Jesse trudged in eventually after seeing to the cows and chickens and horses. Covered with sweat and dust from a full day of work, he announced his intention to head for the stream for a swim and a bath.

"Going to get yourself all prettied up for Dee O'Malley?" Louisa teased, with the impish grin that brought out her dimples.

"What makes you think that?" he retorted, coloring up furiously.

"I know you're sweet on her. Just like Cal's sweet on—" She broke off, clapping a hand over her mouth as her gaze flew to Melora.

Cassie, setting the baked pie on the windowsill to cool, threw her little sister a woeful look.

"Don't you go telling tales on Cal." She sounded far more grown-up than her nine years. "And you're embarrassing Melora. That's not polite. She's our guest."

"No, she isn't," Louisa declared stoutly, her eyes still sparkling. "She's Cal's girl."

"I am not Cal's girl," Melora said firmly. "He doesn't even like me much," she added with a dry laugh and a shrug of her shoulders meant to appear breezy and unconcerned.

"Oh, yes, he does," everyone chorused. Even Jesse, who paused in the doorway to give her one of his lightning-bolt grins.

"How can you tell?" Melora despised the blush flooding her cheeks but didn't have a clue how to stop it. "I mean, if he's never had a girl before—"

"We can tell," Will chimed in, nodding sagely, and everyone laughed in perfect agreement.

· · ·

CAL rode into Deadwood alert for any signs of danger. But when he checked again at the Glory Hotel, as he had that morning, he was told that no one named Rafe Campbell had yet registered there.

He even checked under the name Wyatt Holden, on the chance that Campbell was playing some kind of game, but the clerk shook his head at this too. The weasel simply wasn't there.

He'd come, though, and soon. Cal was dead certain of it.

Campbell wouldn't let him get away with stealing Melora Deane right out from under his nose. His pride alone wouldn't tolerate it.

And that pride, that arrogance, Cal thought as he entered the general store, *is what's going to bring him down.*

Melora's slender golden image kept dancing into his mind's eye as he looked over the available store-bought dresses. She'd look good in any one of them, he thought, picturing her vibrant face, the rich fall of sunshine hair, her firm breasts filling out the bodice of each one of the various gowns Mrs. Hamilton displayed for his perusal. Actually, he concluded, his muscles taut as he remembered the delicate, tantalizing shape of her in his arms, she'd look good in all of them, be they calico, silk, or twill. *Hell, Melora could tempt a preacher even when she's only wearing my old flannel shirt and denims three times too big for her.*

But she'd look even better in nothing at all, Cal

decided, suppressing a grin as he pointed to the dress he wanted.

Not that I'll ever see her that way.

He didn't notice how the eyes of several young women in town followed him about the store as he made his purchases. He was oblivious of the admiration and the blatant invitation some of them showed as they smiled at him or deliberately bumped into him, attempting to start up a conversation.

Cal knew only that Melora Deane was dominating his thoughts more and more when he ought to be thinking about her less and less. He ought to be reviewing and analyzing his plan, working out all the possible hitches, eliminating any potential mistakes.

There was the timing to think of. Marshal Brock's presence at his showdown with Campbell was crucial. But though he'd sought Brock out at his home on the outskirts of Deadwood on two occasions, he'd been turned away both times by the housekeeper, who informed him that the marshal was not there.

Cal couldn't afford to make his move without Brock. Even when Campbell showed up, he'd have to hold off until everything was in place for the confession.

This all had to be done just right.

So quit thinking about Melora and start thinking about getting Campbell exactly where you want him.

He forced his thoughts to focus on his plan as he paid for his purchases and carried them out of the store. As he galloped Rascal east toward the farm, leaving the dusty, crowded streets of Deadwood behind, another rider entered the town from the west.

Coyote Jack spit into the street as he impassively
studied his surroundings. With his hat pushed back
and his bandanna loose around his neck, his hawklike
eyes scanned up and down the streets for some sign
of his prey.

He paid no heed to the cloud of dust at the far
edge of town, a dust cloud kicked up by a horse and
rider too far distant to be clearly seen, headed at a
fast gallop into the dense green of the hills.

His gaze pierced the face of every man he saw,
and every woman. He knew that sooner or later he
would recognize the faces of the two people he'd
been hired to find.

He was skilled at his job, and years of success
had given him a sure, swaggering confidence. He
knew he would find them. It was only a matter of
time.

BY the time Cal returned home, Melora had settled
herself in a chair with Lou and a spelling primer on
her lap. Patiently she was helping the girl with her
lessons. She stayed right where she was as Cal came
through the door, hefting several large packages.

"You went to town?" Cassie ran forward in surprise. "Deadwood or Cherryville?"

"Deadwood." He set the packages down on the
kitchen table.

"What for? Part of your plan, Cal?"

"Nope. Nothing to do with that. I went to buy
presents."

"Presents!" Louisa squealed, and the joy on her
face as she jumped from the chair and raced toward

the table reminded Melora of Jinx on her birthday when Pop would come in with a pile of presents for her. She turned her head so that no one would see the tears misting in her eyes.

"Did you get one for me?" Lou cried, her little hands trembling over the pile of packages, not knowing which one, if any, was for her.

"Yep. And for everyone else too. Simmer down, Lou, and you'll get yours first."

He had bought Lou and Cassie each some ribbons for their hair, a brightly colored spinning top, and a bag of peppermints. For Will there was a windup tin man and a shiny new whistle and several sticks of licorice. Cal handed Jesse a dark blue silk neckerchief. There were grins all around, gasps of delight, hugs, yippees, and thank-yous.

Then Cal reached for the largest parcel, a long white box.

"Who's that for?" Lou demanded. Then suddenly her gaze flew to the gold-haired young woman who'd been watching the proceedings and murmuring happily over everyone's good fortune.

"Melora," she said. "The biggest present is for Melora!"

"Hush." Jesse poked her arm lightly, his gaze fixed with satisfaction on Melora's astonished face.

Melora felt everyone staring as Cal held the box out toward her. She regarded him blankly. "It isn't really for me," she stated flatly.

"Well, I reckon it won't fit Jesse."

To her discomfort the children chortled and elbowed one another. Silently she took the box from him, her heart pounding, though she tried to appear calm. As she lifted the lid, white tissue paper rustled. She pushed it aside and lifted out a dress so light and pretty her heart skittered and a sweet gladness rushed up inside her.

The dress was perfect. It was the glorious blue of summer flowers, a soft buoyant blue, with a low-cut neckline frilled by zigzag white lace. Black piping and lace frothed at the tight-fitting sleeves, and a single row of jet buttons marched primly down the front, contrasting with the sensuously full and graceful skirt.

It was a lovely dress, as simple and charming as the larkspur growing in profusion on the hillsides.

"You bought this for me, Cal?" she asked. The room suddenly felt hot and close.

"Reckon I didn't steal it." His sardonic grin flashed when she threw him an exasperated look. "See here, Melora, we can't have you staying home while everyone else goes to the barbecue. It wouldn't be right."

For a moment she didn't hear the excited babble and laughter of the children and was oblivious of Jesse's ear-to-ear grin. All she saw was Cal standing across the table from her, his green eyes no longer cold as creek water. They gleamed into hers with a warm, quiet intentness that made her skin grow hot, and her pulse flutter.

"I accept—with thanks," she murmured, and he nodded.

"You ladies had best start getting ready for this shindig," Cal said gravely. "Or we'll be late, and all the pies will be gone."

"They will not," Louisa retorted tartly, but she skipped off, clutching her ribbons and her top, followed by Cassie with the bag of peppermints, while Melora carried her lovely dress toward the second bedroom.

She glanced back once, suddenly feeling that she hadn't thanked Cal properly for this extravagant and very thoughtful gift, but he was gone, he and Jesse and Will, probably to wash up at the pump and change their clothes in the barn, and she was left to ponder why he had gone to the expense and trouble of buying her this dress.

Because he wanted her to go to the barbecue.

So that he could dance with her?

A shiver of hope tingled through her. Perhaps Cal wasn't quite as impervious to her charms as he would have her believe.

The idea of dancing with him stirred something deep and delicious inside her, something a woman who'd been on the verge of marrying another man shouldn't feel.

We'll see, she muttered to herself as she closed the bedroom door and tenderly laid the dress across the bed, studying its pretty lines and fancy trim. *It appears to me we'll just see about everything, Mr. Wyatt Calvin Holden.*

16

The night was abloom with stars. Festive music and merriment rocked through the the lantern-festooned yard behind the rambling O'Malley farmhouse, where a half dozen families in their Sunday best laughed and mingled and danced to the tune of three fiddlers beneath a velvet sky and a burnished yellow moon.

The O'Malleys were warm, welcoming people. Quinn O'Malley was the red-haired, stern-eyed father of seven whose great height and girth were a direct contrast with his dainty, tinkly voiced wife. When Jesse introduced him to Cal, he pumped Cal's hand, took his measure with a shrewd, flashing glance, and invited him and his "missus" to make themselves at home.

"My Fiona hasn't stopped baking in three days,"

he declared, shaking his head. "So each one of you had better eat at least four slices of pie. Especially you, ma'am, since I hear you're eating for two," he told Melora with a slight bow.

"Ah, there she goes blushing. My Fiona stopped blushing after the third one came down the pike. Now let me introduce you folks to some of our neighbors. If you don't meet 'em now, you most likely won't get the chance for quite a spell. Once winter sets in up here, we won't none of us be seeing much of each other till the spring thaw."

If any of the neighbors to whom he introduced them thought it strange that Cal, the oldest brother and the one responsible for his siblings, had been away for some time and was just settling down in the area, having left Jesse alone to run the farm and look after the younger brothers and sisters, they gave no sign of it. The O'Malleys drew Cal and Melora easily into the friendly group, made up mostly of other farmers from the vicinity.

Dr. Wright was also in attendance at the party, and upon meeting up with the Holden family, he stared hard at Melora and stroked his white whiskers. "You're looking mighty fit, ma'am. Feeling a bit calmer than you were t'other day, are you?"

"Why, yes," Melora responded smoothly, not meeting Cal's eyes. "I am feeling ever so much better. We were all so concerned about Louisa that I quite lost my head and forgot to worry about my own condition. But fortunately my husband thought clearly enough for both of us."

Dr. Wright appeared quite interested in her tiny

waistline, accented by the cut of the blue dress. He was trying hard, without appearing to, to discern any sign of pregnancy in the fair, slender creature before him, but Cal distracted him from his professional scrutiny by clapping a hand on the doctor's shoulder and turning the older man to face him instead.

"I'm fairly certain that the baby is going to be a girl, Doctor, the spitting image of her lovely mother here. Heard it told that when a woman scarce shows there's a bun in the oven, it means for sure the baby's going to be a girl. What do you say, Dr. Wright?"

"There's no telling, young man. That's just an old wives' tale," the doctor retorted with some scorn, but before he could continue his examination of Melora or ponder the issue further, Cal swept her up around the waist and whisked her off to dance, leaving the doctor scratching his head as he gazed after them.

"You're quite skilled at telling bald-faced lies," Melora noted as he spun her into the crowd of brightly clad dancers.

"Had to learn a lot about lies lately—just to survive." Cal's expression was harsh. The bitterness she saw in his eyes made her regret the teasing remark. "I'll be glad when this whole damn thing is over, Melora. When my family doesn't have to hide out on a farm in Dakota Territory, because the folks they knew back home in Arizona came to look down on them and think their brothers had turned into no-good outlaws. And I'll be especially glad when justice catches up to Rafe Campbell and he's paid the price for what he's done."

"You still haven't explained exactly how you're going to make him pay, what you'll do to get his confession when he finally gets to Deadwood."

"That's right, I haven't."

"Well, it's time you did. You're not the only one who has a stake in this now." Melora leaned back in his arms and gave him a long, level look. Between the moon and the lantern light her eyes were the color of tea. "I have a few choice words to speak to Mr. Rafe Campbell myself."

"You'll have to get in line, Melora. This is my plan, and I get the first shot at Campbell when he shows up."

Her eyes sparked fire. "A tempting choice of words."

"They're only words. I can't afford to shoot him— at least not right away."

"Just so long as I get my turn." She stuck her chin up, and her hand tightened on his as they danced. "Promise me that much."

"I can't promise you anything, Melora." Cal whirled and dipped her with ease, his eyes fixed coolly on her face. If he didn't care much for dancing, that didn't stop him from being good at it, she noted with reluctant admiration. "Life isn't always easy, and it doesn't always go according to plan."

"You don't have to tell me that." She flung the words back at him irritably.

Who was he to tell her that things didn't go according to plan? All her own plans for the future had gone up in smoke, and she was left with nothing, nothing but worry for Jinx and the ranch, a dull sense of humiliation at her own gullibility, and a burning need to fire buckshot into Rafe Campbell's backside.

And there was something else that hadn't gone according to plan. Tonight she'd planned to stun Cal Holden when she came out of her room to take his arm for the barbecue, to dazzle him dizzy when he saw her in this dress.

But it hadn't happened.

After coaxing Louisa's and Cassie's tresses into pretty topknots and helping them wind their new ribbons through the strands, she'd worked carefully for the better part of an hour on her own hair, brushing it until it shone like wildfire and dressing it in tight, perfectly coiled curls to frame her face. She'd taken a few tucks and nips in the gown, studying it assessingly until she was convinced it fitted her figure to perfection, and she'd donned the silk stockings and satin shoes she'd packed for her honeymoon. She'd set creamy pearl earbobs on her earlobes. And stroked flower-laced French perfume at her throat and between her breasts. She'd *thought* she looked rather beautiful in all that finery, at least beautiful enough to attract Cal's notice. And perhaps even to draw a compliment from him.

But Cal had scarcely batted an eye when she'd walked out of the bedroom, well aware of everyone watching her.

"We're late," he'd said in that brusque way of his, and had taken Cassie's arm instead of hers, leaving Melora trembling with angry disappointment as she stomped out to the buggy alongside Jesse.

Now I know why he's never had a girl, she told

herself irately as the dance came to an end. *He no more knows how to treat a woman than a dog knows how to climb a tree.*

As the music stopped, they glared at each other. "I'm going to sit down," Melora announced sulkily, and Cal touched two fingers to his hat.

"Suit yourself."

After he had watched her walk away, he drank down a cool glass of elderberry wine and then stalked to the edge of the O'Malley yard. Plunging off into the darkness beyond the farm buildings, he sought the open solitude of the night.

Behind him the music drifted, faint and rousing on the breeze. He felt removed from the gaiety of the barbecue, locked inexorably in the tangle of his own dark thoughts.

It was damn near impossible to be near Melora and not want to touch her, to wind his hands through her hair and pull her into his arms. And though Cal had learned patience the hard way, sitting in a bug-infested five-foot jail cell day after day, waiting to hang for a crime he hadn't committed, framed by an enemy he'd thought was a friend, tonight he had no patience for anything. His calm, his facade of detached control were fraying ragged. He was beset with a driving ache that couldn't be soothed or calmed or pushed aside.

When Melora had glided out of the bedroom tonight wearing that amazing blue dress, he'd had to fight like hell not to go to her, pick her up in his arms, and carry her right back in there, to lay her down on the bed and make love to her until dawn.

She'd looked enchanting. And he'd wanted her, every silken inch of her. The delicate beauty of her face had beckoned to him, the curve of her lips had mesmerized him. Hell, he'd started to sweat just noticing the way her pearls gleamed at the base of her pretty little earlobes.

And the lushness of her body had been apparent in that splendid dress; it had cried out to a primal part of him. Begging to be touched. To be kissed. To be claimed.

She'd looked like a floating blue vision, alluring as the sea, and every bit as unpredictable and seductive.

What's stopping you? he asked himself angrily. *If you want her, why don't you just go after her, claim her, see what lies behind that smile she gives you sometimes, if she feels as much as she seems to the times you* have *kissed her or held her in your arms?*

But something kept him back. Two things, really. He didn't want to make a fool of himself. Many were the men who had probably made fools of themselves over Melora Deane, and his pride argued against letting himself be added to that list.

And there was something else.

The woman was grieving, whether she realized it or not. She'd lost the man she loved. She'd found out her fiancé was a fraud, that his name wasn't even Wyatt Holden after all. *And now*, Cal told himself, staring out at the great gleaming burnishment of the moon, at the sky that stretched above him to infinity, *it would be a low-down thing to pursue her when she was confused and hurting. And vulnerable.*

When she might not know exactly what she wanted, or what she was doing, or even care with whom.

It wouldn't be right, and it wouldn't be fair. And after everything he'd put her through already, he couldn't stomach the notion of taking advantage of her.

But damn it all to hell. Cal closed his eyes for a moment, letting the cooling wind fan his hot face. *It was sheer hell to resist her.*

It didn't help that he'd noticed every man at this barbecue eyeing her. He couldn't blame them. If things were different . . .

Hell, he told himself, opening his eyes and turning back to stare hard in the direction of the festivities. *For tonight, just for tonight, things are different. You're playing a role. She's supposed to be your wife. Your pregnant wife. If you don't get back there and start paying some attention to her—just for show—it might attract notice. And talk.*

He couldn't afford that, not now when he was so close to bringing his plan to a successful conclusion.

Go back and dance with her. Talk, laugh. Try to behave normally and keep the gossipmongers at bay. It was the sensible thing to do.

He stuck his hands in the pockets of his neatly pressed gray trousers and started back toward the house.

"SHH. Here he comes," Louisa warned, tugging on Will's arm as he capered beside her in the O'Malley parlor, chattering nonstop.

"Hush up, Will!" Swallowing hard, Cassie fixed him with her sternest glance. "Hush up this instant or he'll hear you!"

The other guests were swarming toward the feast-laden long tables lined up in the dining room, and no one was paying the least heed to the three young Holden children.

"Cal! Cal!" Louisa darted toward him as he skirted around a buxom young brunette who flashed him an encouraging smile. Trying hard to school their faces, Cassie and Will ran after her.

Cal frowned down at Louisa when she tugged at the bottom of his black silk vest. "Quick, Cal! You have to help her!"

"Help who? Louisa, what's wrong?"

Lou's eyes were as huge and round as pennies. "Melora!" she cried. "She's gone off crying. She won't talk to anyone. And we can't get her to come out."

"Come out of where?"

"The barn." Cassie gazed up at him woefully. "She's sad and upset. Jesse tried to get her to come out, and so did I—"

"And so did I!" Will chimed in, his little cheeks red with excitement.

Cal looked from one to the other of them. "Locked herself in the barn?" he repeated blankly. "Why would she do a fool thing like that?"

"Because she's upset." Cassie stamped her foot. "I don't know, Cal, but she was crying real hard—"

"You'd better be telling me the truth." His sus-

picious glance flicked over each of them, assessing
Louisa's openmouthed dismay, Cassie's quiet dis-
tress, the restless shifting of Will's small feet.

"Show me where she is." Tension twisted through
his gut as he thought of Melora so distraught she was
sobbing alone in the O'Malleys' barn.

Was it because of the way he'd treated her tonight?
He'd hardly been sociable when they'd been dancing,
and then he'd all but deserted her. But there could be
something more to it than that. She might be upset
over Rafe Campbell, he thought, stabbed by a sharp,
incisive pain. Or maybe she was missing her little
sister.

Whatever was going on, he had to find her, help
her.

"Hurry up, you slowpokes," he urged as he led
the little group outside once again. Everyone else was
trooping inside in search of supper, but Cal, Cassie,
Lou, and Will made their way through the soughing
wind toward the shadowy outline of the farm's outbuildings.

"It's not this barn, the new one; it's the next one,
the old barn," Will sputtered as he tried to keep up.
"That one up ahead."

Jesse stepped out of the shadows as the group
raced up to the weathered old structure, but he gave
Cal no chance to ask him any questions.

"Quick, you've got to do something. She's in real
bad shape," he told Cal.

Deirdre O'Malley materialized right beside him. In
that instant Cal saw that she was a pretty, freckle-

faced girl whose strawberry blond hair was coiled in one smooth braid, but before he could do more than nod a greeting to her and then turn toward the old dilapidated barn with its weathered shingles, Jesse suddenly slid the bolt back on the barn door and promptly shoved Cal inside.

"What the hell?" Even as he wheeled around, the door slammed shut, and he heard the bolt rattle into place.

"Jesse! Jesse, what the hell did you do that for?" Cal stopped yelling and whipped around toward the barn's interior when he heard a sound from the hay-scented blackness.

"Melora?"

"Who else?" she shouted. She sounded mad as a whole nest of hornets.

"Where are you?" Cal moved toward her voice, but in the darkness he stubbed his toe on something hard and swore a string of curses.

Melora ignored his tirade. She had been making her way along the rough wall of the barn, toward what she thought was the door, and she began pounding on it with her fist.

"Open up, Jesse! Cassie, Lou!" Frustration and fury throbbed through her voice. "Do you hear me? Will! Jesse! This has gone far enough. I said open the door right now!"

"Are you telling me they've locked you in here?" Cal demanded. From his voice she could tell that drawn by the pounding sounds, he was moving closer to her.

"That's right," she said bitterly, continuing to bang with her fist. "They told me that you were here, that you'd been hurt."

"They told me you were in here crying."

"I haven't been crying. I've been yelling, pleading with them, ordering them, shouting at them to let me out."

For a moment there was silence. Melora stopped her pounding long enough to sigh, rubbing her sore hand.

Cal leaned against the wall of the barn, groaning as he realized how blindly he'd walked into their childish trap.

"Damn it," he growled, raking a hand through his hair. "I'm going to turn every single one of them over my knee. They won't sit down for a month. And Jesse, I'll whup him good."

"Fine, if we ever get out of here," Melora grumbled.

He was very near to her. He could smell the sweetness of her hair, of the perfume she was wearing, like a cloud of flowers. He could sense the warmth and vibrant femininity of her in the darkness. Moreover, his eyes were adjusting, and he could just barely discern the shape of her less than three feet from him.

"We won't be staying long," he said harshly. "I'll break the door down."

"Be my guest."

Cal discerned her shape and the shimmer of her hair just ahead of him. He bumped into her deliberately, not hard, just hard enough to throw her slightly off-balance. He seized her securely in his arms as she started to stumble. "Sorry. Can't see a damned thing in here."

"I can," she retorted icily, glaring up at him. "I can see the smug grin on your face. It's perfectly clear. Now let me go and do something useful."

"Such as?"

"Break down that door."

"First answer a question, Melora."

She gritted her teeth. Through the darkness she could smell the clean scent of him, a scent like that of the pines and the sage-carpeted prairie, a warm, muskily male, thoroughly reassuring and arousing scent. The grip of his hands upon her arms reminded her of his strength—but also of his gentleness. She felt strangely alert and keyed up as the darkness seemed to enclose them in a world of sense and musk, far, far removed from everything and everyone else.

And because of this, she suddenly felt trapped. Trapped and used and manipulated.

He wouldn't dance with her or be civil to her at the barbecue, and now he expected—what? That she would fall into his arms? Cry like a ninny? Wait for him to rescue her from the big, bad barn?

"Ask your stupid question, Cal, and then help me break down the door!" she snapped.

Faintly she saw him grin. "Why did you say you came out here to the barn?"

His breath was warm against the top of her head, rustling her curls. One hand let go of her arm and slid up to trace the delicate line of her jaw. She bit her lip.

"They said you were hurt, that you needed help—
Oh, never mind," she cried crossly. "It doesn't matter."

"It might," he muttered softly.

Confused and irritated beyond all patience, she
broke away from him then. But as she whirled back
toward the door and began pounding and trying with
all her might to shove it open, Cal came up beside
her, joining his efforts to hers. For several moments
they shouted and banged upon the wood without
speaking to each other.

Then Cal rammed his shoulder against the door.
Over and over again. But the old weathered barn held
fast. Quinn O'Malley had built it solid.

"I give up." Cal grimaced, rubbing his bruised
shoulder. "Unless we can find something to batter it
down, we'll have to wait until they decide to come
back for us."

"I refuse to sit here and do nothing. Help me tinder
a light so that we can see what we have to work
with!" Melora demanded.

"If you want to tinder a light, go right ahead," Cal
invited her grimly. "Just don't tinder a fire. As for
me, I think I'll rest a bit. My shoulder hurts."

"My hero!" Her eyes flashed scorn.

She yelped as he swatted her on the bottom.

"Cal Holden, you stop that."

"Who's going to make me?"

"I am. Oh, you . . ." She struck out blindly at him
as he swatted her again, but Cal, laughing, caught her
wrists.

"Come on, Melora. Might as well give up fighting

and just wait for them to come back.'' He began dragging her across the barn, slowly, since neither of them could make out where they were headed. ''Here, sit down and take a load off.''

He hauled her down on his lap, atop a bale of hay, and she immediately tried to roll off, but Cal grasped her firmly and held her pinned between his knees.

''I said take a load off,'' he repeated in a steely tone, wrapping his arms around her so that she had no hope of escape.

''Since when do I take orders from you, Mr. Cal Holden?'' she gasped furiously, struggling against him, even though she knew it was useless.

He was strong. Far stronger than she. And the feel of his thighs pressed against her, of his arms encircling her, made her weak. Her hairpins loosened, and several thick gold curls tumbled free, cascading around her face and brushing against him as she struggled. He held her tighter.

She felt hot and dusty and helpless—and more than a little furious. She tried to ignore the heat streaking through her, to concentrate on her annoyance. Surely by now her beautiful blue dress was covered with bits of hay and was hopelessly wrinkled and crumpled.

''You do know how to show a girl a good time,'' she panted. ''No wonder you've never had a girl. You have no idea how to go about—''

Before she could finish, he rolled her over and covered her body with the full length of his, his weight and strength imprisoning her against the hay. Gasping, Melora fought a wave of alarm. Maybe she'd gone too far. Maybe she'd taunted Cal about never having had a girl once too often. She wriggled helplessly beneath him, peering upward, trying to discern his hard, stern features through the blackness.

"Cal, what do you think you're doing—" she began furiously, but he silenced her with his mouth. The kiss was not gentle. It was sudden and fierce, a kiss so hungry and shattering that her breath caught in her throat. She whimpered as his mouth took hers, not with tenderness but with violence. A wildness tore through her, rolling through and through as his mouth devoured and bruised. Yet through the violence there was an undercurrent of something else, something she could not name. Her whimper turned into a moan, not a moan of dismay, but one of pleasure, of passion as he continued to deepen the kiss. He was teasing her, tormenting her, doing it expertly, without mercy.

Melora felt herself drowning in that kiss, even as it ignited her. She didn't want to respond this way to Cal Holden. He was rude. He was infuriating. He didn't know how to treat a woman.

But he surely knew how to kiss one. Against her will, trembling from her shoulders to her ankles, she felt herself respond. Her lips defied her, softening, opening to welcome his, blossoming beneath his mouth like the petals of a rose.

Cal tangled his hands in her hair. Need blazed through him. He knew he should stop now, while he still could. He'd made up his mind to steer clear of Melora Deane, to keep his distance. For both their sakes. Yet all his resolutions had gone up in smoke the moment he'd pulled her down on his lap. That unplanned, thoughtless act had brought a rush of responses that he knew he would regret. But he couldn't regret this one kiss, one wild, unfettered, ferocious kiss. She tasted sweeter and deeper than wine, hotter than whiskey. His fingers tightened on her hair, crushing the velvet curls, winding through them as if he would bury his hands in the smooth, glowing strands that flowed past her shoulders like wild golden honey. She was in his blood now. Maybe one shattering, all-encompassing kiss would get her out.

Melora quivered as Cal's tongue glided past her teeth, snaked inside her mouth. Oh, what he was doing to her. She felt a low, rich explosion of pleasure. Then a cry broke from the back of her throat as Cal began to explore her mouth, his tongue slipping in and out, slowly, purposefully, then increasing the rhythm with ever sharpening primal thrusts. An ache burst inside her, spreading warmth and an odd tingling tightness. It swept from her breasts to her nipples and downward past her hips to the core of her womanhood.

He was driving her mad. She'd never felt like this before. Wyatt's kisses had been warm and pleasant—she'd enjoyed them, savored them—but with Cal it was different, a far, far cry from anything she'd experienced before. Or anything in her innocence she'd imagined.

"Melora, you're wrong." Cal's voice was deep and husky when he at last allowed both of them breath. "Dead wrong."

Dazed, she could only gaze at him for a moment with eyes that were smoky with passion. "About what?'' she managed to say at last in a voice so faint she wondered if he could hear the words. She was dizzy from the kiss. Dizzy and confused and thick-headed. Her chest rose and fell, her breasts pushed helplessly against the warm, muscled wall of his chest, and beneath the soft gown her nipples felt hard and tingly.

In answer he brushed a thumb gently across her cheek, smoothing back a strand of flyaway hair. Then he shifted his weight slightly upon her, draping his legs more firmly across hers. The hardness of his male arousal was all too apparent to her as he held her sprawled beneath him.

"It may be true that I've never had a girl. But I've had a woman. Many women. Don't think I'm a ten-derfoot when it comes to making love."

"I don't . . . I didn't . . . I wouldn't . . . I never—"

"Thing is," he said, kissing her eyelids very gent-ly, then leaning back to gaze intently down into her wide eyes, "I wonder if you've had many men . . . any men."

"I'm not going to answer that question." Indig-nation and alarm made her struggle anew. "Cal, let me up right now."

"Sure," he said easily, his breath warm on her cheeks. But he made no move to let her go. Instead he nibbled at the corner of her ear, sending a flame of sensation through Melora that seemed to her would set the hay on fire. "If you want me to," Cal added smoothly.

A wild, throbbing ache took possession of Melora as Cal's mouth branded kisses across her helpless throat. It was torture, sweet torture. She had to get away from him, so she could think, so she could wrest back control of her own body, which was betraying her as it never had before. "I want you to," she gasped. "I do. So let me up. Right now . . . right this very—"

But he cut her off with another kiss, this one gentle, teasingly gentle. His lips cradled hers; his tongue traced the curved outline of her full lips. She moaned with the pure sweetness of it, and her kiss answered his with a fervency that betrayed her. When he lifted his head, she could see the gleaming intensity of his eyes. They pierced even the darkness.

"Melora . . ."

"Wh-what?"

"There's something I need to tell you."

"Wh-what?"

"Something you've probably heard before."

She moistened her lips, a sheen of sweat glistening on her forehead as he continued to press those kisses upon her bare flesh, first her cheeks, then her nose, then covering her mouth again while at the same time his hand slid to her breast, making her gasp with a dazed pleasure as he cupped it with warm, gentle fingers.

"Cal . . ."

"This is what I need to tell you. I think you're beautiful, Melora. The most beautiful woman I've ever seen."

"You do?" she whispered, flabbergasted and immensely pleased. And immensely distracted by the things he was doing to her.

"I know you've heard it a thousand times, but—"

"I've never heard it from you," she said softly, then drew in her breath with a start as his thumb caught and caressed her nipple.

Intense pleasure soared through her. She was drowning in it. In the darkness they stared into each other's eyes. Cal swallowed hard, trying to remember all his noble resolutions where she was concerned. Desperately he reminded himself yet again that he'd made up his mind to stay away, to protect her from her own vulnerability. And to protect himself from being a fool.

But right now all those reasons and tensions and arguments were fuzzy and dim. Right now all he could see was the shimmer of hair that made sunshine look pale, the glow of eyes so huge and compelling he could not have torn his gaze away to save his life. He felt her exquisite body tremble beneath him. Melora breathed softly, pulsing with sensuous warmth, with a feminine vitality that drew him inexorably to her, that made his groin ache and his blood boil.

Easy, he warned himself. *Go easy*. He summoned up the shreds of his usual self-control and forced himself to speak calmly, deliberately, despite the urgent hunger sweeping through him.

"Say so now, Melora, if you want me to let you go." He kissed her roughly. "I will, if you tell me to—but, Princess, tell me right now."

"Don't," she whispered.

Cal sucked in his breath. "Don't what?" he asked in a low, harsh tone.

"Don't let me go," she said softly, and then she was swept up into arms that threatened to crush her but didn't, and the tide of emotions that broke through her was like nothing she'd ever felt before.

"Don't ever let me go," she begged, fervent and desperate as his mouth descended upon her again, and her breasts tingled beneath his touch.

"Not a chance, Princess. Don't even think about it."

Melora was beyond thought. Her arms encircled him. They wrapped around his shoulders, gripping for dear life, her fingers scraping, digging into muscle. His body moved over hers, arousing every inch of her as she felt the hardness and power of him.

There was no more thought. No more hesitation. Just the sweet, blinding urgency that made the very air in the dark, hay-scented barn quiver. Melora felt wonder as Cal's fingers slid swiftly over the buttons of her gown. He flung them open with the ease of a man who'd had much practice doing such things, all the while locking his eyes with hers and sipping urgently from her lips. As her bodice fell open, his eyes darkened to green slate.

"Did I say beautiful?" he muttered, nearly yanking the camisole off her. "Melora, sweet, you're exquisite."

Her breasts were creamy, full, and generous; her nipples dark and taut, rigid beneath his fingers. Cal lost himself in the pleasure of touching her, of learning the secrets of her body, of watching the silken desire slide through her eyes, glisten, and glow.

Her breasts throbbed with a sweet pain that would

have been agony if it had not been bliss. The way he looked at her, touched her, the intent gleam of his gaze sent a ripple of desire through Melora that was so fierce it hurt her throat and her eyelids. As Cal's hands did magical things to her breasts and his mouth tantalized her lips, she suddenly felt a stab of jealousy toward all the women he had known before, whoever they were, wherever they were.

Hungry to block them out, to make him hers, she was swept up suddenly then in need that shook her to her core. With a small sound she reached for him; her fingers tugged his shirt from his trousers and yanked it off almost as recklessly as he had removed her camisole.

Cal grinned, then took her by the shoulders. "Eager little devil, aren't you?" he murmured against her lips. Their mouths clung; tongues danced. While their mouths played, Cal unbuckled his belt.

Melora couldn't help the blush that rushed into her cheeks at his words, but she was already leaning back, staring through the dimness at his wide, magnificent chest. She wished it were daylight so that she could see him, all of him. But the darkness was welcoming, too, splendid and musky and mysterious, with just the two of them and the magical touch of him, and the scent of him, and the way he made her body sing.

Her eyes had adjusted enough now to the lack of light so that she could make out what she wanted to see. Her hands swept out to caress the crisp mahogany hair across his chest, her fingers shyly traced his nipples, played across his muscles.

Her throat felt dry as Cal caught her to him again,

filled his hands with the fullness of her breasts, swept small, hot kisses across her face, down her neck, down her arms.

A hunger trembled through her, grew, intensified. It was a hunger she didn't fully understand, but as Cal lowered his mouth to her breast, found the taut crimson peak, and tasted it, she moaned with starvation. With a craving that increased as his hands skimmed her body, exploring, massaging, as his mouth teased and tasted, as his eyes burned through hers.

"Don't be afraid," he said, his breath warm upon her neck.

"I'm not. Only a little."

It was true, she thought as she raced with him to some wild, unknown destination that beckoned tantalizingly just beyond reach. The fear was there, but it was small compared with the need. Trust flowed through her, encouraged by his every gentle, pleasurable touch. This was Cal, who had cradled her during the storm, who had rescued her from Jethro and Strong. What flowed between her and Cal, what had always flowed between them, was not the stuff of fear. It was wild, sweet, powerful. As powerful as the earth and the mountains. And every bit as natural.

White fire raged through her as Cal's rough hands stripped her naked and found their way to every inch of her, all the soft, secret places that no man had ever touched before. She quivered as his hand brushed between her thighs, nestling there, probing and discovering while all the while he kissed her, his mouth hot and demanding upon her lips. Melora thought the fire he stoked would singe her to ashes, but the fire did not destroy; it shimmered and burned like the splendid rays of the sun.

Cal groaned low in his throat as she wound slim arms around his neck and pulled him closer, arcing against him. His whole body was taut with hunger for her, even as he fought the fierce driving need. Impatience lashed him, but he fought it, chained it, for fear of hurting her.

With the whores he had known, there had been pleasure—easy, grunting pleasure. But nothing more. Only the simple, uncomplicated pleasure of animal satisfaction and release.

With Melora, each touch, each kiss, the sensation of her perfumed hair tickling his skin as he bent to kiss her, the skimming of her long, slender fingers down his back all aroused feelings so deep and intense they rocked through and through him, grinding him heart and soul.

When she reached out trembling fingers that brushed down his torso, past his hips, to touch his manhood shyly, Cal groaned and went still.

"Ohh. Oh." She jerked her hand back in shock, and he felt the hot blush stealing through her entire body.

"Go ahead, Melora. Yes, that's right. Go ahead, Princess, that feels good. So good."

She wanted him to feel good, as good as he made her feel. More boldly she reached out again. She smiled, pleased and eager as she heard his sharp intake of breath. While her lips groped for his, sweet and giving, she glided her hand over his hot engorged shaft, caressing and exploring the length of him. Her breath came in short gasps as he strained against her and his own hand guided hers, teaching her the rhythm.

Love for Cal flowed through her. It was sure and it was magical and she wanted to be even closer to him somehow than she was; she wanted to wrap herself around him, to hold him and devour him and to be held and devoured. Yet when Cal's powerful body shifted, moving deliberately over hers, and when his knee parted her legs, Melora tensed with expectation. She'd shivered and writhed at the delicious stroking of his hand between her thighs, but as his manhood thrust against her and began to slide inside, she gasped with instinctive trepidation and tried to draw her legs together.

"Cal, I'm afraid."

"You said you weren't."

"I am now," she whispered throbbingly, trying to struggle up, but he pushed her back, pinning her down beneath him, his eyes gleaming firmly into hers.

"I'll try not to hurt you, sweet. Don't be afraid—"

"I am afraid."

"Trust me."

Trust. Yes, she felt trust. She gazed up into his lean, sweat-sheened face, met his carefully appraising eyes. And she nearly drowned in the rush of love that flooded up through her,

"Yes, Cal," she whispered, her arms twining

around him, her legs sliding apart. Her fingers curled through his hair; she pressed an ardent kiss to his chest, her whole body trembling. "I do trust you."

Red-hot fire surged through him then. Urgency. Need. A pumping heat that had Cal spreading her legs, pushing into her. She wanted him. Needed him. *Trusted him.*

Even after all he'd done.

Closing her eyes, gasping, Melora braced herself, trembling as he slid deeper, deeper. . . .

Pain spasmed through her as he broke through cleanly; then he went still inside her as she cried out, a sob rising in her throat. But Cal kissed her cheeks, her eyelids, and then her quivering mouth, and the warmth and strength of his body seemed to take control of hers, hypnotizing her even through the pain.

Cal tangled his hands in her hair as he began to move inside her. "Come with me, Melora," he muttered against her lips. "Stay with me, ride with me. Faster and harder than you've ever ridden before."

His thrusts accelerated. Melora mewed against his shoulder as a pounding pleasure filled her, stirring her to a slow, building frenzy. Cal's hips dug against hers, his body crushing, grinding, but there was no longer any pain, only blinding delight, a searing heat, a need that built and built and became so unbearable she bucked beneath him, wrapping her legs around his, clawing his back.

Wild joy tore through her. She cried out his name; she arched her hips, frantic, frenzied, trying to take him completely into her, to embrace him deeper and deeper, to hold him forever. . . .

The barn darkened, brightened, darkened again as Melora clung to Cal. A soaring ecstasy shuddered through her, arced through both of them in a fierce explosion as if the sun and the moon and the stars had whirled together in a white-hot blast that clenched them and shook them and at last released them like a pair of shooting stars.

They shuddered together amid the fragrant hay and grew still at last in each other's arms. Only the sound of their breathing broke the quiet. Until they both heard the bolt rattle on the barn door and the rusty creak as it slid open.

"Cal, Melora?" A tiny crack of light shattered the darkness. Louisa's voice, unexpectedly timid and concerned, wavered through the barn.

"Jesse said to leave you be, but Will and I are worried. Are you all right?"

17

C al shot upright, glaring through the gloom. "We're fine. Get back to the party. Right now."

"But what about Melora? Is she mad at us?"

"No, Lou." Melora managed to reply in a voice that shook only a little. "I'm not mad at you."

"We're talking." Cal grimaced and briefly closed his eyes. "Making up. We'll be back at the barbecue soon."

"Kissing and making up?" Will asked eagerly. He stuck his head into the duskiness of the barn, and Melora instinctively snatched up her dress and held it across her nakedness, a gasp of dismay and laughter trembling on her lips.

It was Cal who answered Will. "If you and Lou

don't want to get walloped for this prank, you'll make tracks pronto and leave us be. You hear me?''

"Yep!" Will and Lou chimed together, sounding as merry as two chipmunks prancing in a barrel of nuts, and then the door thudded shut again. This time there was no sound of the bolt sliding into place.

Melora was certain Cal could see her cheeks flaming in the darkness. Her throat ached suddenly, and she wasn't sure if she was on the verge of laughter or tears. Imagine if those children had walked in a few moments earlier and discovered exactly what kind of kissing and making up had been going on! She peered through the blackness, trying to discern Cal's expression. Shyly she reached out to touch his shoulder, still dazed by that explosion of passion that had passed between them, by what she felt, by what she knew now in her heart about the two of them, what she'd guessed for a very long time but had finally admitted without reservation.

She loved him. Fully, with all her heart. She loved Cal Holden, this tall, hard-jawed man who'd taken her here in this haystack, who'd stripped away her decorous innocence with strong, gentle hands, who'd replaced ignorance with knowledge—the knowledge that magic truly exists, that souls can touch, that love can stir you to the marrow of your bones.

She wanted him to do all of it all over again.

"Cal," she said, smiling in the darkness as she reached for him, "I wish we hadn't—"

"I know, Melora. I wish we hadn't too."

Melora's hand froze inches from his shoulder. Then it dropped to her side like an anvil. The darkness around them seemed to grow deeper, blacker. She'd been about to say, "I wish we hadn't been interrupted." But Cal had cut her off before she could finish. *I wish we hadn't too.*

He wished they hadn't made love? She started to tremble and fought against it. But something lovely and sweet sank sharply through the pit of her stomach.

"I don't understand . . ." she murmured, feeling sick.

He spoke in a tight voice that sent a chill piercing through her. "This was a mistake."

"A . . . mistake."

Cal had sprung up and was reaching for his trousers. "Guess I just lost my head, Melora. Sorry."

She was cold, shaking. "Sorry?"

"This was damned stupid. And it was all my fault. Not that I didn't enjoy it. I did," he said quickly, feeling like a complete fool. Enjoy it? He'd done a hell of a lot more than enjoy it. The memory seared him clear through. He remembered every sweet inch of her, each kiss, each pleasured mew she'd made. Every single thing. The weight and softness of her breasts, the outline of her hips, the way she'd thrashed against him, crying out with a need as deep and blinding as his own, yet somehow one that was infinitely more affecting, a need that made him sweat and burn and vow to never hurt her.

He was probably hurting her now, he thought. Tripping over his stupid tongue. Saying all the wrong things. Just as he'd done all the wrong things, all the things he'd vowed not to do.

He tugged on his trousers, cursing under his breath.

Hell, he'd planned to go slowly, to give Melora a chance to accept the idea that her fiancé was a scoundrel, to stay away from her—and the next thing he knew he was making love with her in a haystack.

Nice going, he thought, his fingers flying over his shirt buttons. *That's the way to court a lady: drag her down in the hay and don't give her a chance to think twice.*

"This wasn't something I planned." He went on doggedly, aware that she was very still, very silent.

"*I* certainly didn't plan it," she snapped, her voice high and cold, totally unlike the way she usually spoke.

"I know that. I'm sorry. I don't know exactly what happened. I wasn't thinking straight, but I guarantee you it will never happen again."

Unless you want it to. That's what he wanted to say, that and so much more. He wanted to haul her up against him, stark naked as she was, and touch her all over, nibble on every delicious inch of her. He wanted to tell her that she was beautiful, amazing, that she took his breath away.

Instead he buckled his belt and wished he had some idea what you say to a woman at a time like this when you've taken advantage of her being confused and vulnerable, when you've behaved like the lowest kind of snake, when you know she's going to end up hating you.

He wouldn't make excuses to her. He'd just leave her alone.

"I'll wait for you outside," he said curtly, and then risked a glance at her. She looked like a frozen block of ice. Half sitting up, her arms braced upon the hay, she was beautiful, a shapely statue carved from alabaster. Her skin gleamed pale in the darkness, her hair was sexily mussed, rippling past her shoulders and her breasts with sensuous abandon, her eyes staring at him, wide and filled with—what?

He couldn't see what was in her eyes.

Through the darkness he thought he saw the glimmer of tears.

Then she sprang up with a cry and began to dress, twitching her clothes on even faster than they had come off.

"Don't you worry about me," she told him with a taut, icy dignity that made him flinch. "I'll be right outside—in just a minute. Don't give me another thought. Just go on back to the party."

"I said I'd wait for you outside."

"I said don't bother."

Cal wrenched her around to face him just as she'd slipped her chemise over her head and his eyes narrowed as he saw the filmy fabric glide down to conceal her breasts.

He wanted to yank it off again.

Instead he forced himself to peer into her eyes, trying to read what was beneath their hard sparkle.

"What the hell is wrong with you? I know you're angry, but—"

"Angry? *Angry*?" Melora choked on the words. Her voice whistled out high and clear and throbbing with the rage and hurt that shook through her like a cyclone. "You're damn right I'm angry, Cal. How dare you? *How dare you* treat me this way?"

His lips thinned. "I said I was sorry. It was wrong, I know—"

"Get out! Just get out! Don't you ever touch me again, do you hear me, Cal Holden? If you do, I swear I'll kill you!" she shrieked. "Do you understand that? Do you?"

"I may be a fool, but I'm not an idiot, Princess."

He picked up his hat, stuck it on his head, and turned on his heel.

She waited until the barn door slammed shut behind him, and then, when she was alone, she threw herself down in the hay and let the tears come.

They were tears of mortification. And tears of pain such as she had never known before.

Cal regretted it. He regretted what they'd done. He felt—*Lord, help me*, Melora thought in agony, her hands covering her face—he felt he'd made a *mistake*.

He doesn't want me.

She'd given him all that she had within her, she'd given him her innocence, her virginity, her absolute love and trust, and the hopes and dreams that sailed along with it, and it had meant nothing to him. Nothing.

He didn't want her.

She sobbed out, wrenched out, thrashed out all the bitterness and pain, but when she thought it all was gone, more welled up inside and overflowed.

She'd thought Cal had felt what she had. She'd

thought he cared for her, maybe even loved her. He'd been so gentle.

But he never said it. He never said anything like it.

She felt like the world's biggest fool. She'd given of herself in a way she never had before, and he was turning his back on her, apologizing for his mistake, walking away from her.

And she wanted him. All she knew was that she wanted him.

"To hell with him," she whispered, and then she bent her head and wept anew, her tears soaking the hay, because Cal Holden was in her blood, in her heart, in her soul, and she knew she would never get him out.

THEY didn't speak to each other all the way home from the barbecue, or afterward, or the next day. Cal made himself scarce, tending to farm chores, staying away from the house. As Melora went about her own solitary way, helping the children with the household tasks and tending the small patch of vegetable garden, she noticed the worried glances exchanged among Cassie and Will and Louisa, and she knew they thought their matchmaking prank had backfired.

They were desolate, and she tried her best to appear cheerful and unconcerned around them, but when Jesse came in at noon for a supper of cold sliced ham and bread, she saw the concerned glances sent her way, and Will and Louisa kept coming over to hug her knees, while Cassie kept telling her how pretty she'd looked and asking Melora to teach her how to

coif her hair in the style she'd adopted for the barbecue.

This is ridiculous, Melora snapped angrily to herself that afternoon, when for no reason at all she
found herself sniffing back tears, and Will, seeing, ran
to hug her for the dozenth time.

*You're Melora Deane, not some pathetic ninny.
Have a little dignity. Don't let the whole world, especially Cal, see you moping around like a lovesick
calf. Where's your backbone? Your pride?*

She could almost hear her father's voice commanding in her ear: *Buck up, girl. Put a good face
on it.*

So she tried. And she managed fairly well, tucking
her flannel shirt into her rope-belted trousers, brushing her hair, forcing herself to smile when she strode
in for breakfast the next day, though she and Cal
stiffly avoided glancing at each other. She concentrated all morning on becoming immersed in small
chores, in cooking and sweeping and reading aloud
to Will and Lou, trying not to watch out the window
for Cal's return or to glance up every time she thought
she heard someone coming, and soon she did begin
to think about other matters—matters, she told herself, of far more importance than Mr. Cal Holden.

For one thing, there was her sister.

She was sorely worried about Jinx. And she missed
her every time she looked at Will and Lou and Cassie.
How Jinx would have loved to be here in this cozy
farmhouse, playing with these children. An agony of
worry overtook her as she remembered that her sister
still thought her the prisoner of unknown desperadoes,

that poor Jinx, who couldn't even walk, was probably worried sick about what fate had befallen her sister.

She went into the bedroom and picked up the note she'd composed explaining to Jinx that she was safe and would be home soon. As she stared at it, an idea formed and grew large in her mind.

Why should she wait to give Cal her message for Jinx? She didn't need him. She would go to Deadwood and send the wire herself.

Only she'd best not go to Deadwood, she reflected, pursing her lips. She had to steer clear of that town just in case Rafe Campbell was already there. He might spot her, and *then*, Melora thought, *I'd have no choice but to confront him.* Confront him?

She'd shoot him. It was what he deserved.

But reason quickly prevailed over this tempting notion. No matter how upset she was with Cal, she couldn't risk spoiling the plan he'd devised to clear his name. He needed to set Campbell up, to arrange Marshal Brock's involvement in order to gain a valid confession. She'd have to avoid Deadwood—for now.

But I can ride to Cherryville; it's only five miles south of Deadwood. I'll send the wire to Jinx and come right back before Cal even knows I've gone.

With Cal so damned busy he hadn't even bothered to say good morning or to come in for supper, who was to stop her?

Only Jesse.

Well, she could handle a fourteen-year-old boy. Thinking quickly, Melora folded the note into the pocket of her trousers, then retrieved her Colt from Cal's saddle pack.

He should have returned this to her days ago. She needed it. Who else did she have to rely on but herself? Always herself.

For a moment her throat closed with unshed tears as she realized that for a time, a very short time, she'd thought she could depend on a man who called himself Wyatt Holden, who'd come courting with flowers and gifts, who'd offered to marry her in church before the entire town of Rawhide.

She'd been a fool.

Falling for the lies of a rustling, murdering con artist had been a miserable enough mistake. But then—then she had allowed herself to think, for a few brief moments, that she could count on Cal. That he cared for her, wanted her, maybe even loved her . . .

Fool, fool, fool, she told herself. *After all the men who have courted you, chased you, wanted you, you have to pick a big lug who couldn't care less about you, or love, or anything but getting revenge against Rafe Campbell. Oh, he cares about his family, these children, and his family name, but not about you.*

Not in the way you want him to care.

She wanted to scream, to pound her fist into Cal Holden's handsome, stubborn face, to grab hold of him and tell him exactly what she thought of him, but she did none of these things.

She knelt beside Louisa, while the other children were out back, and gave her a quick smile.

"Lou, honey, I'm taking Sunflower out for a ride. I'll be back in time to fix dinner."

"You going to find Cal?"

"No, Cal's busy. I'm just going for a ride."

"Where?"

She hesitated, then smiled into the little girl's worried eyes. "It's a secret, Lou, but actually I'm going to Cherryville. See this?" She took out the note and showed it to Lou, folding and refolding it. "I'm going to wire my little sister back in Wyoming."

"Jinx." Lou nodded importantly.

"Yes, Jinx."

"How did she get such a funny name?"

Melora grinned. "Because on the night she was born my pop won three hundred dollars in a poker game."

Louisa chuckled along with her, and suddenly Melora reached out and hugged the little girl. "My sister is just about as cute as you are. Only she's a little older; she's nearly twelve. But she had an accident, and she can't walk, and . . . I'm worried about her. I miss her very, very much."

"I'd miss Cassie if she went away on a trip," Louisa said solemnly. "I missed Cal while he was gone, and," she added in a low, sad tone, "I still miss Joe. I think about him most every day."

"I'm sure you do," Melora replied quietly.

"Can I meet Jinx one day?" the girl asked, suddenly breaking free, her eyes shining with excitement.

Melora wondered how to answer. "I'd like that," she said, picking her words carefully. "But we'll have to see. Right now, though"—she went on briskly, recalling herself to her task—"I need you to tell me how to get to Cherryville. Do you know exactly?"

"Course I know."

"Then tell me, if you please, and if you keep my secret, just maybe I'll bring you back a surprise."

"Let me go with you, Melora; then I can show you the trail."

Melora shook her head. "Not this time. Cal might not like it. Stay here and work in your spelling primer, so when I test you tonight, you'll get all the words correct. And then I *will* give you a surprise."

Jesse came upon her as she was mounting from a fence post.

"Hey, Melora. Where do you think you're going?" He ran over and grabbed Sunflower's bridle.

"Riding."

"Anyplace particular?" He squinted up at her and spoke casually. "Cal's down in the north pasture if you're looking for him."

"I'm not."

"Look, Melora, I've got to speak my piece." She waited as Jesse raked his hand through his hair in a gesture so like Cal's a pang struck her heart. "I reckon we made a mistake, locking you two in the barn yesterday. Things didn't turn out the way we expected."

Nor the way I expected. The tightness in her chest hurt, making Melora snap out, "Forget about it, Jesse. Your brother and I don't get along. That's all. He doesn't like me, and I don't like him. Can you blame me? He did kidnap me after all, taking me away from *my* home and *my* sister."

"I know all that, and you know why," Jesse retorted. "But the thing is, Cal *does* like you. Actually he more than likes you. He's sweet on you, Melora." He went on desperately, blushing with the words. "More sweet on you than he's ever been on anyone. Cal's shy with girls, always has been. He's different with you, though."

I'll say, Melora thought with bitterness. *He wasn't shy about kidnapping me or about kissing me anytime he damn well felt like it. Or about dragging me down in the hay last night, undressing me, driving me wild—until he changed his damned mind.*

"Look, maybe you don't know your brother as well as you think." She went on smoothly, her chin up. "He seems like a man who knows exactly what he's doing. He knows how to get what he wants, and he knows . . . more about women than you'd guess," she said, suddenly overcome by an intense hatred of any woman Cal Holden had ever known, particularly the ones who'd taught him to kiss like that or to move his body the way he did, to set a woman on fire. . . .

"Cal isn't innocent, and he isn't stupid. He's known what he's been doing all along. Particularly where I'm concerned." She went on furiously. "To him I'm a pawn; that's all. Someone useful. Someone involved in his life because I have to be. But he doesn't like me . . . or—or care about me, not in the way you mean—"

"The hell he doesn't!" Jesse burst out.

He sounded so sure that Melora paused, staring at him through wide, wondering eyes. Could Jesse be right? No. She'd lived through what had happened last night. Cal couldn't have said all that about everything's being a mistake, about regretting it, if he loved her.

"I'm not going to discuss your brother with you one moment longer," she said coldly, drawing her dignity around her like a heavy wool cloak in the dead of winter. "I'm going for a ride."

"Cal might not like it . . ." Jesse said uncertainly, biting his lip, but Melora grabbed up Sunflower's reins with an oath and kicked the mare to a gallop.

"To hell with him," she yelled over her shoulder, and then she was racing, racing like the wind across the scrabby grass, toward the lofty forest of spruces ahead.

The air had turned chill overnight, making her glad she'd taken Cal's wool jacket, which he'd left on a peg by the kitchen door. Though the sky was a hot, vivid blue, there was a nip in the air that hinted of autumn and of the harsh Dakota winter to come.

Autumn. It was almost autumn, and she had to get Jinx to a doctor back East before the bad weather set in. She had to get the Weeping Willow into the black. She had to straighten out the mess of her life.

And she had to sweep Cal Holden out of her thoughts and her dreams and her heart.

All the way to Cherryville she kept turning over in her mind what Jesse had said. She came to the conclusion he didn't know what he was talking about. By the time she dismounted in front of the telegraph office and tethered Sunflower to a hitching post, she was so immersed in her thoughts that she never saw the tall raven-haired man in the black Stetson emerge from the saloon.

He saw her, though.

Rafe Campbell stopped dead, his jaw dropping.

What the hell? he growled under his breath.

It was Melora; it could only be Melora. Though she was wearing a flannel shirt, a jacket, and trousers, he would recognize that lithe, slender body anywhere, the shimmer of gold hair tied back with a ribbon, the smooth, swinging, confident walk that could turn a man's blood to liquid fire.

He controlled the impulse to run to her, grab her, whisk her off, and ask questions later. He hadn't come this far by giving in to emotion when reason was called for. There were too many unknown elements here. *Had Holden let her go?* he wondered, his mind assessing the possibilities with rapid calculation. Or had she gotten away?

And how much did she know?

Reflex made him duck back behind the false front eatery alongside the saloon while through slitted eyes he watched her enter the telegraph office. And thought.

And waited.

18

"I'm here to see Marshal Brock."

Cal stood hat in hand on the front porch of Marshal Brock's spotless white house and peered once again into the prim, lined face of the gray-headed woman who opened the front door.

He'd spent the morning doing farm chores and repairing harnesses, but before long the urge to come to town and check on developments had been overwhelming. While everyone at home was having the midday meal, he'd gone to the barn, saddled Rascal, and headed to Deadwood in search of Marshal Everett T. Brock and in search of Rafe Campbell.

He wasn't having much luck finding either one.

"So it's you again. Well, the marshal's not here," the woman said in a high, snappish voice that grated

on his nerves. She looked sweet as marzipan in her
starched gingham dress and apron, with her little
cloud of hair wound tightly into a bun, but her small
marble blue eyes were as arctic as the snowcaps atop
the Rockies.

He spoke with cool deliberation. "When do you
expect him back, ma'am?"

"Told you last time. Don't know. He comes and
goes when he pleases. I have work to do."

Cal replaced his hat. "Sorry to bother you." Yet
he hesitated a moment, uncertain whether or not to
leave his name with Marshal Brock's housekeeper.
He knew the phrase "Once a lawman, always a lawman." What if the famed marshal, retired or not,
started looking into this stranger who kept coming by
his door, started checking out wanted posters, names
of escaped outlaws? The Holden name might come
up, and *then*, Cal mused, *I might find myself being
tracked down and arrested by the very lawman I need
to help clear my name.*

"Just tell him I'll be back," he said smoothly, and
turned away. He sauntered down the steps, away from
her glaring eyes and the neat white clapboard house
without glancing back even when she slammed the
door. With long strides he headed up the street toward
the center of town, keeping an eye out for Rafe
Campbell.

Where the hell was Brock? He needed to get things
started. By today or tomorrow he expected to hear
from Campbell—a note left for him at the hotel, as
he'd instructed. Then he could make his move.

But not without Brock.

As Cal stalked down the busy horse and wagon–filled street, glancing this way and that with deceptive casualness, his mood was as restless as the wind that sent tumbleweed skittering down Deadwood's streets and alleys.

It had been sheer hell today trying to concentrate on what needed doing at the farm. To tell the truth, it had been hell trying to concentrate on much of anything; Melora kept getting in the way.

Popping into his mind when he was chopping wood or planting or repairing a harness. Torturing him with the memory of how sweetly her body moved beneath his hands, how her eyelashes curled like honey-colored lace along her cheeks when she closed her eyes, how she stuck her hands on her hips when she was mad about this or that.

Melora Deane. He had to stop thinking about Melora Deane.

It was time, time at last to bring his entire plan to fruition. To persuade Marshal Brock that he was an innocent man who'd been framed, to get the lawman to agree to conceal himself when Cal confronted Rafe Campbell head-on.

Then all I'll have to do is get Campbell to confess to everything: the rustling, Grimstock's murder, all of it, while Brock is in earshot.

And then it will be up to the law.

Part of him chafed at this plan. Campbell had hurt too many people. Cal would have preferred just to shoot it out with him and be done. The snake didn't deserve to live, didn't deserve even the dignity of a trial.

But he had Lou and Cassie and Will and Jesse to think about. He had to get the Holden name cleared once and for all—and Joe's name, too. He needed Brock to be his witness, to help him wipe the slate clean so that everyone would know—in Arizona, all over—that the Holden brothers had done nothing wrong. That Rafe Campbell was the one who deserved to hang for his crimes.

But Brock seemed never to be at home. And Campbell hadn't yet shown his face in Deadwood, though he should have been here by now.

Cal had a bad feeling in his gut as he hurried across the street toward the hotel, and it got worse when Quinn O'Malley suddenly stepped out in front of him as he passed the smithy and put a hand on his shoulder.

"Need to say something to you, Holden."

"Something wrong?" He met the farmer's appraising gaze with a neutral glance that hid his trepidation. Bad news was coming; he could feel it.

"Don't know much about you, Holden, but you seem like a decent fellow. Got yourself a nice wife, a baby on the way, and your young brothers and sisters are a real nice bunch of kids."

"Where's this headed, O'Malley?" Cal was tense, noting the worry that knitted the Irishman's bushy brows.

"Heard something in Hamilton's Mercantile just a bit ago. Bounty hunter's looking for you. Goes by the handle of Coyote Jack. Ever hear of him?"

"I've heard of him." It was an understatement. Everyone in the Wyoming and Dakota territories had heard of him. Cal's jaw tightened. Coyote Jack had a fearsome reputation as one of the most ruthless bounty hunters this side of the Rockies. He'd as soon kill his man as bring him back alive. He captured more men and earned more reward money in six months' time than most lawmen and bounty hunters did over their entire careers.

So Campbell's hired none other than Coyote Jack to find me—and to kill me too, he thought, not without a flicker of satisfaction. But then his mind jumped ahead: *No, he won't kill me. Not until I tell him where to find Melora.*

"Appreciate your dropping me a hint about this, O'Malley. Did you hear anyone mention the farm?"

"Not that I could tell. But I asked the storekeeper about it when Coyote Jack left, and he said the bounty hunter had been asking questions yesterday too. You in some kind of trouble, Holden?"

"Nothing I can't handle," Cal told him evenly. He locked eyes with the burly farmer, who seemed to be taking his measure yet again "I've got myself some enemies, but I reckon I'll be rid of them right soon. Thanks for the tip."

"One more thing." O'Malley glanced around and waited as several passersby scurried around them on the boardwalk. "Last I saw, that bounty hunter was headed for Cherryville. Anyone there going to know you or be able to give that hombre a fix on your farm?"

"Don't think so, but I'm not taking any chances. Reckon I'm going to have to hunt up this Coyote Jack in Cherryville and teach him to mind his own business,'' Cal drawled, a hard light radiating from the center of his eyes. His mouth was a thin, dangerous slit, startling O'Malley with the transformation from the quiet, polite young man who had come to the barbecue with his pretty wife last night to this formidable-looking stranger whose carved features were harder than granite.

"Thanks again, O'Malley. I'm beholden to you."

The farmer shook his head. "Don't mention it. Just take care of yourself and that family of yours."

"Count on it." Cal clasped his hand and then swung back toward the post where Rascal was tethered.

Quinn O'Malley stared after him for a moment, watching until Cal had vaulted into the saddle and roared out of town. The look of pure rawhide-tough grit on young Cal Holden's face almost made him feel sorry for Coyote Jack and for whoever had set the bounty hunter on his trail.

But he shook his head as the ribbon of rising dust blurred the horse and rider. He'd once seen Coyote Jack shoot three outlaws before any of them could get off a shot. Cal Holden would have to be damned good—or he'd wind up just as dead as those Bailey brothers.

And they'd been mighty dead indeed.

19

Jinx Deane perched desolately in her chair and stared out the window of the Gold Bar Hotel in mute, miserable frustration. She couldn't see much of the town of Cherryville from here; the large back room Wyatt Holden had stuck her in overlooked only a narrow, garbage-strewn alley, though beyond she could just make out a square of the distant Black Hills, its forested peaks looming dark green against the vivid blue sky. She wished she could have looked out over the town, been able to see people going in and out of shops, children and dogs and chickens in the street, riders and wagons and stagecoaches coming and going.

But all she could see was rotting garbage littering the dusty alley, where now and then crows swooped down to grab leftover scraps dumped behind the hotel's dining room.

The gloomy view only added to her sense of unease.

There's no reason to be scared, Jinx told herself. *Stop being such a baby.*

But she was scared, even though logic told her this was silly. She was with Wyatt, her sister's fiancé. He'd already explained that he believed Mel was someplace close by, that he didn't think she was in danger, that she would be with them very soon.

"My men will be combing the area every day until we find her," he had said that afternoon when he'd come to the Weeping Willow and spoken to her privately while Aggie was away, driving into Rawhide for supplies.

"How do you know where she is?" she'd asked, hope bounding up inside her like a released spring.

"I know. You must trust me on this, Jinx. You do trust me, don't you, honey?"

"Ye-es."

Wyatt Holden had smiled then, a smile of gentle warmth. He'd knelt so he was at eye level with her as she sat in her invalid chair with Speckles in her arms and Dot and Blackie mewing on her lap, and he'd talked to her as if she were a grown-up, making her feel very important and very intelligent.

"I only want what's best for you and for Melora, Jinx. As far as I'm concerned, when your sister promised to marry me, that was the day that we became family. You, me, Melora—we're all family, Jinx. And Aggie too," he added. "I don't think either of us could have gotten through this trouble without Aggie, do you?''

"No. Do you think . . . can Aggie come with us while we go look for Mel?"

"I'd sure like that, but it's not the best plan, honey. Someone needs to stay here and run the ranch while we're gone. Your foreman's a good man, but Aggie knows this place nearly as well as your pop and Melora; the hands need her to cook for them, and keep the books, and make decisions. With Melora gone, and next you and me, someone has to keep things in order here. I don't know who else I'd trust with it but Aggie."

"Me too." Jinx stroked Speckles's fur, staring down into the green marble eyes that lifted so trustingly toward hers. "All right." She took a deep breath. "It's the sensible thing to do."

"And your pop taught both of you girls to be sensible," Wyatt had said approvingly, patting her arm. For some reason the touch of his fingers always sent a shiver through her, though she tried not to show it.

"But can we tell Aggie that you think you know who took Mel and that you've got a good idea whereabouts she is?"

"Better not get her hopes up. Besides, she'll be bound to ask a lot of questions about how I found out and what I'm planning to do, and that'll take time to explain—time we don't have." He'd sighed. "The important thing now is to get to the Black Hills and find Melora—and that you be there when I get her back. She'll want to be reunited with you right away, honey, and just the sight of you will cheer her up.

That's what we want, isn't it? To get Melora back safely and make her happy. Then we can all get on with our lives.''

Jinx didn't really understand why they couldn't tell Aggie the good news about having a lead where Melora was, but she agreed to the story he'd proposed.

They would tell Aggie that Dr. Emerson of Philadelphia was traveling in the Dakota Territory and Wyatt had arranged for Jinx to meet with him, that he was an expert on limb paralysis, and would be able to give them some valuable information on Jinx's condition.

Jinx wasn't used to lying. Pop had always taught her that it was wrong to lie, even for a good reason. But Pop was gone, and so was Melora, and now she had to rely on Wyatt Holden.

But more and more, as she sat alone in the Cherryville hotel room these past few days since they'd arrived, she'd begun to feel worried. Her room was pretty, with its amber and white flowered quilt, its blue painted walls, and its solid mahogany furniture. There was a large fireplace with a carved mantel, and a tall crystal vase of flowers set upon it, and there were pretty gilt-framed seascapes displayed upon the walls. But she didn't want to be here in a strange town, alone, waiting for Melora. She wanted to be with her sister back home at the Weeping Willow.

Soon, we'll go home soon, she told herself each night as she lay upon the large cool bed in the strange room and stared at the shadows on the ceiling.

One thing that made her uneasy was that ever since they'd arrived, Wyatt Holden didn't seem to have time for her; he wouldn't even explain how it was he knew Melora was somewhere in the vicinity. He sent a maid up several times a day with her meals and to help her with whatever she needed, but he was always away, looking for Melora, he explained one morning, when he did stop in to urge her to be patient just a little longer.

Jinx was lonely and worried and restless. Sometimes she stared at her legs. What weak, spindly, despicable things they'd become, stretched uselessly before her as she sat in her chair. She hated them; she hated the chair; she hated herself for not being able to walk, to go out and somehow look for her sister herself.

She missed Aggie and the Weeping Willow, missed her kittens and her own cozy room with its books and dolls.

Why don't you try to walk? something inside her whispered.

Try, right now. No one will know if you fail.

She remembered how she had fallen in the kitchen, how Wyatt Holden had scooped her up and carried her into the parlor the night Melora had disappeared. She hadn't tried since.

Don't think about that. Try. Your legs aren't broken. They don't even hurt. You should be able to do it.

Jinx closed her eyes. She thought of the derring-do of the Knights of the Round Table, of the pirates and princesses who had grand adventures and performed feats of bravery in her favorite storybooks. They were strong, courageous, agile.

She couldn't even walk over to the bed.

Try.

Hands trembling, she placed them on the arms of her chair. She pushed herself up, forward, placing her weight gingerly upon her booted feet as she slid them toward the floor.

She was shaking all over. Her feet pressed to the ground, and then suddenly her knees buckled, and so did her courage. With a gasp of terror she threw herself backward, thumping down into her invalid chair and gripping the arms with desperate clinging fingers, like someone trying frantically to keep from being thrown off a horse.

I can't. I never will.

The tears came. The ache of frustration that choked her combined with the loneliness inside her, and her sobs grew louder, harder. They echoed pitifully around the four blue walls.

"Mel," she whispered at last into the empty, pretty room. "Mel, I m-miss you. I need you. Where are you?"

MELORA slipped out of the telegraph office well pleased with herself. There. She had wired a message to Jinx, and Mr. Rappaport at the telegraph office in Rawhide was bound to see that her sister received it. Jinx would not have to worry about her anymore.

A thin smile curved her lips as she closed the door behind her and headed to the hitching post where Sunflower was tethered.

There, Cal Holden. So much for you. I can still

*take care of my own business by myself and you don't
have a thing to say about it—*

Suddenly, strong hands grabbed her, hauled her
clear off her feet and around the corner of the building. She found herself in an alley, a narrow dirt alley
that was rank with the odor of rotting garbage.

Melora spun to face whoever had grabbed her, her
hand reaching instinctively for the gun tucked inside
her jacket pocket.

But she froze as Rafe Campbell seized her wrist.

"Howdy, Melora," he said gently.

"Y-you!" she spluttered, fighting to quell the
shock that was tying her tongue and her thought proc-
esses into knots.

"It's me all right." A strange smile played around
the corners of his full, handsome mouth. "And,
honey, I've never been more surprised or happier to
see anyone in my life." He smiled broadly at her
then, a wary smile, she thought, one that reflected
oddly in his eyes, and suddenly the realization came
thudding to her.

*He doesn't know what I've been told. He isn't sure
if I know who he really is or what he's done.*

"Wyatt," she croaked. "Wyatt, *darling*," she
cried, trying to infuse breathless joy into the stunned
expression she knew was still frozen upon her face.
"I've been so . . . afraid. Terrified. You can't know.
Thank God you found me!"

Rafe Campbell was watching her closely. Melora
peered up into his eyes and grasped him by the shoulders. *Here goes nothing*, she thought, bracing herself

as she leaned eagerly toward him and kissed him on the lips.

They were the same lips she'd kissed countless times before, but this time a bitter chill wisped through her as her lips pressed momentarily against his. His mouth felt warm, moist, almost sticky.

"How did you find me?" she asked, hoping she looked suitably grateful and very much in love.

"Just lucky, I guess. Honey, are you all right?" His arms wrapped around her, clasping her to him in a powerful embrace that was intended to appear protective and warm but that felt stifling. And imprisoning.

"I'm fine now that I'm with you."

"But what are you doing here? What happened to you?"

"I got away," she babbled. "And I sent you a wire ... just now ... you and Jinx ... oh, Wyatt, thank God you're here. I had no idea you were in Cherryville, looking for me."

She saw the wariness fade a little from his eyes. It was warring with relief. *He wanted to believe her*, Melora realized, her hope spiking. He wanted to be able to continue the charade of their engagement, to take her back to Rawhide, marry her, and get his filthy hands on her ranch.

Damn you. Melora controlled the savage hatred jolting through her, and gave him the most dazzling smile she could summon up. "Wyatt, please tell me, is Jinx all right? And Aggie? I've been so worried about everyone!"

"We've been worried about you, honey." His arms tightened. "Real worried. You haven't been hurt?"

"No, he didn't hurt me—"

"Who's he? Melora, who the hell took you?"

He knows it was Cal. If you deny it, he'll know you're lying.

"A man named Cal Johnson, a terrible, angry man. There were two others with him, but Cal was the leader. Wyatt, it was awful. He wouldn't tell me why he kidnapped me, wouldn't answer any of my questions. I was so frightened, but he just kept telling me that I didn't need to know what he was doing. Oh, Wyatt," she gasped, allowing her lower lip to tremble. "Please, let's just forget about him and go home. I really need to go home."

"Sorry, Melora." Wyatt shook his head. His eyes were the same piercing blue as the sky. "We can't do that." He lifted a hand and stroked it against Melora's cheek, a feather-light touch. "No man is going to steal my woman and get away with it. We're not going anywhere until I track down this Cal Johnson. And by the time I've finished with him, you can bet every acre of the Weeping Willow that he'll never bother anyone else ever again. Tell me where he is."

"I . . . don't know exactly."

His eyes sharpened on her. There was a pause. "How is that?"

"Well, I got away from him and . . . Wyatt, please. Can't we go somewhere that's quiet and safe and private to talk? Isn't there a hotel? I need to rest, and

I'd like some food. Please, I'll tell you everything, but let's get out of this alley and go someplace where Cal Johnson won't stumble upon us.''

Slowly he nodded. His eyes remained fixed and steady upon her face. ''Sure, Melora. Whatever you say, honey. But I want you to know you don't have to be afraid of Cal Johnson. I won't let him or anyone else hurt you ever again.'' His hand cupped her chin, tilting it up, high, higher. Melora felt a tiny strain along her neck. ''You're mine, and no one touches what's mine. Do you understand?''

Her throat dry, she nodded.

''Hell and damnation, sweetheart''—he grinned— ''you're sure a sight for sore eyes.''

He drew her closer. Melora held her breath, trying to smile, trying to melt against him as she once had, though every bone in her body screamed for her to jump away and to run as far from this lying snake as she could get.

''Oh, Wyatt,'' she murmured. *I'd love to cut out your heart with a bowie knife,* she thought, and all the while she gazed limpidly into his eyes and brought her hand up to caress his smooth-shaven jaw lightly.

He was smiling that strange smile again, his eyes studying her. They inspected her the way a prospector would look over a nugget of gold to see if it was the real thing or fool's gold.

He doesn't believe me. Not completely. He senses that something's off, but he's just not sure, and he's not ready to call me on it yet.

There and then Melora made up her mind. There

was no way she'd set foot in a private hotel room with this man. She wasn't going anywhere with him. She couldn't keep up this charade much longer; the very nearness of him made her skin crawl and made her want to spit in his crystal blue, lying eyes.

She kissed him. Somehow she forced herself to kiss him. And while his arms slid around her, and his mouth fastened upon hers, she reached ever so slowly toward the Colt tucked inside the pocket of her jacket.

"Don't move or I'll blow your damned head off," Melora whispered sweetly. Then she cocked the trigger with a loud click and jumped back out of his arms in one swift, graceful leap.

Seconds ticked by. Campbell stared at her, not even a muscle twitching in his smooth, suddenly white face.

"Have you gone loco, honey?" he asked at last, his tongue scraping against the corner of his lip.

"No. I've come to my senses. I've finally figured out just what kind of a low-down snake-in-the-grass kind of varmint you are. I can't believe I ever let you touch me, much less considered marrying you."

"Careful, Melora." The eyes riveted upon her were as hard as polished stones. "You're not making any sense, and you're saying things you're going to regret."

"The only thing I regret is ever having met you. Don't you understand, you imbecilic weasel? The game is over. I'm on to you, Mr. Rafe Campbell. I know exactly *who* and *what* you are."

A sudden gust of wind rattled the broken weather vane atop the telegraph office and ruffled some papers in the trash heap behind her. Melora thought she heard something and glanced over her shoulder for a brief instant. She saw only the grimy buildings in the alley and the patch of blue sky beyond. Then swiftly she swerved her gaze back to Rafe Campbell.

He hadn't moved. He was staring at her calmly enough, but she saw the anger flashing behind his eyes like lightning against a summer sky.

She might have been afraid, except that she was the one holding the gun.

"I don't know what that two-bit outlaw Cal Johnson told you, but he's obviously fed you a trough full of lies. Don't believe them. Don't ruin what we had, Melora." He sounded oddly sincere, almost passionate. The firm, handsome planes of his face were softened with appeal.

And the throb in his voice was real.

"Please, honey, put down the gun right now. Right now, Melora. Please."

"Go to hell." She spit the words out contemptuously. "You're a rustler, a murderer, and a thief. You're responsible for the deaths of Joe Holden and that poor rancher Grimstock, and you would have let Cal hang for a murder he didn't commit." Rage suffused her, sparking golden flames in her tawny eyes. "And you'd have stolen my ranch . . . wouldn't you? Admit it, you sniveling weasel. You'd have stolen the Weeping Willow, *wouldn't you*?"

"I'm going to have both you and your ranch, Melora," Rafe Campbell informed her with a curl of his lip. "I suggest you put the gun down."

"The hell I will—"

She never saw Coyote Jack step out from the shadow of the building behind her. Never heard the sharp crack of the blow as he brought his fist down on her head. She knew only a blinding pain that exploded in her skull, and she glimpsed watery red splotches swim before her eyes as she crumpled like a rag doll into the dirt.

Coyote Jack shook his head as he stared down at her and then at the man who'd hired him. "The lady wasn't so glad to see you."

"Shut up. Help me get her out of here."

"Sure, boss. Where to?"

Rafe Campbell smiled thinly as he lifted Melora easily in his arms and studied the sculptured beauty of her pale cheeks.

"I know the perfect place."

JESSE and the children all heard the thunder of Rascal's hooves before Cal even came into view through the dense cover of trees. Horse and rider stormed up the path of the farmhouse past the white gate in a blur. They all came running onto the porch as Cal drew up and dismounted in a gliding leap.

"Trouble." He flicked Jesse one terse glance. "I'm going into Cherryville to head it off. I want you and Melora to keep all the children inside. Lock the doors and windows, get out your shotgun, and you and Melora keep watch."

He was covered with sweat and dust from his ride. As he wiped an arm across his eyes, blotting up the sweat dripping down from beneath his hat, the children watched in silence.

He glanced at each of them: Jesse, Will, Cassie, Louisa. "Where's Melora?" he demanded.

Jesse paled. With a hand that shook a little he shoved his mop of long brown hair from his eyes. "She's not here, Cal. She's been gone all afternoon."

"Gone?"

"I thought she was with you." Jesse met Cal's narrowed eyes with a flicker of uncertainty. "She said she was going out for a ride, and I figured that she found you and the two of you were—" He paused, licking his lips and glancing at the intent faces of his younger brother and sisters. "I figured that you two were ironing out your differences."

"I haven't seen her since breakfast. Did she take Sunflower?"

Barely waiting for Jesse's nod, Cal threw the next question at him. "Did she say anything about where she was going?"

"No . . . out for a ride, that's all she said."

Cal's mouth tightened, a white line forming around his lips. He didn't like the sound of this. He whipped around and scanned the countryside in every direction. On a distant ledge several antelope stood like statues in the fading sunlight. The wind tore through the grass and rattled the leaves on the trees. Birds swooped and wheeled.

But there was no sign of Melora.

He knew he had to track down Coyote Jack and deal with him before the bounty hunter found someone in Cherryville who might recognize Cal from the barbecue and tell Jack about the dirt-poor farm where he could find the man on the wanted poster. And he had to do it soon, or Coyote Jack could be snarling down their door by dark. Steel glinted in Cal's eyes as he contemplated this scenario. He'd be damned before he let some money-grubbing bounty hunter get within a country mile of his family.

But where was Melora? If she'd just gone for a ride, she should have been home by now. Unless she somehow got hurt or ran into trouble.

The thought of her lying on the trail somewhere with a broken ankle or worse sent an ice-cold spear through his blood.

He wheeled about in the front yard, searching the faces of his brothers and sisters. "Anyone know where Melora went?"

"No, Cal." Vehemently, his face tight with worry, Will shook his head.

Cassie clutched the broom she'd been using to sweep the parlor floor. "Don't know, Cal."

Lou stared at her older brother silently.

"Lou?" Jesse threw her a suspicious look. "You know something, don't you?"

"I know lots of things, but not that."

"Yes, you do. I can tell!" Jesse stalked over and grabbed the little girl's arm. "You tell us right now! We don't have time for none of your games."

"That's enough, Jesse," Cal said sharply, and his brother let the girl's arm drop.

"Louisa, this is important." Cal took a deep breath and continued steadily, dropping down on one knee to stare into her pale face. "If you know where Melora is, tell me right now."

"But it's a secret. I p-promised I wouldn't tell."

A muscle jumped in Cal's neck, but he kept a calm, even expression upon his face. "Louisa, promises don't count when a person might be in trouble," he told her sternly. "Could be Melora needs our help right now; she could have fallen off her horse or run into a rattlesnake or a bear. I'm not trying to scare you, Lou, but since Melora isn't back yet, we have to start looking for her. So talk, *now*."

"She went to Cherryville!" the little girl said, her chest heaving as if she'd unloaded a great burden.

Cal felt fresh sweat break out on his brow. He stood up slowly, rigid with anger not unmixed with fear, though he continued to speak quietly. "Did she say what for?"

"To send a wire to her sister, Jinx. Do you know Jinx can't walk?"

"I know that, Lou."

"And Melora didn't want Jinx to be worried about her. So she's sending a wire. There's nothing wrong with that, is there, Cal? Is there?"

He didn't hear her the first time she asked the question. He was staring in the direction of Cherryville. Hell and damnation, he'd never met a woman with more of a sixth sense for running into trouble.

"Did I do something wrong, Cal?" Lou asked in a low, tremulous tone, braving the scowls of Jesse and Will.

Cal answered her at last with steady reassurance. "No, Lou, you didn't do anything wrong. Don't you worry. I'm going to Cherryville right now to find Melora and bring her back."

But he didn't like the feel of this. If Coyote Jack was here asking questions about him, having been hired by Campbell, then it was a good bet that Campbell was lurking somewhere nearby, too. He just hadn't shown himself yet. Wouldn't it be just like Melora to run into him?

And then what?

"I'm coming with you." Jesse started toward the barn as Cal swung back into the saddle and picked up Rascal's reins.

"No." The word froze Jesse in his tracks, but he threw Cal a stubborn glance.

"Cal—"

Cal held up a hand for silence but otherwise ignored him. He fixed each of the younger children with a look that brooked no argument. "Go on inside now and see to setting the table for supper," he ordered. "Will, you help your sisters. I have to talk to Jesse alone."

One peek at his grim face, and they all hurried inside without a word of argument.

The afternoon was fading. The air had changed. There was a gusty chill, an edge, that swept down from the trees and the iron wall of mountains, a chill that hadn't been there during the golden days of late summer. A hint of autumn, maybe, even of the winter to come. Of the beginning of a harsher season.

"Cal, I can help—" Jesse said, starting toward him, arms outstretched in frustration.

"You need to stay here and look after them."

"But you said there was trouble in Cherryville; you said that even before you knew Melora was gone. You might need help, Cal. Let me help." He stuck out his jaw. "I helped you before," he reminded his brother proudly. "You know I did."

Remembering Jesse's courage and resourcefulness in breaking him out of jail, Cal wavered. He studied the boy before him, his gaze flicking over the long, lean limbs just beginning to shoot up toward manhood. Jesse could be of help; he could save Cal some time. While Cal hunted for Coyote Jack, Jesse could search for Melora and at the very least find out if she'd made it to the telegraph office.

"There's one problem: We can't leave Will and Lou and Cassie here alone."

"Let's take them over to the O'Malleys'." Jesse's eyes were bright as he practically hopped from one foot to the other. "Their farm runs along the trail between here and Cherryville. I don't think Mrs. O'Malley would mind a few extra mouths to feed for one night. Deirdre said she always has plenty of food on the table."

Cal frowned, considering this. Then a grudgingly admiring smile touched his lips. "You're got a real good head on your shoulders, Jesse. I'm going to take you up on your plan. Two of us can comb Cherryville a lot faster than one. But if you run into a bounty hunter named Coyote Jack, you steer clear of him, understand? Stay out of his way; then come and find me pronto."

"Why?"

"I'll explain everything later. Round up the others while I hitch up the wagon. And don't forget to bring your shotgun. Come on, Jesse, hurry," Cal called over his shoulder as he dismounted and sprinted for the barn. "We've got to *ride*."

20

Pain crunched through Melora's head like heavy boots through sand as she came slowly, dimly awake. Dark, eerie stillness surrounded her. But as her eyelids fluttered and a moan escaped her lips, dull forms took shape. The light grew, pulsed. Figures became defined.

Then she groaned softly as thin shafts of sunlight pierced her eyelids.

"Good, you're awake." The voice of her former fiancé came out in a low, satisfied rumble, but it struck her eardrums as ominously as thunder.

She opened her eyes fully and realized she was lying on a bed. Not just any bed, a big, sumptuously appointed four-poster bed appointed in red velvet and heaped with black fringed pillows of gold and red sateen.

Melora pushed herself up to sit dizzily, one hand to her aching head. Rafe Campbell lounged at the mantel, a drink in his hand, watching her. Another man, with long, greasy gray-black hair and a long, snoutish face, who wore buckskins, a black hat, and a sneer, sat sprawled upon a spindly gold-cushioned chair. It appeared to Melora that at any moment the delicate chair might splinter into pieces beneath his weight.

"You had me mighty worried, Melora." Campbell studied her over the rim of his glass. "Coyote Jack hit you harder than he should have. You went down hard and didn't wake up. But you're going to be just fine, honey. Why don't I pour you a brandy? A shot of this stuff will do you good."

"Don't bother," she muttered as he set his glass down on the mantel, crossed to a small lacquer table bearing a crystal decanter and goblets, and poured the dark liquor for her. "I don't want anything from you. Get—get away from me."

"Now, Melora, is that a polite way to talk to your fiancé? I'm trying to take care of you, honey. Drink up."

Melora's head throbbed so badly she could scarcely focus her eyes without white light dancing before her. She wanted to hurl the brandy right into Rafe Campbell's smug, handsome face, the same face she'd once held dear and now hated, but instead she clenched her fingers tightly around the stem of the goblet and forced herself to take a sip. Then another.

This wasn't the time to let her anger control her. There were two of them, and one of her, and she was too weak and dizzy to beat either one of them to the door. With fear clenching inside her, she knew this was one of those moments Pop had often discussed with her, a time to use her head instead of her temper.

Cal's life might be at stake. And hers too.

"Better?" Campbell inquired, taking the glass from her at last.

"Why should you care?" she replied in a low tone, and sank back against the pillows. The brandy had run down her throat like perfumed fire, warming and soothing her, helping clear her head. Now that she'd had a moment to observe her surroundings she realized that she was in a large, opulent, overly furnished room. Everything about it, from the gold-flocked wallpaper to the ruby carpeting and the heavy red drapes swathing the windows, seemed more suffocating than elegant. She'd never seen anything like the overstuffed black and red velvet settee or the huge gilded mirrors and gold-framed paintings of half-naked women that covered the walls. And a sinuous heavy floral scent, a perfume that was as cloying and exotic as the paintings themselves, pervaded the room.

"Where am I?"

"One of my favorite places." Campbell set her glass down and retrieved his own. He downed the rest of his brandy in one smooth gulp before continuing. "The Peacock Brothel, my dear. Handsome—isn't it?—if a shade gaudy. But it does set a certain mood."

The man in the chair guffawed, and Melora's glance swerved toward him uneasily.

"The owner of this establishment is a particular friend of mine and has let us use one of her own private rooms. We're on the second floor, in the back, where we won't be disturbed. You see, honey, I want us to have a chance for a very private, serious, uninterrupted chat."

"Then what's he doing here?" Melora jerked her chin at the other man. "Do you think you need protection from me, Campbell?"

She saw him stiffen at her sneering tone and the mocking insinuation. His sharply chiseled face flushed a mottled ugly shade of red that nearly matched the carpet. *Oh, so I've pricked your pride*, she thought with satisfaction. *Good.* Yet the fine hairs at the back of her neck quivered at the glacial expression that shot into his eyes.

Melora swallowed, her fingers curling upon the red velvet bed covering. It was difficult to believe that this was the same man who had wooed her with sophistication and elegant restraint at the town dance and had spoken with such commanding eloquence at the cattlemen's association meetings.

It now seemed that a veneer had been stripped away. She saw so clearly beneath the handsome features, the deep, vivid eyes, the assured authority with which he spoke and moved. All was revealed to her now, mirrored in those eyes, naked in his face.

His greed, his cunning, his ruthlessness.

She tasted hot, pure fear, metallic and tingly on her tongue. And rage, a building, flowing rage, when she

thought of all the grief and pain this man had caused
Cal—and Jesse and Will and Lou and Cassie.

He'd taken their brother from them. And their
name, their family honor.

And he'd almost taken the Weeping Willow from
her and Jinx.

"Did you ever love me?" she heard herself asking,
her voice low with anger she was struggling to control.

"Of course, Melora." He shook his head scorn-
fully, as if amazed she could even ask such a question. "I still love you. I'll always love you. And
you're the first woman I've ever said that to, believe
it or not."

"I don't believe it. I don't believe anything you
say."

"That's too bad. Because now I have another score
to settle with Cal Holden. He's turned you against
me."

"No, you've done that all by yourself."

"Either way, it looks like it's up to me to change
things back. To win your trust again, to calm your
fears. Melora, how can I prove to you that what I've
done, what I'm doing, I'm doing for us? For you and
me—and our future."

"You want my ranch."

Something shimmered beneath the glassy surface
of his eyes. "I won't deny it. I do. But I want you
along with it. Just as much. Maybe even more," he
added softly, wonderingly.

Suddenly he moved toward her, quick and catlike.
Even as Melora flinched backward against the fringed

pillows, her arms flying up as if to ward him off, he sat down on the edge of the bed and grasped her by the shoulders.

"Don't ruin this for us, Melora. Help me, be my partner, a true, loving partner, and I'll make you a queen. Marry me, follow me, and together we'll have everything we ever dreamed of: wealth beyond counting, power, influence, a life of dazzling luxury such as you can't possibly imagine."

Melora placed her hands on his and shoved them off her shoulders. Though her head still hurt from the blow she'd sustained, it was much clearer now. She was no longer dizzy, and the anger singing through her blood sharpened her mind.

"I can't possibly imagine why I ever wanted to marry you. You disgust me."

Campbell drew back his arm to backhand her, then scowled and dropped it again. "You're trying my patience, Melora. But I'll make a deal with you. You tell me where I can find Cal Holden, and then you and I will take our time straightening out all these loose ends between us."

Melora spoke between clenched teeth. "I have no idea where Cal Holden can be found, and I wouldn't tell you if I did."

"You'll tell me all right." Campbell grasped her face in his hand, his fingers cruelly pinching her skin. Melora bit back a yelp of pain, but as she tried to wrench his hand from her face, he grabbed her wrist and twisted it.

Her gasp of pain brought a smile to his lips.

"You want me to let you go?" he asked quietly.

"Yes!"

He twisted her wrist harder. Melora felt tears sting her eyes. "Sure, honey." Campbell went on slowly, watching the moisture form at the corners of her eyes. "You're the one making this hard on yourself. Tell me what I want to know, and I won't lay another finger on you—until you ask me to, that is." He gave her a smug, harsh smile.

"I don't know!"

The other man, the one who must have hit her from behind in the alley, came to his feet. He didn't look like the type to sit still for long in one place, and now he shambled toward the door, shaking his shaggy head. "It's getting dark, boss. Why don't I just amble through town again and ask some more questions? Maybe I'll stumble into our boy, or someone will give me a handle on where to find him."

"No, I have something else for you to do right now. Something more effective." Campbell released Melora suddenly and got up from the bed. She rubbed her wrist, biting back a moan as he paced to the window, stared out a moment, then turned back toward her. The dying rosy sunlight bathed his face with an eerie glow as he gave her a cold, knowing smile.

"Melora, honey, I know how much you miss your little sister. And I'll wager you're worried about her. How'd you like to see her?"

See Jinx? Melora's mind raced dazedly. What was he talking about?

"What do you mean?" she asked, her fingers tracing the bruise that was already forming on her skin.

"She's here in Cherryville. Right here in town. I brought her here myself."

In one leap Melora surged off the bed. Ignoring the pulsating pain that immediately rushed through her temples, she dived at him and grabbed his arm. "You bastard, where is she? Tell me where she is!"

"Sure, honey." Campbell spoke soothingly, his other arm sliding around her waist, yanking her close. He clenched her to him like a bulldog grinding his jaws around a bone, and Melora, recognizing that she was trapped, felt a sickening panic rise within her. She'd made a terrible mistake in coming this close to him without a weapon in her grasp.

"Just as soon as you tell me where I can find Cal Holden, I'll bring you to your sweet little crippled sister."

The red and gold room blurred and tilted as she was engulfed by waves of fury, hot, lashing waves that threatened to drown her.

"I don't believe you," she cried. "You've lied about everything else. How do I know you're not lying about Jinx, too?"

Now Rafe Campbell loosened his grip and turned his head slightly to glance at the bounty hunter, who'd paused near the door.

"You know where to find the little girl, Coyote Jack. Bring us a note from Miss Jinx Deane. A note addressed to her sister. And one of the boots from her dainty little feet; she doesn't need them for walking anyway," he added with a malicious smirk.

Melora drew her hand back and slapped him as

hard as she could. Campbell backhanded her then, sending her spinning against the wall.

"I'll be back, boss—in less time than it takes to pee in a barrel." The bounty hunter shuffled out the door, slamming it behind him.

Rafe Campbell studied Melora as she lay dazed and weeping upon the rich ruby carpet. He sighed and combed his fingers through his hair.

"You're too damned beautiful for your own good," he said softly. He gave his head a regretful shake. "It's made you spoiled, headstrong. You need a bit of taming, my sweet Melora, but don't you worry, I'm just the man to do it. When this is all over, we'll begin again in San Francisco. That was my plan all along, to take you to San Francisco. I wanted to sell the Weeping Willow and the Diamond X, to take the money and set up the most magnificent gaming establishment San Francisco has ever seen. As my wife you'll preside over everything. You'll have gowns from Paris, jewels from the far corners of the earth. The finest champagnes to drink, and the best carriages and mansions that money can buy."

He walked toward her, slowly, deliberately, as she ceased crying and lifted her head to stare at him. "I've amassed a small fortune already through careful investments and some shrewd wheeling and dealing. You'd be amazed how quickly a man can grow rich in the West, Melora, if he knows what he's doing."

He ignored the choked cry that came from her and continued without pause. "And the sale of our two ranches, Melora—to a most eager buyer, who has already made a generous offer—will be all that is needed to set up the place I have in mind. A place that will make this Peacock Brothel look like a two-bit tent, a hovel, a place that will make Rawhide's biggest saloon look like nothing more than a barn. My place will have elegance, class. We'll attract all the best people, the wealthiest, most powerful and important people. And you will be the queen of San Francisco within six months, I guarantee you.''

Melora staggered up from the floor and hobbled toward the bed. Her lip was cut, her cheek bruised, but her eyes blazed with pure, hot hatred.

''If you've hurt my sister, I'll kill you,'' she whispered.

''Of course I haven't hurt her. I've invested too much time finding out about hospitals for her. And while the doctors back East are examining her and treating her and making her well, you and I will be establishing ourselves on the Coast.''

''You're loco if you think I'm going anywhere with you.''

He watched her crawl onto the bed, dazed and battered. He went to the decanter and poured her another drink. ''You're the one who's loco, Melora,'' he said gently. ''You're loco if you think I'm going to release you before I've tired of you. I won't. Come hell or high water, I won't. And to judge from the way I feel about you and the effect you have on me, that day won't come for a very long while.''

21

As amethyst sunset ribboned the sky above the Black Hills, two riders bent low over the manes of their horses, streaking toward the town of Cherryville.

Cal and Jesse Holden shared the same determined expressions, and both rode with practiced ease and grace. Tension crackled through them at the knowledge of what lay before them. Both knew that the time was drawing near to avenge their oldest brother's death and that they had one chance to see their family honor restored.

They couldn't fail in this dual mission they were embarking on. If somehow they both were killed, their younger siblings would be orphaned and might be separated, sent to live far and wide, subject to poverty and the whims of others.

The responsiblity for the children weighed on both their minds.

Cal knew that Melora's life might be at stake too. And that if she came to harm, it would be his fault.

Urgency whipped through him. The fear he felt on her behalf made a muscle pulse in his jaw, made him clench Rascal's reins with hands that were unaccustomedly sweaty.

Melora wouldn't be in this mess if not for him. He'd brought her into danger. He had to get her out.

The fact that he loved her had nothing to do with it and everything to do with it. She was his responsibility now, just as Will and Lou and Cassie and Jesse were. But more than that, far more than that, she was his heart, his life.

One thing had become clear to him when he'd returned to the farm and learned she was gone: He loved her and wanted her and meant to win her. He wasn't much good at courting women, hadn't ever had much practice or much luck, but hell and damnation, he would learn.

He'd give her time, let her sort out her feelings, but one way or another, he would find a chance to show her how he felt. Wooing women might not be his specialty, but he'd learned to shoot quicker than lightning could strike a tree, to ride like hell with his guns blazing in both hands and a knife clenched between his teeth, how to lasso cattle, how to beat nine men out of ten at poker without breaking a sweat, and how to soothe and tame the wildest mustangs on earth. He could learn how to woo Melora Deane.

"We'll start at the telegraph office. That'll tell us

if Melora did reach town and send that wire to Jinx.'' Cal studied the narrow streets of Cherryville with grim eyes. ''If she did, we'll have to split up and search. I'll take the north end of town; you take the south. Keep your eyes peeled for any stranger who might be that bounty hunter; if you see him, come and find me. Do you hear me, Jesse? Don't do anything yourself! You're a pretty darn good shot, but you're no match for Coyote Jack.''

''What about you, Cal?'' Jesse licked dry lips. His fingers wound through his mount's bristly mane as he twisted in the saddle to study his brother's face. ''Do you think you could beat him?''

''We'll sure find out if it comes to that,'' Cal replied coolly, then saw the anxiety on Jesse's drawn face and flashed the boy a reassuring grin. ''It's my job to worry about *you*, pardner, not the other way around,'' he told him wryly.

''What if you run into Campbell?''

''Then he'd better say his prayers.''

''But your plan—you need Marshal Brock for a witness—''

''Jesse.'' Cal reached out and grasped his brother's shoulder. ''The most important thing right now is to find Melora before it gets dark; you let me worry about Campbell and Coyote Jack!''

Before they even reached the telegraph office, they spotted Sunflower tethered to a post. The brothers stared at each other in silent apprehension as the horse whickered a greeting. As one, they moved toward the office. The telegraph clerk was just coming around his desk, ready to hang his Closed sign in the window, when Cal pushed open the door. He ignored the balding little man's sputtering protests and took the sign out of his hands. After one glance at Cal's hard, determined countenance the clerk gulped back his indignation. When Cal questioned him, he rattled off answers rapid-fire and punctuated them by bobbing or shaking his head.

Yes, the man confirmed, a beautiful, fair-haired woman had come in several hours before; yes, she'd indeed sent a wire to Rawhide. And then she'd left.

"I never saw her after that. I swear to you, mister, I didn't!"

Cal scowled, turning away. He and Jesse exchanged glances as they reached the street. "We'd best start searching," Cal told his brother, fighting the fear knifing through his belly. "Be quick and be careful. I hope to God she didn't run into Campbell."

The thought filled him with cold fear. What if she had, and then hadn't had sense enough to swallow her temper and pretend she didn't know what kind of animal he was? That could prove damned dangerous.

Knowing what he did about Campbell, having glimpsed the vicious, utterly single-mindedly ruthlessness that Melora had never seen, Cal couldn't shake the worry that knotted through his insides like chewed-up twine.

He started at the dry goods store at the far end of town, asking questions, watching, listening, alert for some sign of Melora, Campbell, or Coyote Jack.

He just prayed he wouldn't find all three of them together.

. . .

JESSE had just slipped inside the Gold Bar Hotel, the shotgun tucked beneath his arm, when he recognized the bony red-haired boy sweeping the floor of the lobby.

It was Eddie Newell, a boy of about nine who was a schoolmate of Cassie's. Eddie was known among the children for throwing spitballs and hiding spiders inside the teacher's desk.

"Hey, there, Eddie," he said, coming up and giving the boy a playful punch on the arm. "I didn't know you worked here."

"Mr. Duncan, the owner, is my uncle." Eddie grinned, showing widely spaced white teeth. He stopped his sweeping and leaned jauntily on his broom. "What're you doing here, Jesse? Want a room?" He chuckled, his grin spreading across his face from ear to ear.

"Not exactly. I'm looking for someone—" Jesse said, but before he could continue, Eddie interrupted him, his brown eyes glowing with excitement.

"Well, we got somebody in here right now who's pretty important," the boy said. "But you don't want to run into *him*. You ever hear of Coyote Jack?"

Jesse went still. "You mean the bounty hunter?" he asked casually.

"Sure, that's who. Well, guess who just went upstairs!"

"He did?" Jesse swallowed hard and shot an involuntary glance at the thinly carpeted staircase. "What for? I mean, is he staying here?"

"Nope, don't think so. It's kinda peculiar, but—"

"Tell me," Jesse said, drawing a stick of peppermint out of his pocket, breaking it in half and offering a piece to Eddie.

The boy accepted eagerly. "Well, he just came in not more than a few minutes ago and started up the stairs, and my uncle, he was at the front desk and said, 'Excuse me, sir, can I help you?' And then he saw it was Coyote Jack. He knew because he'd seen him shoot a man once in Cheyenne—right between the eyes—and—"

"Hurry up, Eddie!"

"Well, anyway"—the boy continued, taking intermittent licks on the peppermint stick—"he just gave my uncle a look that could kill a man faster than a bullet and said, 'Mind your own damn business!' And he kept on going."

"You don't know where?"

"Sure I do." Eddie's grin stretched across his thin, freckled cheeks. "I followed him."

"And?"

"And that's the funny part. He went to room two-oh-five. That's the little girl's room. The one who can't walk."

Jesse grabbed Eddie's shirtfront. "What's her name?"

"I dunno—Oh, yes, I do. It's kind of a strange name. Lucky. No, no, that's not it. Jinx. She's Mr. Campbell's niece, and he has all her meals sent up to her on account of she can't walk at all. Has her own room next door to his and—hey, where are you going?"

But Jesse was already bounding up the stairs three

at a time. At the landing he took a deep breath and studied the row of doors. Then he headed as quietly as he could toward 205.

"WHO are you?" Jinx stared in fright at the buckskin-clad giant who suddenly burst through the door of her room, his coal black eyes fixed on her intently as a wolf's. "M-mister, I think you're in the wrong room."

"This is the right room. You're the kid who can't walk, aren't you?"

Her cheeks grew pinched as alarm flashed through her. "What do you want?" she quavered.

He didn't answer her, just smiled in a way that made her hands fly to the throat of her calico gown. Her heart was pounding as he closed the door behind him and walked very slowly toward her. He was a frightening man. His hair was dirty and hung past his shoulders, his face reminded her of a wild animal's, and his two big guns slapped against his thighs as he approached her.

This was no ordinary cowboy or rancher; he looked like an outlaw. Or a bounty hunter, the type of man she'd come across sometimes in Rawhide, but when she'd been with Pop, doing errands in town, she'd only been curious, never afraid.

It had been impossible to be afraid of anything when Pop was around.

But now she was alone. Jinx couldn't imagine what this man was doing in her room, but she knew it couldn't be anything good.

Where was Wyatt? He'd been gone longer than

usual today, and right about now, even though she didn't like him much and he wasn't very good company, she'd cry out with thankfulness if he walked through that door.

But the door remained closed. And the big man had now reached the little table by her window and was smiling down at her.

"Get away. Tell me what you want." Jinx tried sounding as authoritative as Melora, but her voice came out in a low squeak.

The man laughed. "My name's Coyote Jack, little girl. But that's not important. You can quit looking like you're about to get bit by a rattler, because I'm not going to hurt you. Your friend Mr. Campbell sent me."

"I don't know anyone named Mr. Campbell!"

"Oh, yeah. I mean, Mr. Holden." He scratched his chin. "Mr. Wyatt Holden."

"Wyatt sent you here—what for?"

"He found your sister." Coyote Jack grinned. "I reckon you're mighty happy to hear that."

A thousand questions flew through Jinx's brain. Why hadn't Wyatt brought Mel here to see her himself? Where were they? Was something wrong?

And why would he and Mel send a stranger to tell her the good news—especially such a mean-looking stranger, one with eyes that Pop would have called buzzard eyes.

"Where is Mel?" she asked, her hands sliding down to grip the arms of her chair, her delicate knuckles turning white with the force of her grip.

"She's here in town, and you'll be seeing her real soon. But Mr. Holden thought you'd want to write her a note. Here." He picked up the sketch pad and one of the charcoal pencils lying on the table beside her and held them out to her. Jinx could smell the rank body odor that permeated his clothes, and something else—the smell of garlic and whiskey on his breath.

"Go ahead and write your big sis a nice little welcome-back letter."

Something was wrong. Jinx didn't know what it was, but she felt it quivering in the air of the suddenly stifling hotel room. She stared at the pencil and the paper and then at the man leaning over her. He was breathing hard, his eyebrows twitching, watching and waiting.

"Take me to her," she said in the bravest voice she could muster.

"You don't give me orders, little girl. Write your sister a note. And then give me your boot."

"I beg your pardon?"

"You heard me. Give me your boot. Just one of 'em. You'll get it back."

Jinx blinked in confusion. It made no sense that he would want her boot. No sense at all.

She fought back the alarm that was rising steadily inside her. Worrying her lower lip between her teeth, she made a decision.

This Coyote Jack was a bad man, a very bad man. He scared her, and he was dangerous—she was sure of it. And she wondered if this was some kind of trick.

Maybe he wasn't really trying to help her and Mel and Wyatt at all; maybe he was the man who had kidnapped Mel—

A thousand maybes rolled through her mind, but one thing was clear: She shouldn't do what he said. Instinct warned her that he was bad.

"If you don't get out of this room right now, I'm going to scream," she cried, the tremble in her voice growing more pronounced with each word. "I'm going to scream so loud that everyone in the hotel will come running to see what happened to me. And the sheriff will come and he'll put you in jail!"

He laughed, a mean, ugly sound, and before she could even flinch away from him, his hand whipped out and grasped her by the hair, his fingers twisting in the bright red-gold curls. "There's no sheriff in Cherryville, little girl, and even if there was, he wouldn't have the gumption to come and put me in jail. So you quit backtalking me, and write something nice to your sister so's I can bring it to her and prove that you're here safe and sound. Use your head and give me the note and one of your pretty little boots, and I won't have to start slapping some sense into you."

"You're hurting me," Jinx whimpered.

He yanked her head back. "This is nothing compared to what will happen if you don't write me that note pronto."

"Stop!" Her voice rose to a scream. "Stop hurting me. Let me go!"

The words were scarcely out of her mouth before the door crashed open.

"Let her go!" a boy's voice shouted.

Coyote Jack was so stunned that he released Jinx's hair. He turned and stared in narrow-eyed fury at the boy who'd bolted into the room. The kid was pointing a shotgun at him.

"Who the hell are you?"

"Jesse Holden. And you're Coyote Jack. Now step away from her before I blow your stupid brains out."

"If I were you, boy," the bounty hunter rasped, his glance flicking with alacrity just behind the boy, "I'd have a look behind me because you're the one about to get his brains blowed out."

Swiftly Jesse jerked his head around. In that split second Coyote Jack went for his gun. He fired, and the room erupted with gunfire and spurting blood.

Jinx screamed. Everything seemed to happen in slow motion as Jesse staggered back against the wall, the shotgun tumbling from his grasp. Blood gushed out all over his clothes.

Coyote Jack reached the boy in two swift strides. He grabbed him by the collar and hurled him to the floor as if he were a pup. Then he kicked the shotgun to the opposite wall and slammed the door shut. When he turned back to glare down at the bleeding, white-faced boy, his swarthy countenance was dark with rage.

"No one interferes with me and my business, boy. Nobody. I'm going to have to teach you that. It's a lesson I guarantee you won't soon forget."

And with the full force of his hefty strength he lifted his boot and aimed a vicious kick straight at Jesse's head.

22

Trapped in the Peacock Brothel with Rafe Campbell between her and the door, Melora made her way shakily to perch upon the red and black settee and tried to think.

She was frantic about Jinx. If it was true that Jinx was here in Cherryville, she'd be terrified when Coyote Jack showed up to demand she write a note. Gnawing at her lower lip, Melora tried to clear the throbbing from her head, tried to imagine how she might escape this monster she no longer knew.

"May I have a glass of water, and a cloth for my lip?" she asked at last in a subdued tone.

Campbell paused while sitting in the chair loading bullets into his gun. He glanced at her, his gaze piercing.

"Sure, honey. Help yourself."

He nodded toward the pitcher of water on the bureau. "And take my handkerchief." He stood and came toward her with it as she eased herself off the settee.

"Say, that cut looks pretty bad." Amazingly his tone held regret. "I'm real sorry, Melora. I didn't want to hurt you. But you made me do it. Next time don't force me to get so rough with you."

She snatched the handkerchief from him, then hurried out of reach before he could stop her. "I'll make a deal with you," she said quietly as she poured water into a glass and then onto the handkerchief.

"Go on."

She drank quickly, then dabbed at her lip with the damp cloth. "If you don't hurt Jinx, I'll do anything you say. Go anywhere you say."

"Not a bad offer," Campbell commented, holstering his gun. He frowned as she continued to dab gingerly at her cut lip. "I like the sound of it, but there's a part missing. An important part. Cal Holden."

"We don't need to bother with him." Melora set the handkerchief down on the bureau and faced Campbell, trying to appear calm and forthright. "Cal isn't important. He's part of your past. And mine. We have to think about the future."

She shivered under his stare. It tried to strip her naked, tried to study what lay beneath her words. Melora kept her eyes clear and focused directly upon him.

"I certainly have no desire ever to see him again after the way he treated me." She continued softly.

"I'd like to forget about this—this entire episode and go on."

"He treated you bad?" His features sharpened. She saw his fists clench, the big knuckles whiten. "Melora, if he touched you, I swear I'll butcher him like a steer."

"No, he didn't. Never," she lied, "not once. As a matter of fact he scarcely spoke to me." Melora hurried on. "But he did kidnap me on our wedding night and ruined all our plans. I hardly thank him for disrupting my life. *Our* lives." She corrected herself quickly. "And now I only want things to go back to the way they were."

"They will, honey. They will. As soon as I kill that hombre and get him out of our hair for good, you and me will get married right here in Cherryville."

Her blood froze. "We will?"

"That's right. Then we'll head back to Rawhide and sell both of our properties. Now, I know you're fond of the Weeping Willow, darling, but all the rustling in those parts doesn't appear to be coming to an end anytime soon. And the ranch—both ranches— will just drain us financially. We can do better, much better, in San Francisco. As I explained before, the profits from the Weeping Willow and the Diamond X will give us a fine start."

She couldn't speak for a moment, could only stare at him. Now, even now, knowing everything she did about him, having been struck and bullied by him, she saw that he expected her to sell the Weeping Willow and go off with him. To sell her home, hers and Jinx's, their birthright, the land they'd grown up on and cherished, so that she could run some gaming establishment with him. He truly thought she'd be his dutiful little wife, his possession, his pretty toy to show off to the important members of San Francisco society.

I'll see you eaten by buzzards first, she vowed silently.

"What about Jinx?" she managed to ask in a subdued tone, needing to know the full extent of his plans, plans he was arrogant enough to think he could really force upon her, just as he would force a marriage.

"Why, Aggie will take Jinx back East. You'll be pleased to know I've found an excellent doctor for her in Philadelphia. Dr. Kirk of the Miller and Peterson Institute. While Jinx is being cured—which might take months, you know, honey, possibly even a year—you and I can make our start in San Francisco."

"With our gaming establishment."

"That's right." He nodded. "There's opportunities galore in San Francisco. You've never seen anything like it."

I've never seen anything like your colossal gall, Melora thought, but she struggled to keep her emotions from bubbling to the surface.

"Will you tell me something?" she asked, turning a gaze to him which she hoped appeared mild and docile. "Cal told me that you were involved in rustling back in Arizona. Is it true?"

"He's a damned liar."

"So it isn't true?"

"Well"—he grinned—"maybe just a little bit of rustling."

The sick bile of disgust rose in her throat. It took all her self-control to keep her voice low and even. "What about in Rawhide? Are you involved *a little bit* in the rustling there as well?"

Campbell didn't answer at first. He strode to the mirror, smoothed his hair, and studied his own handsome reflection before suddenly turning on his heel and eyeing Melora almost belligerently.

"I'll tell you something, Melora, because I'm sorry I hit you and I feel I owe you an explanation. Yes, I have been doing some rustling in Rawhide." He held up a hand as her eyes darkened with a flash of horror. "My little operation there started several months before I officially arrived in town to claim the Diamond X."

"Which you stole from Cal," she croaked. And then moistening her lips, she asked the question that was pounding through her like a sledgehammer, the question that had been at the back of her mind ever since she'd heard about his role in rustling back in Arizona.

"And did you have anything to do with my father's murder?"

He shook his head. "No, of course not. I wasn't even in the territory when it happened."

She desperately wanted to sit down. She felt sick. Sick with rage, sick with grief and overwhelming revulsion. But she straightened her knees and forced herself to remain standing near the bureau. "Was it . . . some of your men who were . . . involved?"

She waited, holding her breath.

"Actually, yes." He crossed to her and would have

grasped her arms, but she flinched away, sucking in her breath so loudly and forcefully that Campbell stared at her and scowled.

''Don't make more of this than necessary, Melora,'' he said. ''My men working the valley had specific orders not to kill anyone. It wasn't my fault that Strong got carried away—''

''Strong!''

''Otis Strong. He doesn't work for me anymore; he's nowhere near the Weeping Willow. Last I heard he'd joined some pards of his robbing banks and had a posse after him. He's probably dead or in prison by now.''

Strong. Otis Strong shot Pop.

''He worked for *you*.'' Her voice was so hushed it took him a moment to register what she'd said.

''Yes, he did, but I told you, I never ordered him to shoot anyone.''

A hot, shimmering redness glittered before Melora's eyes. Her fingers closed over the pitcher, gripping tight as she spun about, lifting it and crashing it down upon his head.

''You bastard!'' she screamed, deadly rage pouring out of her. ''I'll kill you!''

Campbell knocked her aside onto the bed with a sharp blow. There was blood running down his temple from one of the broken china shards. ''You little bitch,'' he rasped. His blue eyes flashed like deadly lightning. ''I've given you every chance, I bent over backwards to be understanding, but now you're going to find out exactly what happens when you cross me.''

He lunged toward her as she lay sprawled on the bed, moving with terrifying swiftness, but Melora rolled off it even more quickly and launched herself toward the window. She raised it in one fluid motion and leaned out.

"Help!" she screamed into the street below, a deserted side street overlooking the flour mill. "Help me! Someone help me!"

Then Campbell grabbed her from behind, one arm snaking tight around her throat. He dragged her backward to the bed, flung her down, and flipped her over.

"I'll kill you!" Melora shouted, fighting him with all her strength. Her teeth clamped down on his forearm, but he immediately hit her with his free hand, a ringing blow that sent a whirling torrent of stars before her eyes.

"I'll tame you, you spoiled, ungrateful bitch," Campbell grunted, and pinned her beneath him. He grasped her breast and squeezed it hard between his fingers, pinching and twisting until Melora screamed in agony.

"There, now. I think you're getting the idea." Blood dripped down his face and stained his clean white shirt, and there was sweat falling into his eyes, but he was surveying her with infinite gloating satisfaction.

"Melora, I've wanted you from the first moment I met you. So you'd better get used to the idea that I'm going to have you, because I always get what I want. Cal Holden learned the hard way that I'll do whatever I have to do to get ahead in this life. I've got plans, big plans. And you're part of them."

She shrieked again as he pinched her nipple between his fingers. Stinging tears sprang to her eyes.

But suddenly he froze. Lifting his head, he went taut, listening. Then, swiftly, he clamped a hand over her mouth.

Melora stopped bucking long enough to try to hear whatever had caught his attention.

She heard deep, throaty feminine laughter bubble up from the room next door, then a man's voice, the words indistinguishable.

"Champagne first!" a woman trilled. "Take off your clothes, lambkins, while I pour!"

"Looks like Miss Lucille has customers next door," Campbell growled, his fingers pressing cruelly against her mouth. "We wouldn't want to disturb them, would we?"

Melora twisted her head and snapped her teeth down as hard as she could on his hand.

He yanked it away, swearing, and in that split second she let out a deafening scream. Cursing, Campbell pressed his fingers into her windpipe, cutting off her air.

"No one's going to pay attention to a woman screaming in a cathouse," he told her. "But I'll be damned if I put up with it. Now listen to me, Melora, and listen good. Are you listening?"

She couldn't breathe. No air could get through to her lungs, and her vision was turning blue, as were her cheeks. With the last of her strength she nodded.

Campbell released her throat. Her hands flew to the tender spot as her mouth opened, and she gasped for air, wanting to kill him, but no longer certain she would live much longer herself.

"I'm sorry about your father," he said, still straddling her. "But that was Strong's doing, not mine. He disobeyed my orders, so you can't hold me accountable."

"I hate you."

"But you'll marry me first thing tomorrow morning. Because if you don't, I can't guarantee the safety of your sister. Where the hell is Coyote Jack anyway?" he muttered with a grimace.

"Maybe you should go and find him. Maybe he got lost," she managed to rasp out past her bruised throat.

"And leave you alone, my sweet little honey pie? Never. Besides, it's only a stone's throw to the Gold Bar Hotel. He'll be back soon enough—maybe too soon."

Melora couldn't speak well at that moment, but she could see. She saw the gleam of lust enter his eyes as he stared down at her, recognized it for the sick, greedy emotion that it was, and she recognized the driving force behind this man she'd once thought she knew and understood.

Rafe Campbell wasn't capable of love, not true love. His soul, if he had one, was scarred and dirty. Diseased. He loved power, money. He wanted to control everyone and everything about him.

No wonder our souls never touched, Melora thought, and then her gaze widened in dismay because Campbell leaned over her once again and cupped her other breast in his hand.

He watched her face as he squeezed painfully, pinching her until she whimpered.

"I've been denied my honeymoon because of Cal Holden. Give me one good reason I should wait any longer."

I've got fight left in me yet, Melora thought on a ragged sob as she struggled anew to escape him. But he pressed his weight on her, and his lips lowered to suck greedily at hers.

She bucked frantically. Kicked. Tried to bite his mouth, to claw his flesh with her nails.

"Damn you, don't fight me, Melora." His voice boomed off the walls, hoarse, throbbing with an odd mixture of anger and arousal. "You can't win!"

Suddenly the door to the room crashed open.

Campbell swung his head around, and his mouth fell open, gaping. Cal Holden filled the doorway, fury cold as mountain snow glinting in his eyes.

"Maybe she can't, Campbell," he said with awful, deadly calm. "But I sure as hell can."

23

Campbell flung himself off Melora in a rolling leap and went for his gun. But Cal tackled him even as he drew it, and they hurtled to the floor with a crash that shook the windows and sent the gun flying.

Melora scrambled up, watching them roll and punch and kick across the carpet, her throat dry with fear. She made a dash toward the gun, but the flailing bodies swerved into her path, and a flying fist caught her shin.

"Get the hell out of the way," Cal yelled.

She dodged them and tried again to work her way around, watching in silent dread the desperate battle that was under way.

There was a savagery to the fight that sickened her and made her skin crawl with terror. The air was thick with the stench of hatred, of sweat and blood. Each blow echoed through the room, and she gasped as she saw Campbell land a brutal right hook to Cal's chin, a punch that sent Cal reeling backward onto the carpet.

But he rolled aside as Campbell aimed a kick at his head, and then Cal was somehow on his feet, his expression grim as he swung a powerful fist that crashed with a thud into the other man's midsection.

At that moment Melora scooped up the gun.

"Stop!" she shouted. "Campbell, back off right now or I'll shoot."

To her dismay neither man paid her the least heed. They continued to fight, their bodies locked together in vicious combat. They tumbled into the bureau, crashed over the settee.

Melora, blinking hard in concentration, tried to maneuver one single clear shot, but there was too much movement; she couldn't fire without the risk of hitting Cal.

And then it was too late because what she saw next froze every bone in her body. Campbell pinned Cal up against the wall, and from inside his boot he yanked a knife.

"Don't move, Holden, or I'll slit your throat."

He pressed the blade tip against Cal's neck.

"Drop it or I'll shoot!" Melora commanded, but he only laughed at her, his gaze fixed on Cal's cold green eyes. With deliberate precision, he edged the tip of the knife across Cal's bronzed skin, drawing a thread of blood.

"You drop that gun, Melora, or your would-be res-

cuer here gets his throat slit in less time than it takes
to say a prayer. Drop it—*now*.''

Shaking, she did as he said. The gun thudded to
the floor. "Let him go," she pleaded, no longer caring how pitifully her voice broke.

"No way, honey. I'm going to kill him and enjoy
every second I watch him die."

"Melora, get out." Cal spoke with iron calm, his
eyes meeting Campbell's steadily. "Go, Princess,
right now."

"I'm not leaving you!"

Campbell's mouth twisted as he heard the passion
in her voice. He made a whistling sound under his
breath. "You should've hanged back in Arizona, Holden. You've got no damn business still being alive."

"Why do you hate him so much?" Melora cried.

"I hate anyone who gets in my way." Campbell
was breathing hard, the exertion from the fight affecting him, taking its toll. Yet he held the knife with
deadly steadiness.

"When he and his damned brother found out about
my little rustling operation, they went straight to
Grimstock. And ruined everything. That was a real
successful little operation I had going there. But did
they hesitate to turn me in? Not for a second." His
voice rose, thick with fury. He slammed his fist into
the wall beside Cal's head. "You were supposed to
be my friend, Holden, you and Joe both. We were
pards, all three of us, but the moment you learned I
was making myself a nice bit of money on the side
you couldn't wait to send for the marshal."

There was no fear in Cal's eyes as they bored into

Campbell's blazing blue ones. There was only anger, but Melora felt enough fear for both of them. She didn't understand how Cal could look so dangerous, so confident and calm when he had a knife at his throat.

"You were rustling the man we all worked for," Cal said quietly, meeting Campbell's glare. "A man who trusted you, just as Joe and I trusted you." There was fury beneath the quiet intensity of his voice, but it was a leashed, controlled fury, no less palpable for its deceptive calm. "So Joe and I went to the law; we did what we had to do."

Campbell scratched the blade at the skin just beneath Cal's ear. Blood ran down, dripping onto Cal's shoulder, staining his shirt. But he never flinched.

"And I did what I had to do." Campbell gave a hoarse laugh.

Melora couldn't keep silent a moment longer. She despised him, longed to throw herself at him, clawing and hitting, but she didn't dare move lest he jab that knife into Cal's throat. Her nails were digging into her hands as she watched in helpless fear. "You're saying you had to murder that rancher? And frame Joe and Cal for it? Couldn't you have merely high-tailed it out of there and left them alone?"

"Not when I could get rid of them and Grimstock in one easy swoop." Campbell laughed again, a smug, ugly sound that stirred a loathing inside Melora that was so intense her stomach roiled. "Sheriff Harper and I had a profitable partnership going. I had no desire to give it up until something better came along, and you provided me with that too, Holden." He mocked Cal with a harsh chuckle. "The deed to the Diamond X Ranch. And that led me to the beauteous Melora."

"And the Weeping Willow," Cal said grimly.

"And the Weeping Willow." Campbell acknowledged it with a broad, triumphant smile.

Then everything seemed to happen at once. The door was kicked in, Melora screamed, and a portly white-haired man jumped nimbly inside with his gun drawn. At the exact same moment Cal slammed a fist into Campbell's stomach and seized his knife hand.

"Stop in the name of the law!" the white-haired man ordered, but just as the two men had done with Melora, they ignored him, resuming their fight with a heightened ferocity.

Cal's fist connected again and again with brutal force. Campbell staggered backward, dazed and winded. Cal hit him again, even harder, his eyes cold and intent. And again. This time Campbell fell over the little gold chair, and crashed to the floor. He landed near the gun he'd forced Melora to drop.

"You're a dead man, Holden!" In a flash he grabbed it, rolled, and pulled the trigger.

But Cal fired first, and Campbell's shot went wide by inches.

Cal's didn't go wide at all. The bullet went straight through Campbell's heart.

Melora watched in mute horror as Rafe Campbell jackknifed backward and collapsed against the carpet, blood streaming from the gaping wound in his chest. The rich crimson stream of it spread across the ruby threads of the rug.

She stared at that river of blood, too stunned to move. How had Cal fired so quickly? His draw was like lightning, as fast as any gunfighter she'd ever heard of or imagined.

Then her knees buckled, and she sank to the floor, covering her face with her hands. The next thing she knew Cal was there, holding her, his arms around her soothing and gentle, so remarkably gentle.

"It's over, Melora. Over. Sweet, he's dead."

She stared into his bruised face, at his cut skin, and gripped him by the shoulders, clinging to his solidness, his strength. Tears ran down her cheeks, tears of joy, of immeasurable relief. She'd almost lost him, she'd almost had to watch him die, and she suddenly knew that if it had happened, she couldn't have borne it.

"Cal, thank God." she whispered. Her fingers dug into his shoulders. "I thought he was going to kill you. He hurt you, didn't he? There's so much blood."

He was bleeding, battered, and weary, but he was alive. There was an intense light in his eyes as he gazed at her, a light that drove some of the chill from her, but as her mind flashed over what had just occurred, she felt her heart rent suddenly in two.

"Oh, no. Cal, you didn't want to kill him; you wanted his confession," she gasped, her eyes wide.

He smoothed back her hair. "Can't have everything we want, can we, Princess?" Gently he laid a finger to the bruises on her face. "You're hurt," he said grimly. "Is it bad?"

"No, no, it doesn't matter. Your plan, that's what mattered, and I ruined it! It's all my fault."

"That's enough of that, Melora. It's done." Sternly he frowned at her, then slid his arms around her and helped her up. There was a low catch in his voice that made her stare at him as he wound his arm around her waist and held her close. "Melora, the only thing that matters is that you're safe. I don't give a damn about Marshal Brock—"

"Someone mention my name?" came a voice from the doorway, and startled, they both jerked around to see the white-haired man still there. They'd both completely forgotten about him. He holstered his gun and leaned a rounded shoulder against the door, his bushy snow white brows knit together as he studied them. Just behind him a young woman with very black, very long, wavy hair and very large breasts gaped into the room from the hall, her heavily rouged face stretched into an expression of horror. She appeared to be wearing nothing more than a feather boa and black garters.

"Who the hell are you?" Cal asked, wiping his bloody face with his sleeve.

The man pushed away from the door, ambled farther into the room, and nudged Campbell's prone form with the tip of his boot. "I told you. The law. Marshal Everett T. Brock, retired, at your service, young man."

"Brock! I've been going by your house every single damned day. What the hell are you doing here?"

"Doing what I like best these days since I retired." Chuckling, he threw a fond glance over his shoulder at the woman in the boa and spoke to her in a jovial tone. "You go on back and pour us some more of that French champagne, Dolly. I'll be there quicker'n you can bat your eye.''

Melora listened dazedly as the marshal moved closer and addressed Cal. ''We were in the next room and couldn't help overhearing, son. Quite an interesting story that fellow had to tell.''

''You heard all he said? What he did?''

''Every word of it.''

Cal gaped at him, then broke into a grin. ''Melora, do you know what this means? I can't believe it.''

But Melora was suddenly remembering something that made her heart stop and the blood drain from her face.

''Cal!'' An anguished cry broke from her throat.

The two men stared at her as she wrenched herself toward the door like a madwoman.

''Jinx! How could I forget? Cal, we have to hurry. Give me a gun! Jinx is at the Gold Bar Hotel with Coyote Jack!''

JESSE managed to twist aside from the kick aimed at his head, but Coyote Jack's next kick caught him in the stomach. He doubled over in pain, trying to breathe as the wind flew out of his lungs and his ribs exploded with agony. Desperately he tried to get up, but Coyote Jack slammed a fist into his jaw.

Jesse went down with a grunt and a crash.

''Stop it!'' Jinx screamed, her small face shining white with terror. ''Stop it, you'll kill him!''

''That's the idea, little girl.'' Coyote Jack chuckled and turned his attention again to the moaning youth on the floor.

Jinx closed her eyes for an instant, unable to bear the horror of the beating the boy was enduring.

Then she opened them. *You have to do something.* But what could she do?

When Pop was killed, she couldn't do anything. She was riding through the grass, and there he was, lying there in the brush. Covered with blood. Dead, already dead. Then Sir Galahad had reared up, and she'd felt herself flying, flying. . . .

There was nothing she could do for Pop.

But there is something you can do now. Right now. Stop him, a voice inside her head commanded. It sounded like Pop's voice. *Stop him now.*

Her gaze fixed itself upon the crystal flower vase on the mantel. She pushed herself up in her chair without thinking. The crystal winked and beckoned. With each grunt and groan and sickening thud that assaulted her ears, its light grew more brilliant.

Everything seemed to be moving in slow motion as she came out of her chair. She didn't feel the sagging ache of her leg muscles, she didn't feel the floor beneath her feet. She only knew that she reached the mantel, reached up, felt the cool shimmer of the crystal in her hands. She only saw Coyote Jack's dirty, shaggy hair sticking out beneath his hat as he leaned over the fallen boy. She hurled the vase.

It struck him square in the back of the head.

He grunted in pain and staggered around, his eyes lighting on her with an expression of astonishment, quickly followed by one of murderous rage.

From the corner of her eye she saw Jesse lunge upward, then everything became a blur of color and motion as the boy grabbed frantically for the gun in Coyote Jack's gun belt. He managed to yank it out of the holster, but the bounty hunter swung back to take it away.

She never saw how the gun went off, she only heard the report, inhaled the acrid smell of gunsmoke, and heard as if from a far distance her own thin, hollow screams echoing through the room, echoing around and around and around.

Suddenly the room was full of people, and they all were watching Coyote Jack sink to the floor, while Jesse Holden stared dazedly down at the smoking gun in his hand, and Jinx clung to the mantel.

Voices jabbered, the room spun. Then Jinx felt herself embraced in soft, clutching arms.

"Jinx, sweetie, it's me. It's Mel. Everything's over now, you're going to be fine. Do you hear me? You're going to be just fine! But how did you get here? You're standing, Jinx. *Standing*."

The little girl gazed up with shining, wondering eyes into her sister's anxious face. Suddenly her legs weakened, the strain of walking after so many months in a chair catching up with her. She gave a slight moan as she slid toward the floor.

Melora's arms tightened, gently lowering her.

Then Jinx threw her arms around Melora's neck as they crouched together on the floor.

"I walked, Mel," she whispered, the joyful words slipping out with breathless awe. "*I walked*."

Melora shook her head. "I know, but how? How?"

"She did it to save me," Jesse piped up, his voice

thin and strained as Cal wound a neckerchief tightly around his wounded arm. "She walked right to the mantel and picked up that vase and threw it at this varmint here."

"Did she hit him?" Cal wanted to know.

"Dead on."

The sisters stared at each other. They might have been alone on the top of Devils Tower or in the parlor of the Weeping Willow Ranch. Tears squeezed from Jinx's eyes and flowed silently down her cheeks. Melora was crying too, sweet tears of happiness that felt as if they would never stop.

"Oh, Jinx, I can't believe it," she whispered. "I can't believe it."

"It was Pop," Jinx said softly, meeting Melora's stare with calm, exultant conviction. "Pop helped me do it. I heard his voice, and he—he made me better. Mel, don't cry. Everything's going to be all right now. Everything's going to be just fine."

24

The rollicking notes of a harmonica floated out the windows of the Holden farm after supper the next evening, wafting over the shadowy Black Hills, serenading the ancient granite cliffs, the regal pines and spruces with its sweet, rousing melody.

"Another one! Oh, please, play another one!" Jinx begged, fixing Cal with such huge, pleading eyes that he laughed ruefully at the little girl sitting on the rug at his feet.

"I won't have any lips left by the time you've had your fill of harmonica music, Jinx Deane!" He reached out and tousled her freshly washed and brushed hair, and she giggled. The sound was every bit as richly delightful as the music he'd made.

Melora's heart turned over as she watched them

together, all of them, not only Cal and Jinx but Cassie, Will, and Louisa. Everyone was gathered around the fireplace, the children ready for bed in their warm flannels, their tummies all full of the redolent stewed chicken, mashed potatoes, and buttermilk biscuits she'd cooked for their supper tonight.

Cal began another tune, this one slow, plaintive, heart-rending. Firelight touched the faces of the children in the cozily lit parlor, faces that were dreamy and transfixed as they listened to the music, and Melora's own cheeks flushed with emotion as she gazed at each of them in turn.

Jinx was so much better now, her legs still weak but growing stronger by the hour. She was able to walk across the kitchen floor or to the little bench Cal had set for her beside the vegetable garden, and she'd shed her sadness like a worn, musty old shawl. Her lovely eyes had their old sparkle back, her lilting laughter rang out with the sweet sunniness Melora remembered so well from happier days, and ever since she'd awakened this morning after a good night's sleep in the same bed as Melora, she'd been talking a mile a minute.

Except when Jesse was around. She was awed and tongue-tied and flustered whenever the boy who'd saved her from Coyote Jack stepped into the room.

Jesse wasn't here just now, however. He'd ridden out after supper to court Deirdre O'Malley, and when Louisa had whispered to Jinx exactly where he was headed, poor Jinx had gone still as a mouse, not even looking up until after Jesse had slipped out the door, saddled up, and ridden off.

Then she'd walked slowly to the window and watched his galloping figure disappear over the rise.

It was clear to Melora that her little sister was suffering from her first infatuation. *Poor Jinx*, she thought, twinges of sympathy winding through her. Jesse was three years older than Jinx and considered her nothing but a child. It was the full-bosomed Deirdre with her flirting eyes and rolling hips that captivated his attention.

Wait a few years, she wanted to say. *The boys will swarm to our door like ants toward a picnic cloth.*

But she knew Jinx would be embarrassed to discover that Melora had guessed her plight, so she held her tongue and said nothing.

It pleased her enormously, though, that Jinx and Louisa and Cassie had become such fast friends. Will followed her everywhere, begged her to play checkers with him, or marbles, or jacks. He'd even brought his rabbit to sit on her lap this morning after she'd murmured that she missed her cats.

"You'll see Blackie and Speckles and Dot soon enough," Melora had assured her while sizzling eggs in a pan as Cassie and Lou set the table. The words were said cheerfully enough, but they had brought a sharp pang.

The Deane sisters were leaving for home the next day on the stagecoach.

So this cool, starlit, lovely evening held both the happiness of celebration and the sadness of parting.

Melora's gaze shifted to Cal as he finished the last notes of the song. How relaxed and peaceful he looked now, surrounded by all the children. Despite some cuts and bruises, he was handsomer than ever. Achingly handsome, she thought, her palms growing warm as an unbidden heat stole through her.

Firelight bronzed the strong lines of his face. A face no woman could ever grow tired of looking at, she thought wistfully, wondering how she ever could have thought him less than stunningly handsome.

At that moment his gaze shifted to her, and the cool fire of his eyes rested upon her countenance.

Her eyelashes swept down to hide her eyes, to hide what naked emotion might show there that she didn't want him to see.

They hadn't had a moment alone together since fetching all the children late last night and returning to the farm. This morning he and Jesse had been busy with Marshal Brock all day, sending wires, filling out paperwork, tearing up the hated wanted posters with Cal's face sketched across them.

And putting out a new poster: one marked by a picture of Otis Strong, now wanted in the murder of Craig Deane.

Before returning to the farm, Cal had purchased Melora's and Jinx's stagecoach tickets.

Perhaps he just doesn't want to be alone with you. Perhaps traipsing across the country with you was enough, or being locked in the barn together. Perhaps he doesn't have anything else to say; it's all been said. And done.

Pain closed around her heart like a fist.

Then she remembered the intensity with which he'd looked at her in the Peacock Brothel after he

shot Campbell and what he'd said to her: "The only
thing that matters is that you're safe."

A flicker of hope smoked up inside her, a wisp so
fragile the slightest breeze could extinguish it.

Melora didn't dare glance at his face again. She
kept her eyes fixed on the scrubbed, shining faces of
the four children.

It wouldn't do me any good to study Cal anyhow,
she reflected bleakly. Never before had she been so
unable to read a man's emotions, to anticipate what
he was going to do or say next.

"Time for all good little children to run along to
bed," Cal announced, setting the harmonica down on
the table. Ignoring the children's groans and protests,
he grinned and wagged a finger at Jinx. "Especially
you, my little princess, you have a very long few days
ahead of you."

Melora saw Jinx beam when he called her "my
little princess." The fist around her heart tightened.

Good-nights were said, cheeks were kissed, hugs
exchanged, and extra blankets added to each bed for
the night, since chill air had wrapped itself around the
mountains.

"Melora, aren't you coming to bed?" Jinx asked,
struggling slowly back up to a sitting position and
hugging her knees as she watched Melora move rest-
lessly around the darkened room.

"Mmm, not yet. I think I'll have a glass of warm
milk. I'm too wide-awake to sleep."

"Tell the truth. You're going to look for Cal!"

Jinx's remark stopped her cold, one hand on the

doorknob. "Of course I'm not," Melora said casually, giving her head a toss. "I'm going to look for a glass of warm milk. Why would you think anything so ridiculous?"

Jinx folded her fingers together primly. "Because of the way you two stare at each other all the time."

Absurdly Melora felt herself blushing. It was certainly warm in this room, despite the cool autumnal air outside. "We don't," she said staunchly.

"Yes, you do. Gee, Mel, I've never seen you act so . . . so—" Her sister struggled for the right words. "So *timid* with any man before. Usually when there's someone you like, the charm and the laughter pour out of you, sort of like sunshine."

Amused and more than a little embarrassed, Melora smothered a giggle. "Nonsense," she managed to say crisply, and squaring her shoulders, she went to the bureau, where she picked up her hairbrush. She began sweeping it absently through her hair.

"But with Cal . . ." Jinx persisted, eyes dancing as she let the sentence trail off.

"I *don't* like him. Not in that way. Not in any way. The man kidnapped me, Jinx!"

"That was wrong," Jinx said with a frown, "but he did have a good reason. And he saved you from making a terrible mistake, marrying Wyatt—I mean, Campbell."

"And nearly got us all killed in the process," she muttered, then bit her lip. That wasn't fair. Cal had rescued her. Just as Jesse had rescued Jinx.

It all had worked out just fine in the end.

Except . . .

Except for the hollowness inside each time she remembered how he had turned away from her that night in the barn, how he'd told her he'd made a mistake.

Ironic, wasn't it? she pondered with a heavy heart. The one man she truly wished would fall madly, ridiculously in love with her and make a fool of himself over her the way countless others had, and write her silly ballads, and bring her armloads of flowers— that man didn't want her. He "regretted" the time he'd spent alone with her in the soft, scented hay of the barn.

"Damn Cal Holden," she fumed aloud, choking back tears. She whirled toward Jinx, gesturing with the hairbrush. "I don't want to think about Cal Holden, I don't want to talk about Cal Holden, and I certainly don't want to *see* Cal Holden."

"Well," Jinx couldn't resist adding, hugging her knees tighter, "suit yourself. But I like him. I like the way he smiles. And the way he takes charge of everything. And the way he looks at you." Suddenly, with a muffled giggle, she threw herself back against the pillow and tugged the sheet up cozily to her chin. "He's *much* better than that *other* Wyatt Holden," she concluded. "And you know it, Mel."

Melora tossed the hairbrush onto the bureau with a clatter and marched from the room. "Warm milk," she muttered to herself as she headed through the silent, deserted parlor toward the kitchen. "The only thing I need is a cup of warm milk."

"That's the only thing? You sure, Princess?"

She jumped a foot into the air as Cal spoke to her

from the chair he straddled at the kitchen table. In the lamplight his eyes held a glinting challenge.

She swallowed hard and lifted her chin, trying not to notice how with his shirtsleeves rolled up she could see the corded muscles in his arms, the fine dark hairs glinting there as he gripped a mug of coffee and raised it to his lips.

"You scared me out of my skin!" she exclaimed crossly, trying to hide how flustered she was just to be alone with him. Never in her life had she been so shaken, so unsure with a man.

"And such pretty skin it is too," he commented.

At this she raised her brows. "Compliments, Mr. Holden?"

"Isn't that what it usually takes to woo a woman?"

"Since when are you in the business of wooing women?"

"Since I met you."

She stared at him. *No, don't do this to me, Cal. You're driving me crazy. One minute you kiss me or hold me or say something so sweet it makes my toes tingle, and the next you're pushing me away or walking away or somehow or other putting up a wall between us.*

"Taking lessons?" she managed to say casually as she started for the door.

He stood up. "Where are you going?"

"To the well house. I'm going to fetch some milk, and then I'm going to heat it on the stove, and then I'm going to—"

He blocked the door as she reached for the knob. "Not so fast. We have some things to discuss."

"Do we now?"

"Melora, what the hell is wrong with you? Back there at the Peacock Brothel I could've sworn you cared about me. I saw something in your eyes when Campbell had the knife to my throat, and I thought . . . oh, hell, I guess I was wrong. Dead wrong," he muttered quietly, and with anguish she heard the fine-edged bitterness in his voice.

"It looked to me as if you cared about me too," she managed to whisper, dropping her gaze. To her dismay he immediately reached out, grasped her chin, and tilted it up so that she was forced to meet his eyes.

"I do, Princess. Lord help me, I do."

"No." She shook her head. "You were only feeling responsible for me, which is quite noble—and quite unnecessary because I've always been able to take care of myself, and I plan to continue to do so."

"Sure you can, Princess, although you must admit you were in a peck of trouble for a while there with Campbell. It was lucky I heard you screeching all the way down the street. And when I burst in, as I recall, things weren't going so well." He paused as she scowled, and he fought the impulse to slide his fingers through the curtain of her hair, to touch those lips that were pouting at him so adorably. "But I know you're a strong woman, Melora, as courageous and self-sufficient as they come," he said, pulling her ever so slowly closer to him. "There's one thing, though."

Melora was trying to keep her back stiff and her eyes off the hard, sensuous lines of his mouth. "What's that?" she asked, trying to sound cool and uninterested. But to her dismay the question came out in a dry croak.

"I don't want you ever to have to fend for yourself, not ever again. I want to be there for you. To take care of you. To take care of you and Jinx."

"We hardly need—"

His eyes narrowed. "Everybody needs, Melora. People just need different things." Cal took a deep breath. "Let me say something I'm damn sure I'll regret, but if I don't say it now, I'll be kicking myself after you get on that stagecoach tomorrow. I don't know how to play courting games. I don't know how to sweet-talk a woman, and I don't know how to make a female fall in love with me. It never mattered much before because there never was anyone I wanted to sweet-talk or to make fall in love with me. Until now."

The heat of his hand gently cradling her chin tingled through her. She felt that flicker of hope inside her igniting into a thin, straight flame, and she tried hard to contain it as she swayed slightly on her feet.

Cal's arm slid around her waist to steady her. The hand that had cupped her chin now strayed to her hair and wound slowly through the silken strands.

"You were saying . . ." She prompted him, noting the slight upward curl of his lip as he grinned at her.

"I was saying that—hell, you know damn well what I'm saying!"

"I'm not sure I do."

"Melora," he grated, and suddenly his hand tightened in her hair. He yanked her close to him, and she could feel the hard strength of him pressed roughly against her own quivering body. Heat jumped between them, and for a moment she read danger in the cool green eyes as they caught and pinned hers.

"If you're playing games with me, I'm going to make you very sorry," he said.

"Games?"

"You look at me with that look in your eyes, the way a woman looks at a man when she really wants him . . . when she really loves him. If it isn't real—"

"How do you know how a woman looks at a man when she really loves him if you've never had yourself a decent woman before?"

"Some things a man knows," he growled, and then he moved so swiftly she never even had time to blink before he hauled her around, switching places with her. Melora found herself spun about with her back against the door, Cal holding her there, hemming her in with his body.

"Before we left that barn the other night, I said some things that hurt you, Melora. I'm real sorry for that. But I was trying to protect you. I knew you were mixed up on account of having just found out the truth about your fiancé. I reckoned you didn't know your own mind. And I figured it was a pretty lowdown thing I did, taking advantage of you—"

"You didn't," she whispered, suddenly feeling that if they weren't honest with each other now, they never would be. Her heart thundered inside her chest, pounding so hard it hurt. "You never have taken advantage of me. I knew exactly what I was doing.''

He stared at her, studying what shimmered within the depths of those glorious gold-flecked eyes, as if he would penetrate the secrets in the hidden places of her soul.

''And what was it you were doing exactly?'' He scowled.

''Making love to you.''

''Why?'' he demanded. ''Why did you want to make love to me? Because it felt good? Because you wanted to feel safe . . . comforted? Because there was nothing else to do in that damned barn?''

''Because I love you, you imbecilic, pea-brained numskull!'' she exclaimed. ''And yes, it felt good, and yes, I wanted to feel safe and comforted, but not just with anyone. With you!''

For a moment Cal only stared at her, his eyes searching her flushed face with harsh scrutiny, his breath lodged in his lungs. His muscles were taut, unbearably taut, and there was an aching heaviness in his loins it was becoming more difficult by the moment to ignore. He saw the passion in her eyes, the truth shining in them bright as gold, and at last, at last, he began to believe.

When he pulled her to him and kissed her, something wild broke free between them. The power of that kiss singed them, seared them, rocked them like a red-hot avalanche, sending feelings tumbling through them, jarring into them like mountain rocks careening over a precipice. But as the kiss deepened, they catapulted beyond caution, beyond wariness and

fear. Unchained passion fused their bodies. Then Cal
was tangling his hands and his lips in her hair, drowning in its texture, in its scent, and in the soft, pliant
feel of her as she melted against him, their bodies
fitting together as if they were vines, sinuously, naturally, desperately wound together.

"Lord, how I want you, Melora." It was such an
understatement he almost laughed. Need licked
through him, hotter and more potent than whiskey, as
he ran his hands down her back, cupped her sweet
rounded bottom, devoured her mouth until she
moaned in pure delight. "I want you so much—all
of you." The words came quickly, between kisses and
touches that set her afire. "Tell me now if you're not
sure, if you have doubts—"

She answered by dipping her mouth to his, her
tongue slipping through his lips, tasting, discovering,
promising. Cal's response left her shaking as he
pressed her against the door, his mouth attacking hers
with rough, hungry greed, and his hands scraping like
sandpaper all over her body.

"Cal, I never knew, I never knew," she gasped
when he wrenched back again and they both gulped
air like drowning swimmers. "I never knew before
what love was. I was so wrong, so foolish. This is
different from anything I felt with *him*. What I want
now, what I feel—"

"I know what you want." His hand was already
unbuttoning her shirt. He was grinning, a hard, dangerous grin that made her pulse rush. But she grasped
his hand as he tugged the ends of her shirt from her
jeans. "Not here, Cal. We can't. The children . . ."

His fingers closed around hers, tight and strong. His grin widened. "Come on then."

He dragged her out the door, then scooped her up into his arms to carry her down the porch steps and past the vegetable garden while all the while their mouths clung.

"Not the barn," Melora managed to say shakily when at last they drew breath as Cal strode with her beneath the cool white stars.

"I know." His eyes gleamed wryly beneath the slanting brows. "Will. And Jesse will be coming back." He tightened his grip on her, his long strides smooth and even despite the darkness. "Woman, you're sure a lot of trouble."

A stifled giggle rose above the excitement sweeping through her. "I'm worth it," she declared.

"You'd better be."

An exultant laugh flew from her throat and winged its way quietly through the night. "Where are you taking me?"

"Someplace where you can't escape me. And where no one will bother us. Someplace that's as wild and lovely as you are."

He carried her past the well house and the barn. The mountain air was cold, but his arms were warm. Above them the stars twinkled against a blue-black sky, tiny gems glowing with pristine fire to guide them.

Melora was trembling with eagerness when they reached a natural hollow in the land and Cal set her down upon the grass. She saw that they were in an exquisite clearing that shimmered like a pewter jewel in the starlight. The grassy enclave was sheltered from the wind by a wall of granite rock. Late-summer flowers and low shrubs made a delicate bower. Pillowy grass shivered in the light wind that danced down from the mountains.

They were some distance from the house and the barn and nowhere near the trail. With a breath of delight Melora turned slowly around and around, surveying the hideaway. They were hidden from all the world by the rock wall and by the spruces and the steep rise that sloped upward between this gentle spot and the farm.

"It's perfect," she whispered, going into Cal's arms as the wind played with her hair. "Absolutely perfect."

"Glad you like it." His embrace was rock-hard, crushing her so fiercely her ribs trembled and her breath caught in her throat. "Because unless you change your mind," he murmured, his mouth brushing tenderly across her eyelids, then dipping down to ravish the length of her throat, "we're going to be here for quite a spell."

"Promises, promises," Melora gasped, closing her eyes, dizzy from the sensations fluttering up wherever his warm mouth pressed. "I won't change my mind," she whispered.

"I'll hold you to that."

"Just hold me."

This time it was different from the time in the barn. This time when they sank down upon the grass and grew lost in kisses, when their clothes were shed with desperate haste and tossed in heedless piles, when their bodies locked in sweet combat, when their self-control snapped and they careened together into a realm of madness, this time she knew where she was headed. As they rolled across the grass, and Cal devoured her creamy nakedness with his eyes and drove her wild with his hands and his lips, this time she knew how to touch him, how to make him as frenzied and needful as she, how to draw from him those grunts of pleasure and of primitive desire that sent a heady satisfaction spinning through her.

She learned quickly. And she loved with all her heart. She gave and she received, arching, twisting, coiling around him with a wanton delight born of release and freedom and trust. The pleasure kept coming, wave after wave. He stunned her, made her shudder as flashes of tenderness warred with rough demand.

Cal was all man, and he made her feel all woman. When he caressed her breasts, and his tongue softly explored their hard, sensitive tips, the craving inside her grew. Unlike the cruel way Rafe Campbell had touched her and hurt her in the Peacock Brothel, Cal's touch was smooth and gentle, arousing wonderful sensations. They were wise hands, wicked hands, Melora thought on gasp after gasp of pleasure. And deliciously loving hands. She kissed his fingertips, then moaned as his mouth slid down the length of her body, tasting and nibbling on its journey.

Despite the night wind, sweat glistened on Melora's skin as she and Cal rocked and tumbled like wild forest creatures across the carpet of grass. When he spread her hair out across the sea of dark green and leaned back, panting, to survey her, her eyes gazed up at him, glazed bright with desire.

"I . . . do love you, Cal," she cried. She held her breath as he spread her legs with his knee and held himself poised above her. Tonight she could see the magnificence of his body, the rough, muscled chest, the corded splendor of his powerful arms and oaklike thighs. The sight of him cut her breath to fevered gasps. "I love you so much, so very much."

"I'm dying from love of you," he told her, his voice hoarse. She was so beautiful he could almost imagine he was dreaming. Her skin was like silk beneath his hands, her eyes more luminous than all the stars. Taking her mouth again, he captured it in one more mouthwatering kiss before he lowered his frame upon hers and slid his shaft boldly inside.

With a soft cry she opened herself to him, opened everything to him. Her body and heart and soul blossomed like a flower, and she clung to his shoulders, whispering, "Love, my love, my love," over and over again.

Cal answered her with powerful thrusts. As he plunged inside her again and again, all restraint disappeared. Faster and harder he drove into her, bringing Melora to a state of wild delirium. A fever raced through her blood. It swept her away, hot and powerful and dark, yet sweeter than any wild honey that had ever glided down her tongue. Cal was inside her, he was one with her, and there was no space for thought, or reason or sanity; there was only she and Cal and the driving fury of a storm so strong, so heated and furious it whipped at their souls, shook

them to madness, shot them to heaven and around the
stars in a tearing blaze of white-hot thunder. Thunder
and lightning, fire and light, sweetness and wildness
tore through them, lifted them, shattered them, and at
last left them sated and exhausted—but wondrously,
brilliantly whole.

IT was hours later that they strolled back to the
house in soft amethyst darkness, arms entwined
around each other. Melora was convinced that no two
people had ever been as close or as happy.

"I almost forgot." Cal stopped short as they
reached the farmhouse door. He kept his voice low,
aware that Will and Jesse were asleep in the barn,
while the three little girls were within earshot inside
the house. "I have something that belongs to you."

"Your heart, I hope." Smiling mistily in the starlit
darkness, Melora leaned against him. Her arms
wrapped around his neck as she raised up on tiptoe
to kiss him yet again.

"Uh-huh, that . . . and this." He pulled a small
pouch from his pocket, and as she watched, he drew
out the cameo he had taken from her that first morning after he'd kidnapped her.

Melora went perfectly still.

"I can't."

"You can. And you will."

She shook her head and stared miserably at the
lovely treasure in his hand. "It was from him—from
Campbell. He stole it from you, didn't he? Otherwise
you wouldn't have made me give it to you that morning."

"That's right, Melora. He stole it, along with so much else. But he can't steal the memories behind this cameo. Not unless I let him."

She studied him in surprise. "Memories?"

Cal's fingers closed around the delicate necklace. "This belonged to my grandmother Grandma Edda Davies Holden. A great lady, Melora. As family-minded and devoted as they come. Before she died, she gave something special of hers to each of her grandchildren, and this cameo is what she gave to me."

"It's beautiful." Melora smiled and touched his hand. "I've thought so since the first moment I saw it."

"Exactly what I thought about you." He rested his gaze upon her, taking in the rippling fall of satin hair, the large, glowing eyes and delicate features. Then his glance shifted down to the fragile cameo in his palm. "Grandma Edda told me: 'Give this to the woman you love. To the one you want to marry. To spend the rest of your life with' " Deliberately he reached out and brushed his knuckles lightly across her cheek. "And that's why I'm giving it to you."

Give this to the woman you love. To the one you want to marry. Marry?

Melora swallowed past a sudden lump in her throat. "In that case," she murmured, trying to keep from jumping to any conclusions, for she was not sure if she had correctly discerned a proposal in his words or not, "I gratefully accept."

She trembled as he clasped the cameo around her

neck. In her mind's eye she pictured Edda Davies Holden handing over this treasure to her grandson. And the question she was suddenly shy with teetered on the edge of her lips. She *thought* Cal had just asked her to marry him, but she wasn't sure. She didn't want to misunderstand something as significant as that. "Cal . . ."

"Hmm?"

He was nibbling sensuously around the delicate shell of her ear. "Does this mean . . . Was that a marriage proposal?"

"Sure was." A tiny pause. "Was that an acceptance?"

"Sure was."

Laughter bubbled from her lips. Cal grinned at her. She didn't have the heart to tell him that it wasn't exactly the most flowery or specific proposal she'd ever heard. It didn't matter. God willing, he'd never have the need to make another one.

And there were more pressing matters to discuss.

"When should we have the wedding?" Melora wanted to know, her arms clasping around his neck. "I need to invite all my neighbors and all the folks in Rawhide to my *next* wedding with Mr. Wyatt Holden."

He caught her around the waist, his eyes gleaming. "You sure you've got the right one this time?"

"Absolutely sure."

"Then let's plan on getting married the first of October."

"*October*?" Dismay washed over her. "That's a whole month from now!"

"It can't be helped, Melora. There's a lot to do first. For one thing I have to sort out all the legalities involving the deed to Uncle Jed's ranch. And then I have to sell the farm and move everybody to the Diamond X, get the ranch running and . . . some other matters. But I wish like hell it could be tomorrow, Princess," he growled, cradling her nape in his hands and kissing her with a hunger that left no doubt of his feelings.

"October," she repeated, pulling back, troubled.

"It's only a month away, Melora."

"It will seem like a year."

His tone was gentle but held an undercurrent of firmness that made her stare. "The separation and the delay will give you a chance to think things over. Make a clean break with the past. Be sure in your own mind."

"Cal Holden, I am sure!" she cried indignantly.

Cal dropped a kiss on the tip of her nose. "Then you'll be more sure," he said matter-of-factly. "It's settled. October first."

"It would serve you right if I did change my mind!" she exclaimed, though she kept her voice low, mindful of the sleeping family members in both the house and the barn. Suddenly she broke free of his embrace and jumped back just out of reach to glower at him.

"Cal Holden, you are infuriating. You're the most stubborn, mulish, irritating, high-handed man—"

"Come here, Melora."

"I will not," she whispered furiously. "If you think I'm going to take orders from you after we're married and go meekly along with everything you say, you have another thing coming—''

''Come here, Melora.'' He grasped her arms as he spoke, hauling her up against his chest.

''I will *not* give in to you on every point—''

''You don't have to tell me that. If I thought you were some mealymouthed little worm, I wouldn't have fallen in love with you. Do you know how adorable you look when you get your back up?''

''Don't try to change the subject on me. I'm talking about this October business—''

''Melora—''

''Why can't we—?''

''Melora!'' He silenced her with a kiss that stole the fight right out from under her. His lips claimed hers with a deep violent heat that completely obliterated all of her anger.

''Oh, very well, I'll give in to you just this once,'' Melora said shakily when she could speak again. ''October first we'll join the Deane clan with the Holdens.'' Her saucy smile teased him, making him want her all over again, as she had intended it to do. ''I suggest we seal the bargain with another kiss.''

''Only one kiss?'' Cal's mouth seared the tender hollow at her throat.

His hand found her breast. His stroking intensified the fresh waves of desire that were already sweeping over her. Melora moaned as her body thrummed alive beneath his hands, and desire waged a battle with responsibility.

''As many as you like,'' she gasped, ''but, Cal, we can't . . . not right here . . . the children—''

"When we're married, I'm building a separate wing for the children," Cal growled. He tugged her away from the door. "Come on, I know another place."

"Where now?" she whispered on a half giggle, running alongside him.

"The well house."

The well house?

It proved to be cool, dark, and quiet in the well house and sheltered from the wind.

They didn't come out until dawn.

Epilogue

❧❧❧❧❧

The hideout shack was cleverly concealed on a hidden shelf deep in Wild Horse Canyon. But not cleverly enough. Cal found it at sunup after five days of concentrated tracking. He left Rascal tethered to a rock some distance away and made his way stealthily down a rocky incline and through a trail of brush and scrub.

Eagles arced beneath the glimmering sun. The cloudless sky was porcelain blue, delicate and smooth and clear in contrast with the harsh abrasiveness of the land.

Cal noticed neither land nor sky, however. His attention was completely focused on his quarry. Otis Strong had apparently found himself some new partners, outlaws no doubt as cunning and amoral as himself.

But Cal wasn't interested in them either.

Two of Strong's companions were saddling their horses in front of the hideout shack when he spotted them. It didn't take long for Strong to emerge as well. He swaggered out the front door with a bottle of whiskey in his hand, and Cal noticed that above his beard, the big man's face still showed bruises from their fight. He was scratching his armpits and taking gulps of whiskey.

With satisfaction Cal observed that he was also wearing his guns.

"Nobody move!" He leaped out from the rocks less than fifteen feet from the three desperadoes, his Colt aimed straight at Strong's belly.

Strong and the other two froze.

"This has nothing to do with either of you," Cal barked to the strangers. All the while he kept his gaze riveted upon the incredulous face of Otis Strong. "You boys stay out of this and you can go to hell in your own good time. It's Strong I want."

"You!" Recognition turned Strong's ruddy skin the color of putty. "You low-down bastard. I'm going to kill you!"

"I'm taking you in, Strong."

"The hell you are."

"You're going to hang for the murder of Craig Deane."

"Like hell I am!" Strong's mouth stretched into a sneer. "You're the one going to die, mister. Right here, right now! Get him, boys!"

Gunmetal flashed in the sunlight. The eagles scattered. And the high rocks echoed with thunder as a hail of bullets sprayed the desolate shelf of land.

It was over quickly, and when the shooting stopped, Cal sprang up swiftly from the dust where he'd leaped and rolled and crouched while firing. He swept a cold glance over the bodies of the three dead men and holstered his gun.

Walking slowly, he crossed the weeds to stand over Strong's corpse, to study it dispassionately. "This is called justice, Strong. Evening the score. Now it's over."

Killing a man had never given him cause for happiness or celebration, but as the pale blue wisps of gunsmoke dissipated in the clear, cold air, Cal's lips thinned into a smile of grim satisfaction.

Now he could go home. To Melora.

It was almost his wedding day, and Cal knew if he didn't make it to Rawhide in time, he might just as well dig himself a grave right here alongside Otis Strong.

EVENING, SEPTEMBER 30

Tomorrow night, tomorrow night, I'm supposed to be a bride tomorrow night.

Cal Holden, if you leave me standing at the altar, I'm going to skin you alive, Melora thought, lamplight casting an amber glow upon her furious countenance as she paced barefoot across her gleaming bedroom floor. Her diaphanous white silk wrapper swished in time to her rapid footsteps, whipping around her legs like a shimmering cloud.

"Don't worry, Melora." Jinx stuck her head in the door with a sympathetic smile. "Cal will make it in time."

Melora's dismay faded at the sight of her sister in her ankle-length blue flannel nightgown. Her eyes softening with pleasure, she watched the girl scamper across the floor and plop down on the bed, Blackie curled comfortably on her shoulder. It was so good to see Jinx well. She was not only walking now, but running, skipping, jumping. A miracle had come to pass.

Not a day went by that Melora wasn't thankful for it.

But at this moment it was difficult to feel thankful, difficult to find a trace of the peaceful contentment that had enveloped her all the past month as she planned her wedding.

"I'm supposed to be getting married in the morning, Jinx," she grated out between clenched teeth. She wheeled toward the window, where the moon shone like her cameo against a sky of deepest ebony. Melora took a quick, panicky breath and brushed her fingers over the necklace, as if touching the cameo would bring her good luck. "All of the town will be there," she whispered dejectedly. "All except the groom! I'm going to be the laughingstock of Rawhide—again!"

Melora resumed her pacing, her hands tearing through her curling, freshly washed hair.

The citizens of Rawhide had found it richly amusing that Melora Deane was planning a wedding for the second time to a man named Wyatt Holden, an altogether *different* Wyatt Holden. The corrals and stores and saloons and offices were full of folks grinning and shaking their heads.

But not a soul had found anything funny about the criminal deceptions her original groom had carried out.

Many of the townspeople and ranchers had met Cal when he'd arrived a few weeks ago to help move Jesse and the children into the Diamond X ranch house. They liked him and warmly welcomed him and his family. And they especially welcomed the fact that they could expect cattle ranching profits to go up and rustling incidents to go down now that at his hands, the rustlers' ringleader, Rafe Campbell, was dead.

But how everyone would roar, Melora fretted to Jinx bitterly, when *she* found herself abandoned at the altar, just like Campbell before. Why, folks would flap their jaws for months about how Melora Deane's second attempt at a wedding had ended in failure.

"Failure? Since when are you talking about failure?" Aggie broke in, following Jinx into the bedroom, her tone crisp as corn. "That man will not let you down."

"But—"

"He's a good man, Melora. I may have made a mistake about that *other* man, but this time there can be no mistaking. Cal Holden will come through for you—always—unless I sorely miss my guess. Besides," she added, her eyes sparkling as they rested on the girl's hopeful face. "I saw the way he looked at you the night the Holdens all moved into the Diamond X and we brought his family that delicious fried chicken supper."

"And *I* saw the way he kissed you in the kitchen when he thought no one was looking!" Jinx giggled.

Melora couldn't hold back a grin. "Cal does love me," she muttered, closing her eyes and remembering how beautifully they fit together. "I know that at least. So I guess I have to dig down deep and find myself a little bit of faith."

But she kept on pacing.

She scarcely heard Aggie urge Jinx to move along to bed. But she shook herself out of her reverie when Jinx whispered from the door, "Mel! Are you *sure* you want to marry Wyatt Holden?"

The same question her sister had asked the night before her other wedding. Now their eyes met with warmth and love and sisterly laughter.

"I'm sure." Melora went to Jinx and knelt. She hugged her tightly, emotion swamping her. "Oh, Jinx, I've never been more sure of anything in my life."

It was quiet when Jinx and Aggie went to bed. The darkness of the midnight sky, the emptiness of the night haunted Melora as she padded to her closet and gazed at her mother's wedding gown, wondering if she would have the chance to wear it come morning. It was so beautiful. Her fingers trembled over the elegant lace veil, the creamy satin bridal slippers, the flowing train . . .

She never saw the man who swung through her window with single-minded purpose. She didn't hear even a footfall until she was seized roughly from behind and yanked against his tall, hard frame.

"Princess, don't tell me you weren't expecting me." Cal's breath tickled warm and enticing against her ear.

He spun her around in his arms and drowned out her shriek of joy with a kiss so fierce it left her weak with happiness.

"Where have you been?" she demanded, clutching him, her lips darkened from the force of the kiss, her whole body melting against his. "I thought you were leaving me at the altar!"

"Never, Melora. Not if I'd had to crawl across the plains on my knees and elbows to get here." He grinned. Then the grin faded, and his features became grave. As he caressed her cheek, every last glimmer of humor left his eyes. "I had business to attend to."

He picked her up, carried her to the bed, and set her down upon it very tenderly. As she drew him down beside her, she studied his serious expression with growing concern.

"What kind of business?"

"Otis Strong."

She bolted upright. Her golden brown eyes widened with a single crucial question.

Cal kissed her cheek. "He's dead, Melora. That hombre's taken up permanent residence in hell."

She nodded, her gaze locked upon his. "Thank you," she whispered.

"You're welcome." This time their kiss was longer, deeper. Cal tugged at the sash of her wrapper, discovering to his intense approval that beneath it she wore nothing at all.

"Now about this wedding tomorrow—" he said.

"What about it?" She had already stripped off his vest, and her fingers were skimming eagerly across the buttons of his shirt, freeing one after the other in rapid succession. She slid the shirt from his shoulders, her lips curving into a saucily tantalizing smile.

"You're sure you're getting hitched to the right fellow this time?" Cal inquired, pulling her down on top of him and wrapping his arms around her so tightly her breasts were crushed against the hair-coarsened roughness of his chest. "I'd hate to see you make any mistakes."

"No mistakes." Her slender finger traced his mouth, rubbing against the smooth warmth of his lips. "I love *you*, Cal," she said softly, gifting him with sweet, tiny kisses. "Only you. Always you."

"That about sums it up for me too, Princess." He grinned, and then the rest of their garments landed on the floor in a heap and there was nothing left to impede their lovemaking, nothing standing in the way of the happiness that swept through them with such passionate intensity that their bodies and hearts and souls burned like fiery spears with the heat of it.

And when their passion had joined them together and made them blissfully one, when they'd touched the edges of heaven and floated back to earth, when the night was nearly gone and a silvered pink dawn was peeking over the horizon, they slept in each other's arms and dreamed of their wedding and their future and their children and their home.

And the angels that accompanied the dawn on its glowing journey across the earth paused that October morning. They glanced in the ranch house window and looked and nodded sagely to one another, for they felt the joy bouncing in the air, the peace and harmony and happiness, the quiet, pinging thrum of souls meeting. Loving. Touching.

And the angels smiled.

The Four of Hearts Checklist

Books by Marsha Canham:
__STRAIGHT FOR THE HEART
__IN THE SHADOW OF MIDNIGHT
__UNDER THE DESERT MOON
__THROUGH A DARK MIST

Books by Jill Gregory:
__WHEN THE HEART BECKONS
__DAISIES IN THE WIND
__FOREVER AFTER
__CHERISHED

Books by Joan Johnston:
__MAVERICK HEART
__THE INHERITANCE
__OUTLAW'S BRIDE
__KID CALHOUN
__THE BAREFOOT BRIDE
__SWEETWATER SEDUCTION

D e l l